PRAISE FOR LUCINDA BERRY

One in Four

"*One in Four* by novelist Lucinda Berry is an extraordinary and fun read from start to finish for fans of psychological murder mysteries having to be solved by an amateur female sleuth. Original, fascinating, and unreservedly recommended."

—Midwest Book Review

If You Tell a Lie

"Another poisonous Berry special . . . The hits just keep on coming. Be glad you're a reader and not a character."

—*Kirkus Reviews*

Keep Your Friends Close

An Amazon Books Editors' pick for

Best Mystery, Thriller & Suspense

"Perfect reading for those who wonder: 'If you couldn't trust your best friend, could you really trust anyone?'"

—*Kirkus Reviews*

Off the Deep End

"As usual, Berry tightens the screws smartly in the opening pages and never lets up, and as usual, her ending is more intent on deepening the nightmare than providing a plausible explanation for it. Warning: The title applies as much to the audience as to the characters."

—*Kirkus Reviews*

"As the suspense mounts, the action drives to a harrowing conclusion. Berry delivers the goods."

—*Publishers Weekly*

"A well-done mystery with a plausible yet surprising ending."

—*Library Journal*

Under Her Care

"The action never wavers, and the surprises are unending. Berry is writing at the top of her game."

—*Publishers Weekly* (starred review)

"It's a humdinger . . . Perfect for suspense fans."

—*Kirkus Reviews*

"Lucinda delivers every time. Unputdownable."

—Tarryn Fisher, *New York Times* bestselling author

"Lucinda Berry's latest, *Under Her Care*, is her best thriller yet! A dark, riveting read that will keep you up late, racing to the chilling end."

—Kaira Rouda, *USA Today* bestselling author of *The Next Wife* and *Somebody's Home*

"Lucinda Berry's *Under Her Care* is stunning, diabolical, and gripping, with one of the best and most gasp-worthy twists I have read in a very long time. Fast paced, fabulous, and enthralling, the pages practically turn themselves. Absolutely captivating."

—Lisa Regan, *USA Today* and *Wall Street Journal* bestselling author

"Creepy and chilling, *Under Her Care* is a tense page-turner that leaves you questioning everything you ever knew about motherhood and the family bond."

—Tara Laskowski, award-winning author of *The Mother Next Door*

The Secrets of Us

"Those looking for an emotional roller-coaster ride will be rewarded."

—*Publishers Weekly*

"Combine Lucinda Berry's deep understanding of the complexities of the human mind with her immense talent for storytelling and you have *The Secrets of Us*, an intense psychological thriller that kept my heart racing until the shocking, jaw-dropping conclusion. Bravo!"

—T. R. Ragan, *New York Times* bestselling author

"*The Secrets of Us* is an unputdownable page-turner with two compelling female protagonists that will keep readers on their toes. Fantastic!"

—Cate Holahan, *USA Today* bestselling author of *One Little Secret*

"Lucinda Berry's *The Secrets of Us* is a tense psychological thriller that explores the dark corners of the mind and turns a mind can take when it harbors secret guilt. The interplay between sisters Krystal and Noelle and their hidden past is gradually revealed, and in the end, the plot twists keep coming. Right and wrong can be ambivalent, and this story explores all shades of gray, from their dysfunctional family to an old childhood friend to a husband who may or may not be too good to be true. Berry's background as a clinical psychologist shines in this novel with a character so disturbed they spend time in seclusion lockdown at a psychiatric ward. Don't miss this one!"

—Debbie Herbert, *USA Today* and Amazon Charts bestselling author

"*The Secrets of Us* is an utterly gripping, raw, and heartbreaking story of two sisters. Berry's flawlessly placed clues and psychological expertise grab you from the first word, not letting go until the last. Compelling, intricate, and shocking, this inventive thriller cleverly weaves from past to present with stunning precision. I was absolutely enthralled."

—Samantha M. Bailey, *USA Today* and #1 national bestselling author of *Woman on the Edge*

"The past and present collide with explosive consequences in this addictive, twisty thriller from an author at the top of her game. *The Secrets of Us* grips from the first page and doesn't let go until the final shocking twist."

—Lisa Gray, bestselling author of *Dark Highway*

The Best of Friends

"A mother's worst nightmare on the page. For those who dare."

—*Kirkus Reviews*

"*The Best of Friends* gripped me from the stunning opening to the emotional, explosive ending. In this moving novel, Berry creates a beautifully crafted study of secrets and grief among a tight-knit group of friends and of how far a mother will go to discover the truth and protect her children."

—Heather Gudenkauf, *New York Times* bestselling author of *The Weight of Silence* and *This Is How I Lied*

"In *The Best of Friends*, Berry starts with a heart-stopping bang—the dreaded middle-of-the-night phone call—and then delivers a dark and gritty tale that unfolds twist by devastating twist. Intense, terrifying, and at times utterly heartbreaking. Absolutely unputdownable."

—Kimberly Belle, international bestselling author of *Dear Wife* and *Stranger in the Lake*

The Perfect Child

"I am a compulsive reader of literary novels . . . but there was one book that kept me reading, the sort of novel I can't put down . . . *The Perfect Child*, by Lucinda Berry. It speaks to the fear of every parent: What if your child was a psychopath? This novel takes it a step further. A couple, desperate for a child, has the chance to adopt a beautiful little girl who, they are told, has been abused. They're told it might take a while for her to learn to behave and trust people. She can be sweet and loving, and in public she is adorable. But in private—well, I won't give away what happens. But needless to say, it's chilling."

—Gina Kolata, *New York Times*

"A mesmerizing, unbearably tense thriller that will have you looking over your shoulder and sleeping with one eye open. This creepy, serpentine tale explores the darkest corners of parenthood and the profoundly unsettling lengths one will go to, to keep a family together—no matter the consequences. Electrifying and atmospheric, this dark gem of a novel is one I couldn't put down."

—Heather Gudenkauf, *New York Times* bestselling author

"A deep, dark, and dangerously addictive read. All-absorbing to the very end!"

—Minka Kent, *Washington Post* bestselling author

HER FIRST LIE

OTHER TITLES BY LUCINDA BERRY

One in Four

If You Tell a Lie

Keep Your Friends Close

Off the Deep End

Under Her Care

The Secrets of Us

The Best of Friends

When She Returned

A Welcome Reunion

The Perfect Child

HER FIRST LIE

A THRILLER

LUCINDA BERRY

Published by Thomas & Mercer, Seattle

www.apub.com

EU product safety contact:
Amazon Media EU S. à r.l.
38, avenue John F. Kennedy, L-1855 Luxembourg
amazonpublishing-gpsr@amazon.com

ISBN-13: 9781662526060 (paperback)
ISBN-13: 9781662526053 (digital)

Cover design by Damon Freeman
Cover image: © Dave Wall / ArcAngel Images; © showcake / Shutterstock

Printed in the United States of America

HER FIRST LIE

PROLOGUE

"I'm not a killer." That's what he told himself underneath his breath as he frantically dug in the dirt. Same as he'd told himself that night. Over and over again to calm his racing heart. Sweat dripped off his forehead. Burned his eyes. Exhaustion seeped into his bones, but he kept working. He had to. He was almost there. He couldn't stop. Not now.

He scraped deeper, choking on the rising scent of rot. His gloves were torn. His palms sore and blistered. Mud smeared down his neck, sweat pooling under his arms. He'd lost track of how long he'd been out here. The sun had gone down hours ago.

The shovel clattered against rock. He swore under his breath and yanked it free. The blanket shifted. A hand slipped out. Pale in the moonlight.

He froze.

The body lay face down in the shallow grave, wrapped in an army blanket. He was slumped like a mannequin. His arms twisted too far back. Jeans half shredded and stuck to his body. A tennis shoe missing.

He'd buried him wrong the first time—not deep enough and too close to the property line. Now the land was flagged for development. A road expansion or a new strip mall. He wasn't sure which. Just something with huge machines, construction workers, and blueprints. They'd already found one body.

They couldn't find this one.

He crouched down and kept digging. Frantic. The cold air turned his breath into fog. His fingers burned where the gloves had torn through. His back screamed as he finally uncovered him.

The boy in the blanket had been dead a long time. Long enough for him to almost forget. Almost. This wasn't part of the original plan. Not even close. The past was supposed to rest in peace.

He worked fast. Grunting and heaving as he adjusted the blanket, pulling it tighter around the boy's legs before dragging him out of the hole. The body hit the ground with a hard thud. The sound wasn't right. Not like it had been the first time, when he was dropping him into the freshly dug hole. Back when it was an accident—when it was self-defense.

But this wasn't about justice anymore. This was about keeping the past quiet. Because if this body came up with the others, people would ask questions. They already were. He'd seen that detective on the news last night. That's why he was here.

He shoveled the dirt back fast and rough. The ground squelched underneath his boots. When it was done, he patted down the soil like it was some kind of apology. Like it would matter. It wouldn't. No one could ever know what he buried here or why.

And that's the way it had to stay.

PART ONE:
The Beginning

ONE

OH MY GOD. That's a baby's head coming out of me.

I gripped the side of the wall to keep from passing out from the pain. Another sharp stabbing contraction throttled me and sent me reeling all over again.

I screamed.

My insides twisted in knots. SO much pressure!!

Severe cramps had kept me on the toilet all night long. Stabbing me from side to side. I thought it was just gas. Guttural sounds exploded from my mouth again. My body pulled me apart. More pressure. A rim of fire twisting and burning, stretching my tender skin until it ripped. Shooting pain.

I can't take this. I'm going to die.

"Aaaah!" Wild, primal noises exploded from deep inside me as I bore down and ejected the baby. I had no control over it. My body just took over. A release of pressure so fast, and something shot out.

Splash.

Into the toilet. An actual baby in the toilet.

I jumped off. The cord was still attached to me and coming out of my insides like I was an alien. Liquid rushed into my mouth. I swallowed hard, forcing it back down.

I grabbed the baby. Scooped it out of the toilet. It was so slimy. And slippery. I almost dropped it back in the bowl. It was all scrunched up. Like an uncooked chicken. Tiny thigh buns.

It wasn't crying. Was it dead? How long had it been inside me?

I flipped it over. Did a quick body scan.

A girl.

It's a girl.

White film covered her tiny face.

I held her with one hand and quickly swiped the goop off, pulling it out of her mouth and nose in thick strings. I flung it on the floor just as she started squalling. Ear-piercing shrieks.

I slowly took a step toward the tub. My legs spread wide, still cradling the baby against my chest. The umbilical cord drooped between us like a jump rope. What do I do with her? Did she really just come out of me? *This can't be happening.*

Another cramp. Quickly followed by another. I keeled over. Gripped my stomach.

I stumbled toward the bathtub. Woozy and dizzy. The baby's cries reverberating off the tiled walls of the bathroom.

"Please be quiet, honey," I begged her like she understood anything. She was only a few minutes old.

My legs jittered. Muscles vibrated.

Everyone was going to hear her if she didn't stop crying. I had no idea how much time has passed. Almost everyone in the dorms went to the Delta Phi party tonight, but there was always a group that came home early. The same ones that hadn't wanted to go in the first place. What if they were all back? Hysteria squeezed my throat.

My T-shirt clung to me, foul with sweat. I held the baby with one arm, wiggled my way out of my shirt, and threw it onto the linoleum floor. My movements made the baby scream even louder. I quickly hugged her back to my chest.

"Shh . . . shh," I whispered to the top of her sticky head. "You have to settle down, sweetie. Please. Someone's going to find us. Please, be quiet. You have to, honey."

Before I knew what was happening, she worked her way to my breast, wrapping her small pink mouth around my nipple. I gasped. A strange pain. Nothing in comparison to what I'd just been through. Slightly sweet.

Suddenly, she was quiet. I breathed a sigh of relief, holding her against me and trying to calm my racing heart and catch my breath. I kept her close to me while she sucked. Was there actually milk in my boobs? Did it come during the last trimester? Was it even my last trimester? She could be early. I glanced down at her again. She was really tiny. Maybe she was premature.

My entire body trembled uncontrollably. Hard and violent like a seizure.

Am I in shock?

I had to sit or I was going to fall down. I gingerly stepped into the tub, doing my best to balance the baby on my boob. Breastfeeding her was keeping her quiet, and I needed her to be quiet.

Because that was the only way to keep her a secret.

TWO

It's been nine days since I gave birth to this baby girl in the bathroom. Nine grueling days without sleep and on high alert. Her shrieks were shrill and constant—as loud as her fresh lungs would go—when she wasn't eating. It was the only time she ever stopped crying, so she was practically attached to me. Nursing sent shooting pains like knives through me every time she latched, leaving my nipples cracked and bleeding from her sandpaper tongue, but I didn't care as long as she was quiet and satisfied. All I wanted for her in this world was to feel happy and loved.

It was so hard to take care of her in my dorm room, though. Harder than anything I'd ever done in my life, which was saying a lot because I haven't had an easy one. I didn't know anything about babies or taking care of them. I was an only child, and I hadn't been around other kids outside of school or my friends. I'd never even changed a diaper. Not to mention the fact that I had no idea I was even pregnant. I was completely unprepared for this and had zero baby things.

But I wouldn't be like my mother, Cerena. She was literally repulsed by the idea that I had even basic needs when I was a kid. Especially when it came to food. Telling her I was hungry might send her into a violent rage. Asking for new shoes had risked getting me banished to the basement for days for being selfish and inconsiderate.

If I decided to keep my baby—and that was a huge *if*—I would be a good mother. A loving mother. An attentive one. Kind. Who smelled nice. Gave you hugs and snuggled you against their chest just because they could. Because they wanted to. That let you brush their hair in front of the mirror instead of swatting you away like you were an annoying bug.

There were so many different things I'd do differently as her parent. I'd let my baby sit on my lap. Tell her I love her. That I'm proud of her. Do everything I could to make her feel secure and safe. Cerena only ever did those motherly things when other people were watching us. She didn't know how to be loving or kind unless there was an audience.

I definitely didn't need to worry about having an audience, because my baby was still a secret. Nobody knew about her. She didn't even have a name. I'd just been calling her *baby* or *sweet girl*. Sometimes *peanut* because she's so tiny. I put her on the bathroom scale, and she only weighed five pounds, two ounces. That's underweight. She could definitely be a preemie. I couldn't wrap my brain around being pregnant for however many months I was pregnant—I had no idea.

How could I not know there was an actual human being growing inside of me, though? How didn't I feel her kick? Or move? Something . . . I still got my period. It was sporadic, but that wasn't anything new. I thought nothing of it. I'd read and heard all those stories before. Watched the episodes on TLC. The women—young girls—who didn't know they were pregnant until they delivered.

I always thought it was the most ridiculous thing I'd ever heard.

Like, no way. Unbelievable. It was impossible to not know you were pregnant. That was what I wholeheartedly believed.

Until it happened to me.

I knew exactly who her daddy was. Not that it mattered or helped with anything, because he was a one-night stand. I didn't even know his last name. That made me sound so bad, but I have the most boring sexual history on the planet, really. Lots of girls in college lied about how many people they'd slept with because they were afraid their body count was too high. There was nothing worse than being labeled easy.

But me? I lied in the other direction. No way I was telling anyone that I was in my twenties and had only been with one person.

That was a ridiculously low number. It made me look like one of those weird homeschooled kids. It wasn't like men and women didn't show me any interest or try to hook up. I'm not repulsive. I've just never really been into it. For a while, I thought that meant I was a lesbian, but I wasn't into women either. I kissed a couple just to see. Maybe I'm whatever it was they called it nowadays? Asexual or something?

Listen to me, sounding like an old lady already, and I've only been a mother for nine days.

Honestly, I didn't even know what happened that night at the bar. I was just trying to prove a point, really. That I could be fun too, and I wasn't a prude.

Percy and Miller had been teasing me again about how I never went out with them after our shifts. They thought it was because I didn't like to drink, but they have weekly allowances deposited into their bank accounts by their parents. They could afford to go out and have a few drinks to wind down after the hospital every night. I, on the other hand, didn't have that luxury. I squeezed in cleaning shifts at the dentist's office whenever I could fit them in my already packed schedule because my scholarship didn't cover my full tuition. Every single penny of my financial aid check was budgeted each month, and it didn't include twelve-dollar drinks on a Tuesday.

Percy and Miller didn't know that, though. Neither did anyone else. But I'd rather they think I was stuck up and conceited than poor. People looked at you differently when you were poor. Like being poor also meant you were dirty. I learned that early on, living with Cerena.

So, I finally went out for drinks and hooked up with some random guy who had bad teeth and pretty brown eyes. They were so proud of me. They still asked about him. But I'd never given him a second thought until now. Should I tell him? I didn't even know how to find him.

I looked down at my baby furiously nursing like it hadn't been forty-five minutes since she'd been in the exact same position. She nursed with her eyes wide open, staring at my chest like she was thinking hard. Babies weren't supposed to do that, were they? What if something was wrong with her? I didn't go out with my friends to drink much because I couldn't afford it, but I kept a couple of cheap bottles of wine in my dorm room at all times. A few nights a week, I sipped on a glass. Sometimes two. I swallowed hard.

What if she had fetal alcohol syndrome? My stomach rolled. I hadn't gotten any prenatal care, and she'd never seen a doctor. I needed to get her checked out soon to make sure she was okay. There could be something seriously wrong with her. Maybe she screamed all the time because she was in pain. She sure sounded like she was, which was why I couldn't just let her cry it out. I was compelled to do something every time she suffered. Constant movement helped, so I bounced her up and down while I paced circles in the room. I probably walked miles.

But if I took her to the doctor, then she'd no longer be a secret. That would mean I'd decided to raise her myself, and I still haven't made that decision. I couldn't even think straight yet. How was I supposed to commit to something so huge when I'm such a sleep-deprived mess?

So many things hinged on my decision. The number one being school. It really weighed heavily on me. I couldn't stay hidden here forever or I was going to screw everything up, and I couldn't let that happen. Not when I was this close to graduating. Only three more semesters to go.

My classes weren't a problem. I could still do most of my work online and submit it to my professors if I needed to, but I couldn't go to my job at the dentist's office that helped pay my tuition or work any of my internship hours at the hospital without leaving the baby. And obviously, I couldn't leave the baby. Not without getting busted. I just wanted to give myself enough time to figure out the right thing to do for my daughter.

So far, I was only skirting by on missing my classes and shifts because I told everyone I caught a bad case of food poisoning and was having serious complications. It was the easiest way to buy myself time to think and catch my breath after such a life-altering moment. I made my symptoms sound terrible. I told my supervisor at the hospital and the one at my job that I'd gotten nasty oozing sores all over my body, especially on my hands. I made it sound like I had leprosy.

But my free sickness pass couldn't last forever. None of this could. I was going to have to do something soon. I just didn't know what. And being all alone in this world meant there was nobody I could ask for help in making such an important decision.

THREE

Tell her. Just open your mouth and tell her the truth. I screamed at myself internally as I sat in the waiting room, anxiously watching the door for the therapist to come get me and bring me back to her office.

But which truth should I share?

The one where I tell her that I have a three-week-old infant in my closet right now? Sleeping in a laundry basket on top of blankets? Who's the reason I'm desperately glancing at my phone every two seconds so I can watch the baby monitor app. Or should I let her know that I have no idea what will happen if my baby starts crying and other students hear her while I'm gone? They'll probably alert the RA, which wasn't going to be all that helpful, seeing as I was the RA. When I first transferred to the University of Illinois, I hated the idea of having a roommate and getting stuck with some random person I might not get along with or who was super annoying. Being a resident adviser got me my own room and bathroom at the far end of the hallway away from everyone else. It also meant I paid less in room and board, which was really important too.

My daughter was still nameless. Technically, she didn't exist. As soon as I spoke her name or told anyone, she became alive. An actual real person. But right now?

I was the only soul on the planet that knew she was alive.

Once I told the therapist—this woman who was already ten minutes late—about the baby, it would change everything. I'd speak my anonymous baby into existence, and I didn't want her to be real. I didn't want her to exist because I didn't want to face the impossible decision of what to do with her. So, I was still pretending she wasn't really here.

The fire station took babies up to thirty days after birth without any questions or legal consequences, according to Illinois's Safe Haven law. I'd looked it up, but I still had so many questions. Like how did they actually know how old the baby was if it was anonymous? Is there a medical way to tell? The no-legal-consequences part worried me too. What if that was just a trick? I didn't want to get in trouble for this. The more time that went on, the more I felt like I might. That scared me.

Plus, abandoning her meant I had no choice in what kind of a home or type of family she got placed with, and if she wasn't with me, I wanted her to be with the best possible family. One that loved her and took care of her properly. What if they put her in foster care while they tried to find her a permanent home? I couldn't stomach the thought. That was the biggest reason keeping me from dropping her at the safe-baby harbor. There was no way I was going to put her into a system that had failed me in such a profound way when I was a kid. I wanted to tell the therapist that, but how was I supposed to tell a stranger something so private?

Maybe I'd just start small. I wasn't good with people. Definitely not intimacy—this already felt way more personal than any first date I'd been on, and I wasn't even in the room yet. I didn't know what to say. How did therapy work? I'd never done this before. Poor people couldn't afford therapy.

Suddenly, the door opened, and a young woman stuck her head out into the waiting room. "Beatrice?" she asked like there was anyone else in the room besides me.

I nodded and stood. "Hi, that's me, but I go by Becky."

"Okay, hi, Becky! I'm Maura. So lovely to meet you," she said, smiling wide. She looked like she'd just jumped out of bed and thrown herself together. Her hair was in a messy bun on top of her head. Clothes disheveled. She motioned for me to follow her into a long hallway, and

I did as she instructed, hurrying so I didn't waste any more of our time. She opened the last door on the left, and I took one more quick glance at the app before nervously stepping inside.

Her office was small and cramped. The opposite of what I'd expected a therapist's office to be. It wasn't at all inviting, loving, or calm. It was devoid of color and whatever else you put in a room to cheer people up and make them less depressed or psychotic. Spill all their secrets to you. Instead, it was like a doctor's office without any of the equipment. There were beige walls. No pictures. There weren't even comfortable chairs to sit in. Just old conference chairs with padded backs and threadbare seats.

Everything about this seemed primitive and basic. Or maybe it wasn't. It could be just like everything else. Poor people got zero bells and whistles, and the only reason I was here was because I couldn't afford to get therapy anywhere else and I needed help.

This clinic was staffed by students that were going through graduate school to earn their doctorate in clinical psychology. They had their master's, but they were still earning their PhDs. They were cheap if you were an undergraduate student. Less than half the cost of what you would pay to see a licensed psychologist off campus. Even with the student discount and the therapist-in-training rate, though, I was still going to have to skip paying my credit cards this month.

At least they were supervised by real psychologists. The camera in the corner let me know everything was being recorded. Something about that made this even more unsettling than what it already was. The consent forms I signed explained that sometimes the videos were used in group supervision.

"So, like, the whole group will watch my session?" I asked, pointing at the camera as I took the seat against the wall. The one pushed up next to the aluminum desk.

She laughed nervously and tucked her curly brown hair behind her ears. "Not the entire session. That'd be too long, and multiple people are trying to present during supervision, so we only watch the important parts or the ones people specifically request feedback on."

This was a teaching university. But the thought of a room full of people watching me made me regret my decision all over again. And now that I was here, I couldn't leave. They had my name. My information. Even worse, my student ID number. What if they thought I was mentally unstable? Could they tell I was harboring a dark and dangerous secret just by looking at me? Read my mind?

Settle down, Becky. They were psychologists, not psychics.

They weren't even real psychologists. They were psychologists in training. Trainees.

My mouth went instantly dry. Face hot. This was a terrible idea. What was I thinking?

That I needed help. That I was in over my head. All of which was true. So just open my mouth. Open my mouth and speak.

Tell her the truth.

I spent all of second grade living out of a bathroom.

Maybe I could start there. See how she responded to those stories. I came here to tell her I needed help deciding what to do about my baby. But I couldn't. Not yet. I had no idea if I could trust her.

Maura cleared her throat. "How are you doing today?"

Her question took me aback. I was expecting so much more. Not just a casual hello.

"Pretty good," I lied, plastering a smile on my face.

I had a baby and didn't know I was pregnant, and now I'm paralyzed with fear about what to do with her. That was the only thought going through my head. I held back from saying it out loud, though, because it wasn't really giving her to another family that I was struggling with. But I couldn't admit the truth. That I actually *really* wanted to keep her, even though she'd been a complete shock and surprise. As insane as that sounded and as big of a wrench as it would throw in my life—part of me desperately wanted her. She was my daughter, and what if I never got another chance to be a mom? Except, I couldn't raise her because I was too terrified that I'd hurt her in some irreparable way, and she was just an innocent baby. I'd come close the other night. That's what put me over the edge and brought me here.

It was three o'clock in the morning, and the baby had finally slept peacefully after having been up most of the night. A rare moment when her face wasn't blotchy and red from crying. One second, I was standing next to the bed watching her sleep, and in the next instant, I was taking a pillow and putting it over her face. She didn't even make a sound. I realized I would barely even have to press down to stop her breathing. I leaned into it. Just a little. To see. She kicked her legs. Let out a small yowl.

I quickly yanked the pillow off her and chucked it at the wall like it was the pillow's fault I'd done what I did. I picked her up and brought her to my chest while she sobbed her eyes out.

"Shh . . . shh . . ." I cooed, rubbing her back and bouncing around in a small circle. She liked to bounce. Constant movement always helped with her crying fits. "It's okay. It's okay. I'm sorry. Oh my god, I'm so sorry, baby." That's all I kept saying, over and over again, until she calmed down.

I hadn't slept the rest of the night or pretty much since. I still didn't even know what happened. Like what in the actual fuck was that? Who does something like that? I was scared to even pick her up now. What if I dropped her? Not because I wanted to. I didn't want to hurt her. I really didn't. I couldn't even let her cry without trying to fix it. But clearly, I had terrifying impulses lurking underneath the surface. That's why I couldn't keep my baby, but at the same time, I couldn't let her go. I had nowhere else to turn, so I looked up student-counseling services on campus, but there was no way we were starting with that story.

"I've been on my own since I was fourteen," I blurted out instead.

(THEN)

"You're going to act like an animal?" Mommy smacks me down to the floor before I can dodge her. "I'll treat you like one." She kicks me down the stairs, sending me crashing to the bottom and landing on the cold cement floor.

I cover my head with my hands. Try to breathe. *Don't look at her. Don't say anything.* I bite the inside of my cheek. *Just be quiet. Don't move.* My ears strain for the sound of her footsteps coming down the stairs behind me. *Please don't let her tie me up to the pipe. Please don't let her tie me up to the pipe.*

"Stay down there all night, you little brat! I can't stand to see your ugly face!" she screams from above me. Then,

Wham!

I jump as the door slams. But she's gone. Thank god. Mommy is gone.

I slowly sit up and rub my eyes in the darkness as they try to adjust. I hate the basement. It's so much worse than the closet or the bathroom. So moldy and wet. Cobwebs hanging from the low ceiling. Makes it even scarier.

I didn't mean to make Mommy mad at teacher conferences tonight. I just said Miss Emily's dress looked pretty. And it did. Bright red, with those white flowers stamped all over it. So, I just blurted out the compliment without thinking. I know better than that, though. But it's not like I didn't tell Mommy she was pretty. I did. All the way there in the car, I said it. How she was going to be the most beautiful mommy in the whole school tonight. Over and over again. At least ten times, but it didn't matter. I blew it at school.

Mommy doesn't like anybody else to be pretty. Only her.

Pew. It stinks down here.

Yuck.

She's going to feed me the dog food again. I just know it. I hope she gives me the Kibbles 'n Bits kind this time. That one's not so bad. I just pretend I'm chewing rock pellets that give me superpowers. Lately, she's been giving me the nasty soft kind, though.

I always try not to eat it, but she leaves me down here for so long that the hunger always wins. You can starve to death if you go without food for too long, and I don't want to starve to death. Good thing I have a method. I plug my nose and pour the food into my throat straight from the bowl. Getting as much down as possible in one swoop. I do math then, so I don't gag and throw it back up.

Two plus two equals four.

Four plus four equals eight.

Eight plus eight equals sixteen.

I keep going. Fast as I can. I'm not super good at math, so sometimes I get too far and don't know how to solve the equation anymore. All the numbers get jumbled. Then I have to start over. But that's okay. As long as I keep it down.

Mommy doesn't like other girls, but she really hates Miss Emily. I love her, though. She smells so wonderful and clean. She's from Papua New Guinea—a place I'd never heard of before—and she laughed when I asked her if they raised guinea pigs there. She has the best laugh and smile. She's so bright. I just want to crawl up on her lap and stay there forever.

I don't know what Miss Emily ever did to Mommy, but Mommy can't stand Miss Emily. Mommy always smiles real nicely at her, though. Bats her eyelashes too. Just like a butterfly.

She had her nice-mommy voice turned on tonight when she was talking to all the other parents and teachers. Complimenting them. Talking about recipes and reading books. But she's just tricking them. Mommy doesn't like cooking, and she only read a book that one time when she was making a video to send to her friends. That's the thing about Mommy, though. She always makes people think she likes them and finds a way to make them feel good about themselves no matter what. She's really good at it. It's one of her special tricks.

She has so many special tricks. I'm jealous.

Her other one is changing into different mommies. There's good mommy. Bad mommy. Inside mommy and outside mommy. Angry mommy. Happy mommy. She does it so fast too. She'll be good mommy one second, all happy and bubbly, talking in a singsong voice. And then—*bam!*—she's angry mommy, and you have to run and hide as fast as you can. Except if she's already seen you. Then you've got to freeze and turn into a statue.

I'm so good at the statue game. Almost as good as Mommy is at switching.

It's because she's a famous actress. I've never seen her on TV, but she's a huge celebrity, and I'm going to be just like her someday. She likes it when I tell her that.

That, and how pretty she is. There's nothing Mommy likes better than when you tell her she's pretty. Her whole body lights up like you plugged her into a light socket and turned on the switch. She gets so happy. I love making Mommy happy, so I make sure to tell her at least twenty times a day how beautiful she is.

I get up from the cement and walk over to the stack of boxes laid flat on the floor in the corner. My marks from where I played tic-tac-toe last time are still there. At least I'm not tied up to the pole with that stupid bike lock. That hurts my butt bone so much. This is better, even if I have to eat the dog food. All I have to do is wait for Mommy to switch. For good mommy to come back and let me out of here. Hopefully, it's not too long this time.

HIM

(NOW)

The file was already open on his desk when Detective Vega stepped into the office. His partner, Detective Santos, sat with one leg slung over the side of her desk, flipping through a stack of photocopied documents like they were old love letters.

"They pulled a body out of a property they're developing in Waldorf," she said without looking up. "You want an unusual one?"

Vega dropped his keys into his desk drawer and sank into his chair. "How weird?"

"An old foster home. The land was flagged for commercial development, and they started digging last week. The crews hit something two days ago. They found partial human remains. Construction is totally halted. CSU confirmed that it's human. Likely an adult male."

Vega exhaled. "So, maybe not weird yet."

Santos smirked. "Give it a minute."

She slid the folder across the desk. He grabbed the file and opened it immediately. There were photos piled on top of the reports. Grainy ones of a sagging white trailer half swallowed by overgrown weeds. An old, dilapidated farmhouse. Field notes were scribbled in blue ink. There was one name at the top of the report: Earl Miller.

"Is he the owner of the property?" Vega asked, pointing at the name.

Santos shook her head. "He used to be, but not anymore. He's a former foster parent. Licensed through the state from '96 to 2009, along with his wife, Helen. They took in at least two dozen kids over the years. Only teen placements, though. They wouldn't take any young kids, and they usually only accepted the hard cases. You know the ones—lots of trauma, a history of running away and drugs, prone to fighting."

Santos had practically described herself. That's why her heart was as big as his was for the underserved and underrepresented. It was also one of the reasons why they worked so well together.

"And?" he asked, because there was obviously more to the story or she wouldn't be making such a big deal out of the case.

"A lot of those kids went missing." She raised her eyebrow at him.

Vega matched her expression. "Define missing."

Santos flipped to the next page and pointed at the list. "Three were classified as runaways. One suicide. Several others with unsubstantiated abuse reports. There are complaints of night visits and kids locked in the attic. Medical neglect. CPS went out there numerous times, but nothing ever stuck. It's all there in the files." She tapped the paper. "CPS closed the case out in '09 when Miller stopped renewing his license. He vanished after that."

He scanned the list of foster kids. None of the names meant anything to him. Yet. "How long's the body been in the ground?"

"Too early to tell. CSU says at least five years. Maybe more. The soil was disturbed before, which makes dating harder. We'll know more in a few days."

Vega tapped the edge of the file. "You think it's Miller?"

"Could be." Santos shrugged. "It could also be one of the older foster kids."

He leaned back in his chair, letting the news settle.

"All right," he said finally. "I'm in. I want full workups on everyone who lived there. Case files, placement records, school reports, and incident logs. If there are gaps, I want to know why."

Santos smiled and tossed her hair back over her shoulders. "Already working on it, boss." She stood and grabbed her jacket from the back of her chair. "You want to go out to the property with me later?"

Vega looked out the office window behind her. Breezy and overcast. The kind of gray that made you depressed after a few days without sun. "Not yet," he said. "Let's see what they find first."

FOUR

I hurried out of the counseling-services building and down the stairs. My face flaming hot. Cheeks red. What just happened? What was all that? Why did I say that?

Immediately confessing to being a homeless teenager wasn't what I'd intended to say, but it's what came out in the moment. I totally panicked.

I was horrified by all the things I'd just told a complete stranger, but also strangely exhilarated. I NEVER talked about my life with anyone. There was stuff I wouldn't even acknowledge to myself. How does that saying go?

I didn't heal—I just kept going?

That was me.

But what just happened in there?

I didn't know, but I just spent fifty-nine minutes talking about my childhood. More minutes than the zero minutes I'd spent talking about it for my entire life.

Cerena has always been off limits, even in my own mind. I just didn't go there. Ever. Partly because it was so painful, but also because I'd been militantly trained to never talk about Cerena or what it was like for us at home. At least not outside of the script. I could never discuss anything that might reveal the real Cerena. The one behind closed doors.

I glanced down at the baby monitor app on my phone as I hurried across the street by the library. Counseling services was on the total opposite side of campus from the dorms. The baby was still asleep. Curled into the same position she'd been in when I left the apartment. I breathed a sigh of relief. Thank god. Still. I picked up the pace.

I shook my head at myself. I hadn't said a single thing about the real problem. The current one happening in my life. But it just felt so good to talk openly about Cerena. Like slicing open a wound and finally being able to let it drain. I already felt some of the fucked-up-and-flawed energy leaving my body. It didn't matter that Maura's office didn't look like a therapy room—something about being there automatically made me start talking like they'd pumped truth serum into the room.

"Since you were fourteen, huh?" Maura had commented with the most impassive and unreadable face after I blurted out that I'd been living alone since then.

Her next question might've been the most therapist-like response she could've made. It must be the first thing they taught you in therapy school.

"Do you want to tell me more about that?" she'd asked, leaning forward in her chair.

"Cerena—my mother—sorry, I haven't called her that in a very long time—is a monster." Everything inside me had flinched as soon as I said it out loud. Instinctually bracing for punishment. I'd never told anyone how awful she was. Not even all those social services people that kept digging around and asking me all those questions. Cerena would've killed me.

"A monster? That's a very strong word choice to describe someone," Maura said, shifting in her seat and trying to keep a blank expression.

"It's true. She likes to hurt people on purpose. There's nothing she likes better or that brings her more joy than watching other people suffer. Well, except winning. She loves to win too. Almost as much as she likes hurting people."

"What about your father? Was or is he in the picture?" she asked next, because that's what you do in therapy—talk about your childhood. All the ways your terrible parents messed you up for life. Everybody knew that. Because why else would I be here? Why else would I be keeping a baby in a laundry basket in my closet right now?

"I don't know who my dad is," I told her. "Never met him, and Cerena refused to tell me anything about him no matter how many times I asked her. For some reason she gave me his last name, even though he wasn't even on my birth certificate. In the space for father, it just said *unknown*. It was always just me and her. Cerena hated her own family. Supposedly, her family was really wealthy and privileged. They kicked her out when they found out she was pregnant with me, but see, that's the thing about Cerena. You can never trust what she says. There's no way to know if it's the truth. She's a liar. Always has been."

"That must be so hard. Are the two of you in contact now?"

"No, I haven't spoken to her since I was seventeen. I don't even know where she lives. Or if she's even alive. She might be dead for all I know." Or cared. But I didn't say that part out loud.

If Cerena was alive, she was most certainly at work on her next conquest because Cerena was a Venus flytrap for married men. And not just any kind of married men—the ones with families. The more children, the better.

When I was young, I thought she was out shopping for a husband when she'd disappear for days a time. Trying to find me a new daddy. Someone who could take care of us.

And that was the thing.

She could've easily had any of the rich men that she lured into her snare. She loved reeling them in. The thrill of the chase. How they threw themselves at her. All the expensive gifts and lavish weekend trips.

The way they love bombed her at the beginning. She had that effect on people. Men. Women. It never mattered. Her energy was magnetic when she turned it on you. Everything quickly disappeared in the background behind you. All else fell away under the beauty of her spell. Cue the music. End of scene. Like some kind of messed-up fairy tale. They so easily fell under her magic.

I was seven when I figured out that it was all a game for her. She lured them in only to let them go with delight. She wanted to steal them from their wives, but she didn't want to actually keep them.

Everybody called Cerena boy crazy, but that couldn't be further from the truth. She didn't care anything about any of the men she dated. Not one. She cared about getting them to leave their wives. That was the chase. Sure, that's what most mistresses wanted, wasn't it? Their man to own up to his promises and leave his wife for them. Not my mother. Oh no. Because the moment they left their wives and families?

That was the moment she was no longer interested in them. It went the same way every single time. She never really wanted them to leave their wives. That was the game. Revenge against the wives and traditional marriage. To prove men were liars and couldn't be trusted no matter what. Even after they'd achieved the American dream. Nothing made her happier than completely ghosting the men she'd enticed to leave their wives and families to be with her. She loved the discard almost as much as the chase.

"Don't you feel bad?" I asked her once when I was first starting to get brave. That's what happened when I turned twelve. I'm not sure what changed, but I just stopped being afraid of her and started plotting ways to get out.

"Bad?" She'd thrown her head back, flipping her long blond hair over her shoulders. "They're cheating on their wives."

"Because you make them think you love them. You lead them on," I cried, jumping up and down.

"Oh honey." She'd pat my head like a puppy, and I wanted to bite her hand off. "Someday you'll understand," she said in her patronizing voice, like she was feeling sorry for me.

She was wrong. I'll never understand her viciousness or her cruelty.

I'd told Maura all about that too. And nothing bad happened. I couldn't believe it. I was still shaking. Even though I'd lived free of Cerena's clutches for years, I still felt like she could hurt me. Punish me the way she used to. The way she swore she'd do if I ever told.

"Your mother sounds so horrible," Maura said as we were finishing up. I couldn't believe how fast the session had gone.

"You wouldn't think that if you met Cerena, though. Nobody did. If you met her, you'd think she was absolutely wonderful. She was so charming and beautiful—the celebrity kind of pretty. But you could only admire her from a distance, though, because she was like an exotic pet. If you got too close, she might attack, and unless you made her center stage, you were worthless to her. She paraded me in public when it served a purpose, but the moment people weren't around, the performance stopped."

Me and Cerena always lived two lives. The one in public where we were on stage performing as best friends and the one behind closed doors where she hated me. It always felt like we were actors when we were around people, but I didn't mind, though, because I loved our characters.

"We're just like the *Gilmore Girls*," she always said. That was our story. Absolute besties. Just like Rory and Lorelai Gilmore. Cerena was the single mother who did everything for her daughter. That's who we were to people in the outside world.

Cerena was always so proud when I remembered my lines. Ad-libbing as necessary. Dropping jokes at the right time. Not missing a step when she changed things up or forgot her lines. She would've been furious with me today, but I didn't care.

My entire life I'd been a shape-shifter. I didn't have any other choice if I wanted to survive. I've never been free to be the person I was on the inside. It wasn't safe. It was one of the reasons I preferred being by myself—I didn't have to wear a mask. But see, that was the problem. Why people's love never reached me. Because they were just loving the character I presented to them. The one on the outside.

But today?

I was just me. Who I really was on the inside. And I told the truth. I might not have figured out what I was going to do about my baby, but for the first time ever, I'd bled some of Cerena's toxicity out of me, and it felt amazing. I didn't know if I was going to keep my baby, but I was definitely going to keep my therapist.

FIVE

I raced across campus. I was drowning trying to take care of this baby and keep up with school at the same time. I had McDonald's ketchup packets mixed with water for dinner last night. That's how broke I am.

The baby monitor app went off during my physics class just seconds ago. As soon as the professor turned around to write on the board, I grabbed my stuff and bolted as fast as I could. The app was on mute, but she was obviously screaming at the top of her lungs. Most babies woke up rested and happy no matter how upset they were before going down for their nap. But not mine. She woke up crying as loud as she was when she was falling asleep.

I picked up the pace, practically sprinting in my baggy sweats and fake UGG slippers. I looked ridiculous, but I had to get there before anyone heard her and figured out that I'd kept a baby hidden in the dorms for over a month now. I couldn't believe it'd been that long already. How was that possible? I kept my head down as I reached my housing row. I didn't want anyone to see me in case they tried to talk to me and ended up walking with me to my apartment.

Somehow, I'd managed to keep my daughter a secret. I still hadn't made any decisions other than that I had to go back to school or I was going to fall so far behind I'd never get caught up. I'd devised a brilliant plan and had been leaving her alone in my room just like I had when

I went to therapy. So far, it'd been working. She'd only woken up once before this. The baby monitor app alerted me immediately. Last time, I'd gotten home before anyone heard her. Hopefully, it'd go the same way today.

I hurried around to the back of the building. I was the only one with keys to the back door, so it was super easy for me to sneak in and out undetected. That's how I lived these days. Like a strange fugitive.

I could hear her crying from the stairwell, even though she was in the closet. That's where I always left her. I'd padded all four walls with egg crates and blankets. I kept music going loud in there and set a white noise machine right outside the door to muffle the sound even more.

And then I'd done the unthinkable—given her something to help her sleep. It was only Tylenol. Not an actual drug. Technically, you weren't supposed to even do that, but they gave it to babies in the ER if they had an infection. They just monitor them closely. And if they felt it was safe enough to give it, then it couldn't be all that bad. The number one side effect was excessive sleepiness. Which is exactly what I wanted. That's why I started using it in the first place. It gave me a four-hour window of time to get things done.

How had I let things spiral like this? I didn't even recognize myself anymore. I shoved the thoughts down and eyed my surroundings.

The hallway was empty, but I waited to make sure nobody was coming before opening my apartment door. I barely cracked it, doing my best to contain the crying sounds, before quickly sliding through and dashing inside. I locked the dead bolt behind me and raced through the living room to the hallway closet. I flung open the door.

The baby lay in the laundry basket, covered in spit-up. I quickly leaned over and scooped her up as she wailed. Her onesie was crusted to her body with sour milk.

"Shh, shh, it's okay, sweetie. I'm here now," I cooed, trying to hold her against me, but she pushed my hands off. She didn't want to cuddle or be comforted. She just wanted my boob. There was no way she'd wait to eat until after I cleaned her up, so I lifted my shirt and brought her to my chest.

I rubbed the top of her head while she nursed. Her hair was silky soft. It was like petting a kitten. Poor thing obviously had some type of acid reflux going on. Everything I'd read online said you should switch them from breastfeeding to a special formula for babies with acid reflux. I was all for it until I saw how much it cost. There was no way I could afford formula. Not at that price. I had to do something, though. I couldn't keep living this way.

It wasn't lost on me that I was repeating the exact same cycles I'd spent my entire life determined to break. Cerena used to lock me in the closet to punish me. She'd turn off all the lights and leave me in there. Sometimes for hours. Other times for days. I wasn't doing this to punish my daughter, though. This was out of necessity, but still . . . right now, staring at her like this, it didn't make me feel any better.

After she was finished, I changed baby girl's diaper for what felt like the millionth time, because you couldn't leave her wet. Oh no. The millisecond that urine touched her skin, she screamed like you were tearing her arms off. How had nobody heard her, and why did babies go to the bathroom so much? Or was it just her? I had no idea what was considered normal for an infant and was constantly worrying that something was wrong with her. Looking things up only scared me more. I just wanted her to be okay.

I gazed down at her, and she locked eyes with me. Big blue eyes gazing back at me. Tiny fists waving in the air. Her skin was pink and perfect. I smiled at her, and she kicked her legs, like she was excited to see me now that she was full. Her little mouth forming an O as she cooed.

Just like that, I whispered her name—the one I never told anyone. I hadn't planned to name her. It'd make me too attached. But it was too late.

In that moment, she was mine. And I was hers.

"Janie," I whispered it again, louder this time.

All the motherly love I'd kept at bay immediately flooded me, along with the acceptance and recognition that we belonged together. It's why I fought so hard to take care of her. Why I couldn't tolerate her being in pain. The way it physically hurt my body when she cried, and I was driven by an unrelenting compulsion to make it stop. How she looked at me like she recognized me too. As if she already knew me. And she did. Probably better than anyone else. She'd shared my body for nine months.

I picked her up and carried her into the bathroom, turning on the tub faucet. My body felt the relief at having finally made the decision. It'd taken me so long to get here, but what did I expect?

I'd gone from having absolutely no idea that I was pregnant to being a mother within minutes. Seconds, actually. The moment I felt her head coming out of my body. I'd never forget that feeling or the realization. Up until then, I really thought I was having the worst constipation of my life. The whole time I was worried about getting hemorrhoids from pushing so hard or rupturing something on my insides, because it felt like I was being stabbed. Like the hardened stool was compacted shards of glass. I definitely didn't think I was pushing out a baby.

So, I'd barely had time to adjust to the idea of it, let alone the reality of it. And now that I had? I wanted to be her mother. To be the one who raised her right. Who saw her take her first steps and learn how to talk. I wanted to be there for every other milestone along the way too. I didn't want to miss a second of her life.

The only thing I'd ever wanted to do was escape the childhood hell I grew up in. That'd been my primary focus always. To create a different life for myself. I'd never stopped to consider whether I wanted someone else to be a part of it, especially not a child. This didn't fit with anything I had going on in my life, but lots of people found a way to be students and parents at the same time. I could do this. I was the queen of forging my own path, and I would be *such* a better mother than Cerena.

(THEN)

Mommy loves starving me. Probably better than anything else. Especially since she can't make me cry anymore. Nope. No more crying like a baby. Those days are gone. I don't care if she hits me. Bites me. Spanks me. Shoves my head into the toilet and tries to drown me again. I won't cry. That's the point of all her games—knowing she hurt me. As soon as I figured that out, I stopped crying when she hit me. I don't even flinch anymore when the belt cuts into my skin. I just bite the inside of my cheek whenever I want to scream. Sometimes I bite so hard that it bleeds. But I don't care as long as Mommy doesn't know she hurt me.

You can touch my body, but you can't hurt me. I'm not the me inside the body. The day I learned I could flip a switch and leave? Just step outside of myself like I was taking off a wet swimming suit? That was the day of the real miracle. Mommy couldn't stand it when I stopped crying—it made her furious—so she had to find other ways to hurt me.

Starving me is one of them. The only time she ever buys groceries or does anything in the kitchen is when I'm not allowed to eat. She cooks elaborate meals then. The entire apartment fills with the smell of freshly cooked meals. The way only a good home-cooked meal could make a place smell. The way my friends' houses smelled. The way I'd imagined a real home would.

After she's done, she always forces me to join her at the table while she eats. Making each bite as dramatic as possible. Never giving me one.

Tonight was no different.

"This is *so* good, Becky," she said, then took another bite of the chicken tacos she just made.

My mouth watered. I practically drooled. You can't play uninterested. Not when you're starving like me. It physically hurt not to eat. Nine days without food. She took away school too. My safe place. That's what she does sometimes when she's really angry. Not because of how much I love it there, even though I do, but because they feed me at school.

All this because I said hello to Mrs. Carter at the grocery store. Last time I didn't say hi to one of the women from church, Mommy slapped me in the car for being rude and disrespectful. That's why I'd made sure to do it this time. I still don't know why she was so furious. She won't tell me, and she acts like I should already know.

"I'm sorry for disrespecting you," I said again tonight, like I'd been apologizing for the last three nights. That's what she called it when she raged at me the night it happened. The welts on the backs of my thighs still haven't healed. They've moved into the purple-and-brown stage. A few more days and they should be yellow.

"How could you disrespect me like that, you ungrateful little bitch!" she screamed at me that night, all red faced and bugged-out eyes. She stormed through the apartment slamming drawers and throwing things against the wall after we got home from the store.

"I'm sorry, Mommy. I'm sorry," I cried, cowering in the living room. That's what I always said during her rage storms. You didn't ask questions. Didn't justify. You just said sorry. *Sorry, Mommy.* But sometimes that didn't work. Mommy still stayed mad.

This was one of those times.

She locks the cupboards and the refrigerator at night, making sure I don't sneak down there to eat while she's asleep. I used to do that until she caught me. She pulled me outside in the snow without a coat or socks on, and made me stand there in it for hours. I thought that was the end of my life for sure. The big toe on my right foot still has no feeling at the tip. Pretty sure the nerves are permanently fried.

Why is Mommy still so mad?

I act like she needs reasons. Sometimes she punishes me for fun. Just because she can, and once she starts hurting me—she can't stop. Those times are almost worse than when she thinks I've done something bad.

Last night I ate the toothpaste. As much as I could eat without her noticing. I just needed something to fill the aching hole in my gut. Feels like worms are eating my insides. I don't want to have to eat paper again. That hurts so much coming back out.

She licked her lips and set the fork down on her plate. "Delicious. I really am an amazing cook." She smiled like she was so pleased with herself. Clearing enjoying my agony.

I swallowed my glare. Forced my face to wear no expression. "Would you like me to do your dishes?" I asked. Tone flat. Eyes down.

"Oh certainly, darling. Why don't you?" she said in some weird accent, like she's an aristocrat. For the longest time when I was little, I believed her stories about being an actress. Now I know those were all lies too. She picked up her napkin and brought it to her nose, doing a long, thick blow of snot into it and wiping across her nose multiple times after she finished. She crumpled the napkin and put it on the plate. An evil glint in her eye as she moved the nasty tissue around on the plate, making sure I'd be too grossed out to touch any of the leftovers on it. She's always one step ahead of me.

I squeezed my fists together. I wanted to grab the fork and stab it into her eyes.

Evil mommy.

She doesn't even try to be good mommy anymore.

And I hate her.

But I make my eyes dead inside. Holding on to the one piece of power I have.

SIX

I sat in my usual seat, waiting on Maura. If our sessions were dates, we've been on seven. That was a long time to get to know someone. Which was weird. She knew all these things—intimate things—about me, and I knew absolutely nothing about her. Except that she was always late.

Just like today.

Thankfully, I didn't mind, because it gave me a chance to gather my thoughts and settle down from the race across campus, and maximize every second away from Janie. I assumed things would get easier once I accepted that I was raising her and officially transitioned into motherhood, but things have only gotten worse instead of better. I was even more worried and paranoid than I had been before, now that I was truly responsible for her.

I'm so afraid something awful is going to happen to her. These totally irrational fears come over me, like the onesie zipper is going to get caught on her skin and cut her throat or the nipple of the pacifier is going to pop off in her mouth and she'll suffocate on it. Other weird things keep happening too. I've started hearing Janie cry, even when she's not. That's been the strangest experience so far. I'll hear her crying and rush to check the app or check on her wherever she is in the apartment. Only to find her sound asleep. It's not good. I can barely sleep because of the phantom crying, and I feel like I have to stay awake to keep her alive.

It was only a matter of time before I failed out of school, and I couldn't let that happen. Not after I'd worked so hard. From the moment I left Cerena's house, I swore two things:

1. Never to go home again.
2. Never to be like her.

Never being like her meant that I needed to go to school and get a good education.

What was I going to do if I got kicked out of school? I would lose all my scholarship money. Everything I'd worked so hard for. I had to become a doctor. I didn't care if it was a doctor that looked at feet. Doctors were never out of jobs, and they were rich. It didn't matter what kind of medicine they practiced. I'd take whatever I could get as long as I had an MD behind my name.

Maura popped her head into the room, interrupting my spiral. "Hi! I'm so sorry I'm late. Are you ready?"

Such a weird question, since I was on time, but I just smiled back at her and headed into the hallway behind her. We meet in the same room every session. That's one thing I liked about coming here—the predictability and routine of it all. I also liked *her*, surprisingly. She was so easy to talk to, and I'd never had anyone in my life that was easy to talk to before.

It felt nice.

Our therapy sessions made me feel better, and I kept hoping I'd work up the courage to tell her that I needed help. That I was in way over my head, taking care of Janie. All my fears about being her mother. My terrorizing thoughts. The concerns I still had about her development.

"How are you today? You look a bit stressed," Maura said, jumping in immediately as soon as we took our respective seats. We never switched. Both of us creatures of habit.

"I failed my biochemistry class. I've never failed a class in my life," I said. *I also don't have enough money to buy groceries because I'm spending all of my money on diapers. I can't leave my house for more than a few hours because I've got a baby asleep in my closet.* That's what I wanted to add, but didn't. I never did. Even though every single time I was on my way here, I told myself that I was going to tell her about Janie.

"That must feel like a big disappointment, but one poor grade shouldn't drag down your entire GPA. Was it a particularly hard class?" she asked, switching to her neutral therapist voice.

"Not really. I just have a lot going on," I said.

"How do you feel about all this?" she asked.

"I feel overwhelmed with all of my responsibilities . . . and, um . . . ashamed that I got a bad grade and that I'm not keeping up with the class. Working hard is super important to me, and I'm not someone that gets bad grades." I rubbed my hands against my jeans and let out a long, slow breath. "But mostly I just feel scared."

"Scared of what?" she asked, with her most concerned face.

"That despite everything I've done and how hard I've worked, I'm still going to end up like my mother."

There. I'd finally said it out loud. My biggest fear.

"Do you think you're like your mother?" Maura volleyed the question back at me, another one of her favorite tactics.

"I hope not . . . I try really hard not to be. Cerena completely rejected society. Her every move was a deliberate fuck-you to the world, tracing all the way back to her mother—my grandmother—Lillian. You could feel Cerena's hatred toward her even in the way she said her name. She lived and breathed to show her parents how much she hated their world. Despised its existence and rules. But me?" I shrugged and gave her an apologetic look. "I don't think the regular world is all that bad. Sure, there's rules, and some of them I don't like very much either. But one thing I know? I don't want to live anything like she did."

"And how did she live? Outside of the men she was dating?" We'd beat that subject to death already.

"She made us live like total savages. In and out of cheap hotels and Section 8 housing. Sometimes we were homeless, living in cars. Once we lived at Balboa Park and slept in the bathroom there for almost nine months. She loved a good trailer court, though. Those were her favorite places to stay," I said, instantly remembering some of the shitholes we'd lived in. "But I always wanted a nice house growing up. One with electricity and hot water. Shoot. I would've settled for a full refrigerator. Not to have to sneak into the cupboards and eat flour by the spoonful just to fill up my stomach. I'd have given anything not to starve."

"That must've been so hard," Maura said.

I nodded my head in agreement. "There were so many awful parts, and I hated it. I never had my own clothes. I was always in hand-me-downs, even though Cerena's clothes were brand new and usually designer. Do you know what it's like to live your whole life smelling like other people?" A lump of emotions lodged in my throat. Frozen tears. That's what Maura called the experience. She said one day, when I trusted her enough, I'd let them go, but I guess I still didn't trust her enough yet, because just like that, I swallowed them down and they were gone. Back to my logical brain. That was one way I was different from Cerena.

I reasoned with logic. Not emotion.

"The worst part was the way she could turn on the charm and her ambition whenever she needed to. I saw her do it so many times. She was fully capable of being successful. She could do anything if she wanted to. She scammed her way into so many different private schools for me. Worked for weeks at a time if she had a good reason. Mostly when she needed a new outfit or if she was trying to go on a trip. She had no problem landing jobs then. I'd watched her transform into the belle of the ball at parties a million times at all those private school functions we attended. That's when her real wealth came out. She carried herself like she had money. Practically oozed it the way only truly rich people can do, so I know that's how she grew up."

"Did she ever talk about her childhood?" Maura's eyebrows furrowed the way they did when she was really interested and listening hard.

I shrugged. "Every now and then. She'd talk about growing up in their huge house and the full staff that waited on her. Their beautiful gardens. The elaborate parties her parents threw. Apparently, her favorite part of her childhood was the huge dollhouse she had in her bedroom. She took the girl doll with her when she got kicked out. She loved telling me the story of how she'd taken her doll and left the parent dolls sitting in the chairs at the kitchen table with their heads pulled off." I sighed. "It just wasn't fair, you know? She rejected that lifestyle, but I'd never been given that choice. We could've lived so differently."

Go to work! That's what I'd wanted to scream at Cerena so many times over the years. *Get a goddamn job!*

Every time the shutoff notices started showing up in the mail. When the three-day eviction warnings were posted on the front door.

She only went to work when it served her. That's the only reason she ever did anything. She never went to work so that I could get new tennis shoes for PE. Or sheets for my bed, so I didn't have to sleep on the itchy mattress and wake up with hives every morning. Money to the school so that I could go on the field trip and not have to sit in the library all day, missing out and feeling embarrassed. Food. The list of things we needed was endless.

While she rocked all the latest styles, I was stuck in other people's leftovers. In fifth grade, I only had one outfit for the entire year. I'd never been so humiliated. Of course it didn't take the other kids long to notice. I skipped most of my fifth-grade year because I couldn't stand it. Even if they weren't teasing me, I still burned with embarrassment.

Being a good mother meant putting your child's needs above your own. You had to take care of the family that you'd created, no matter what. Cerena couldn't do that for me, but I could do that for my daughter.

I cleared my throat and looked Maura straight in the eye. "There's something I've been meaning to tell you . . ."

HIM

(NOW)

The CPS records division was tucked away in the basement of the county building on Main Street. The files were behind a broken vending machine and two locked doors. The clerk at the front desk didn't bother to look up as Vega tapped on the glass.

"My partner submitted the file request yesterday," he said, in case she wasn't the one Santos had spoken with. "Foster license: Earl Miller. Waldorf County. Cases closed between 2005 and 2009."

The clerk leaned forward and squinted at her computer monitor. She tapped the keys with deliberate slowness. "I see the request, but most of that's still on paper." She raised her eyes at Vega.

He shrugged. It wasn't his fault that no one had entered the case into the computer. "We've got to do it."

The clerk rolled her eyes and disappeared behind the doors to retrieve the records. Vega caught up with emails until she emerged from the back room carrying two cardboard boxes stacked shoulder high. She dropped them onto the counter. Dust scattered.

"No sign-outs," she said. "You scan what you need."

He nodded in agreement, grabbing the boxes and bringing them into a conference room down the hallway. The one with the huge printer. By noon, he was on his third cup of bad coffee and his third CPS incident report. All of it was disturbing:

INTAKE REPORT ID: IA-0589204-2021
DATE/TIME OF INTAKE: 06/14/2005—4:36 PM
CHILD NAME: Kristen Mulvaney
INTAKE SPECIALIST: Olga Tanon

Allegation: *Child seen with bruising on upper arms and legs. Round fingertip bruises on left side. Child currently in foster placement.*
Reporter: *School nurse*
Outcome: *Unsubstantiated. Child refused to confirm. Case closed. (see attached summary)*

INTAKE REPORT ID: IA-0782201-2079
DATE/TIME OF INTAKE: 03/24/2006—1:22 PM
CHILD NAME: Unknown
INTAKE SPECIALIST: Betsy Raver

Allegation: *Child being locked in basement for extended punishment. Child claims was a foster child in Miller home for three months. Refused to give name. Says others undergo similar abuse.*
Reporter: *Anonymous hotline*
Outcome: *Home visit completed. No visible signs of abuse on any of the children in the home. Children present were interviewed and denied mistreatment. (see attached summary)*

INTAKE REPORT ID: IA-0872202-2043
DATE/TIME OF INTAKE: 1/04/2005—10:15 AM

CHILD NAME: Ebony Walters
INTAKE SPECIALIST: Thomas Gunderson

Allegation: *Sexual abuse during overnight hours.*
Reporter: *Former foster sibling (aged out). Sister has frequent visits with child and claims child reported Earl Miller was sexually abusing her.*
Outcome: *Referral dismissed. No current placement in home. (see attached summary)*

Each report followed the same pattern. There was a complaint followed by a brief investigation. There was no action taken. Not once. Never even a follow-up. There were so many red flags. But that's not what chilled Vega the most. It was all the gaps and missing pieces.

The names on old placement logs that disappeared from school records without any explanation. Kids marked as "runaway" who had no prior behavioral history. Ones who'd never been in trouble before. There were transfers that were never logged in the central system. Vega wasn't sure if it was the Miller house or the system that had swallowed them whole, but there was no mistaking that something had.

All the children interviewed refused to confirm any of the abuse allegations. But that wasn't unusual. Children rarely confirmed abuse—they almost always denied it. That's what happened when your very survival was dependent on the people hurting you.

There were so many names to follow up on, but Vega was committed and continued to go down the list one by one. Trying to determine how the children had fared once they reached adulthood, since all of them were adults by now. Most of the searches led nowhere. There were a few promising dead ends. A handful of former residents were in prison, but that wasn't unusual. Being locked up as a teenager was a huge risk factor for being locked up as an adult. There were two confirmed suicides.

He wanted to get through all the files today, but that wasn't going to be possible if he wanted to make it home in time for dinner. There were just too many kids and incident reports. He was going to have to come back tomorrow. Then, he found Charity Greene, and she stopped him in his tracks because she was still local. He quickly texted his husband that he'd be late for dinner before diving headfirst into all her reports.

She was one of those foster care kids with a huge file. She'd been in the system since she was six years old up until she aged out—a true lifer. She was the daughter of two parents with intellectual disabilities and schizophrenia. They'd gotten pregnant while living in a group home together. At first, they'd tried to raise Charity, but there were too many limitations, and after getting reported to social services numerous times by multiple sources, Charity was permanently removed. All their parental rights terminated.

Charity bounced in and out of foster care until being placed in the Miller home in 2007 when she was thirteen. There was a very brief note that she'd been removed nine months later under emotional-disturbance codes. She was placed in a group home and stayed there until she was eighteen. No further placements. No current record. But there was a forwarding address from a therapist's referral. It was local and still active.

He quickly tapped out the number.

SEVEN

My tiny studio was a mess. The walls were cracked and peeling paint. The toilet never stopped running, and black mold circled the right side of the tub, slowly climbing up the wall. Bunched up clothes lay in piles on the floor next to crumpled-up fast-food bags filled with half-eaten burgers and old french fries. Diapers were piled so high in the corner they spilled out of the broken Diaper Genie. You could smell us from the end of the hallway the moment you walked into the building.

It'd been three months since we'd moved out of the dorm and into this apartment complex downtown. It'd only been a matter of time before someone heard Janie in the dorms. I was surprised we lasted as long as we did. I blew off the students the first time they said something about hearing a baby cry. I told them it must've been the TV in the other room and not to worry. They listened to me. After all, I was the RA.

A couple of weeks later, I came home from my shift at the hospital to find the same three residents standing in front of my door. Their ears pressed tight against it. Arms folded across their chests.

"You can't keep your baby in the dorms with us," the girl with the red glasses said the moment she noticed me coming down the hallway. She'd been the most vocal when they confronted me about it before. "It goes against the policy and rules of having no children in the dorms."

The girl standing next to her shrugged sheepishly and mumbled an apology underneath her breath.

The other one shrieked, "But like, is that your baby? Oh my god. I didn't even know you were pregnant! How'd you stay so skinny?!" She reached for my stomach like she was about to rub it. I jumped back.

"It's not my baby. It's my sister's." The lie was out of my mouth before I thought twice. The same way I'd lied when I told Maura about Janie. I told Maura I'd kept my pregnancy a secret, but I didn't share that her existence still was, and I felt so ashamed for the primary reason—I couldn't afford day care or a babysitter. Once people knew about her, they'd expect me to care for her properly, and I just couldn't do that. Not yet. Not to mention that I didn't trust other people with the most precious thing to me, anyway. I didn't know how I'd ever leave her with anyone else.

I was still trying to figure out a way to make this new life work, and I was drowning. Buried so far under the pressure and responsibilities of school and Janie that it didn't feel like I'd ever dig myself out of this hole. I was completely unprepared and ill equipped to raise a child, obviously. Doubt was creeping into my mind.

Poverty clung to me like I was never going to get it off. A heavy anchor pulling me down into the depths of despair. Tears filled my eyes as I stared at Janie. Overcome with shame for all the ways I felt like I was already failing her. Her face was still blotchy and red from earlier.

She's teething and going through these unbelievable crying fits, which made things even more difficult. She's regressed back to being a few weeks old instead of almost six months. She never stopped wailing unless she was latched onto me, and she refused to take a bottle. No matter how many different kinds I tried. I even tried to force it into her mouth once when I was super frustrated, but she'd clenched her jaw like a pit bull. That's when I gave up. I didn't have money to waste trying all those expensive bottles, anyway. Sometimes it felt like she was torturing me, and then the guilt immediately assaulted me for even thinking that way. Because of course she wasn't doing that. She was just a baby.

I'd missed so many classes and failed two finals, so I was officially on academic probation. I received the notice last week. Unreal. What was I going to do? My scholarship required a 3.2 average to keep it. Grades have never been a problem for me before, so this was completely uncharted territory. I've never gotten anything less than an A since they started giving grades in middle school. Not even junior year, when I was sleeping in the janitor's closet at the YMCA.

But Janie—this baby girl. Right here.

I stared down at her lying on her pink bath mat. She'd changed everything. All my plans. My grades. My years of hard work. They're all gone. Just like that. I've become a person I didn't recognize. One I swore I'd never be. And all I could think about was Cerena.

"I wanted to kill you. Did you know that? You're a botched abortion." That's what she always said when she was really angry with me. Peering into my face. Breath rank and rotten just like her insides. "I tried getting rid of you. Believe me—I tried. I took the pills those doctors gave me. Just like they said. Even bled. Apparently not enough to bleed you out, but I sure thought I did. That it was over with. Problem solved." She wiped her hands together like she was wiping her hands of me. "I didn't think anything of my first missed period. The doctors at the clinic told me that could happen. How your body takes a while to regulate hormonally after you've been pregnant. But then I missed my next one. And guess what? By then it was too late. I was eighteen weeks. Nobody will get rid of a baby at eighteen weeks." She snorted. "I even tried throwing myself down the stairs. That didn't work either."

As awful as Cerena's words were, for the first time ever in my life and as much as I didn't want to admit it—I understood them. Still so heartless and cruel to say to a little girl just trying to earn her mother's love, but I'd derailed her life in the same way Janie had derailed mine. Some days it was hard not to be angry about that, especially when I kept failing classes because I couldn't go.

I'd stopped giving Janie Tylenol to make her sleep, which meant she pretty much had me strapped to the apartment, especially during the day. She rarely took naps, and on the rare occasion when she did, they were so short that I didn't have time to get to class. Things had been easier when we lived on campus, but we were almost fifteen minutes away. So, I used the tiny window to dart to the grocery store or Target.

I've never felt anything like this. Whatever was happening to me. Even though I loved Janie, it felt like I was unraveling, and I didn't know how to stop it. There was constant pressure behind my eyes as if there were a thick rubber band wrapped around my head and cutting off my circulation. Any second, the rubber band might snap, and I didn't know what I'd do then.

It was scary to feel so out of control.

What am I going to do?

I couldn't stop being afraid of Janie getting hurt or killed. It's part of the reason I still kept her inside. Nobody could take her. She was contained.

Except it wasn't other people that I was the most afraid of—it was me.

Before her bath, Janie cried for three hours straight tonight. The unconsolable, screaming kind, and her wails drilled holes straight through my skull. My chest felt so tight, like my ribs were pressing inward, crushing my heart. I tried everything, and absolutely nothing worked. She wouldn't eat. Refused to be comforted. Just screamed.

I stood in the middle of the living room holding her against my chest as she cried, red faced and scrunched up tight like I was killing her. That's when the thought came: *What if I shook her?* Just one sharp jolt to make her stop. I gasped out loud the second the idea hit me—like someone else had dropped the thought straight into my brain and it'd burned me.

"Oh my god." I immediately held her away from my body with both hands, stiff armed. I was terrified to even have her near me. "Oh my god," I said again, twirling around in the living room, disoriented and dazed.

I walked over to the mattress in the corner, slowly and purposefully, like I might drop Janie at any second. I barely breathed, like even the air from my lungs might hurt her or, worse, set me off. I gingerly placed her on the blankets and pillows as gently as possible, like she was an egg that might break. As soon as she was safely on the mattress, I darted into the bathroom. I slammed the door like I was being chased and locked it behind me.

I burst into tears and slid down the wall to the cold tiled floor. I put my head between my legs and sobbed harder than I've ever cried in my life. Loud enough to drown out the sounds of Janie's cries from the other room. I stayed there for ten full minutes until my hands stopped shaking.

That's when I got up and called Maura. I left a message and told her I didn't trust myself to raise Janie. I hadn't seen her in over three months, but I had to find a way. Because I couldn't keep living this way or something terrible was going to happen.

(THEN)

I kept my face straight. My emotions off. Ice-princess face.

Mommy's eyes drilled holes in mine from the front seat of the car while we waited for the light to turn green. She studied my every move. Scanning for weakness. A break in my armor. But she won't find one. I'm a trained soldier.

She scowled at my expressionless face. It leaves her no clue what I'm doing next. She hates feeling powerless, just like I do, and my fear slips into pride, but I won't let the satisfaction show on my face either.

Give her nothing.

That's how you stay in control.

She narrowed her eyes to slits. The hate I felt toward her mirrored in her eyes. She doesn't know what to do with me anymore. Not since I stopped being afraid of her. She's lost all her power. She might be the meanest and cruelest woman on the block, but I'm the smartest.

She was so furious about the bedbugs. Like I wanted them to burrow their way into our beds any more than she did. They'd been chowing on me for weeks, leaving me with nasty red welts and unbearable itchiness. The need to scratch is relentless. So much worse than mosquito bites. She thought it was funny how the bites formed a trail around my ankles. Almost a full circle. She just laughed and refused to do anything about it.

"Maybe if you weren't such a nasty, filthy girl, you might not have bugs in your bed." That's what she said when I told her. She turned her nose up at me, like I had any control over the way she made us live. She was the pig.

They lay their eggs in your mattress. That's how you know you've got them. I took a spoon and tried to scoop their eggs up, but it was like trying to gather salt and pepper. Impossible. Still, I put them in her mattress, hoping they'd hatch there. Sprinkled some down into her pillowcases. She was the only one that got pillows with cases. I would've put the bugs in her bed too, but they only come out at night. That's when I decided to do a full switch as soon as I could.

I'd switched everything while she was gone the next day—mattresses, bedding, bugs. If she wasn't going to do anything to get rid of them, then she could live with them. Let them feast on her flesh for a few nights and see how much she liked it. Which is exactly what they'd done last night. She woke up this morning with the classic three-bite bedbug trail on her back, and she was furious. But she couldn't prove I'd done anything, so she had no way to punish me.

I've outsmarted her more than once, and there's nothing she hates more. It makes her simmer. The silent, simmering rage sitting right below the surface. I hate to tell her, but I'm only going to get smarter, so she should probably watch out.

Ever since I turned twelve, it's like this switch got turned on inside me. I spent my childhood walking on eggshells around her. Trying not to upset her while simultaneously craving her attention and affection. I was always so desperate and clingy, feasting on the tiniest crumbs she'd throw in my direction every now and then. Sitting as close as I could get to her while she got ready to go out. Wishing for a hug was too much. I would've settled for not getting pushed off the bed. Telling her over and over again how beautiful she was. Just waiting . . . hoping . . . she'd smile.

I was also terrified of her, and all the ways she'd punish me if I upset her. Or even sometimes just for fun. Those were the scariest rages. When she decided to torture me just for a good time. That's exactly what happened three nights ago.

"Get up!" She'd grabbed my arm and yanked me off the pallet I'd made on the floor. She slept on the bed. Even if she wasn't home, I wasn't allowed to touch the bed. I could touch everything else in the room, but that was off limits. It was all hers.

"I don't want your nasty, grimy fingers anywhere on my stuff. Do you understand me?" she'd sneered when we'd moved in, and I'd nodded my agreement, even though she was the dirty one. Her balled-up underwear from weeks ago was still in the corner. Leftover Taco Bell on her nightstand.

She'd pulled me to standing position. Stabbed her finger into my chest while my brain raced to figure out what I could've possibly done wrong. TV was off. Clothes put away. Bathroom clean. Everything tidy. I came up empty handed. I'd been perfect. I was always perfect.

"Don't you say another word," she said, even though I hadn't spoken. Past and present colliding. In the world only she could see. Fighting demons.

Sometimes Mommy just needed to punish something. She has so much volatile rage inside her that it's impossible to contain. She just has to get it out. I used to think it was because she'd been hurt so bad. I actually used to feel sorry for her. I really did. I thought she'd been traumatized so she was reacting like a wounded animal. You couldn't hate a wounded animal. Except she wasn't all that wounded. She was just an animal.

I might be the one whose head always ended up in the toilet, but she wasn't fighting me when she acted that way.

Or maybe it's not that a switch got turned on inside me. Maybe it just got turned off. Because I don't feel anything for her anymore. I'm definitely not sorry.

She's the one that's going to be sorry.

Sorry she ever made me.

Definitely sorry she ever met me.

All I had to do was keep getting bigger, smarter, and faster.

EIGHT

"Your message was really concerning, and please don't worry about paying for this session. I want to help you, so just tell me what's going on, and I'll take care of all the financial stuff. Fill me in on everything that's happening," Maura said as soon as we took our seats in her office.

She'd been out on vacation when I'd left my frantic message, and it'd been another week before I'd been able to see her. I was even more frazzled. She could probably tell just by looking at me.

"I'm really starting to think I might've made the wrong decision . . . I'm doing such a terrible job with Janie already. Totally screwing her up, and it's only going to get worse. I just know it. What was I thinking? I wasn't thinking—that's the problem. I've been so emotional. Like how your hormones go so crazy right after you give birth? That's where I'm at. And breastfeeding too, right? So, I've got all that oxytocin gushing through me at all times." I waved my hands down my body to emphasize my point. I was rambling and talking fast, but we had exactly fifty-nine minutes to talk, and I wasn't wasting a single one. "I'm sure all that influenced my decision. That stuff is so powerful, you know? I think I let my emotions get the best of me, which is so weird because I'm not an emotional person. Not at all. You know that. I just . . . I just . . . it's so hard. I know I keep saying that. But I have no money. I'm failing out of school. How am I going to take care of Janie if I don't finish college? I mean, honestly, what would I have done if I'd actually found out I was pregnant before I had her? I just—"

"Whoa. Slow down." Maura raised her hand to stop me. "I can see that you're really upset and understandably so. Let's just try to take a deep breath and see what we can figure out together. Maybe we can break it down into some manageable pieces."

I nodded at her, doing my best to take a deep breath, even though my chest was tight with anxiety. She gave me an encouraging look as I tried to exhale. I wrung my hands together on my lap as I continued explaining. I wanted her to know exactly where I was coming from so she could tell me what to do.

"Janie's way behind where she should be, and I know it's all because I didn't take care of myself when I was pregnant. I didn't take any of those prenatal vitamins." *I drank wine.* That's what I wanted to add, but everyone's acceptance had a limit, and I didn't want to test hers. I was already pushing it. "I looked through the milestone pamphlet online—responds to name, enjoys peekaboo, sits with support—and she doesn't do any of that."

Maura smiled at me kindly. "There's a huge degree of variability with babies in hitting their developmental milestones. I promise. You really don't even start being concerned until they're two or three."

"It's more than that, though." I shook my head at her. I wished they had one of those observation rooms with the double-sided mirrors, so we could put Janie in it and Maura could watch how she behaved. "She's supposed to be laughing and cooing by now, but she doesn't do any of that either. She's so uninterested in interaction. That's what worries me the most. And it's not like I don't try to engage her and do all the things they say to do. Saying her name. Clapping. Blowing raspberries. But it's always just nothing." I dropped my voice, ashamed. "If I pick her up when I'm not feeding her, sometimes, her body goes stiff like she doesn't even want to be on me. I've actually wondered if she was deaf, so I clapped real loud next to her ear once and she jumped, so now I know she can hear, which kind of makes it worse because it means she's ignoring me. Or maybe she's just autistic? Developmentally delayed or whatever it is the doctors call it?" I shook my head in bewilderment. There were just so many different possibilities. It always made my head spin.

Maura smiled again. Even kinder and softer. "Becky, all of what you're describing sounds like a perfectly normal experience for a new mom. Every new parent wonders if there's something wrong with their child and if they're keeping up with other babies. The comparison is brutal. It can drive you absolutely mad."

I leaned forward in my chair. She didn't understand. It wasn't that simple. This was serious. "Maybe she acts the way that she does because of me . . . like, what if there's something wrong with me? Maybe she can sense that I'm not a good mother or that I'm broken inside from everything that happened to me when I was a kid."

"The first year with an infant is incredibly difficult. So many women struggle and have *such* a hard time. That doesn't mean there's something wrong with you or that you shouldn't be a parent. And not that I have to remind you, but you're doing this alone, which only makes it more difficult."

I shook my head at her again. "I know I've never been a mom before, but my thoughts aren't normal. Not even close."

"Can you give me some examples of what you're thinking so that I can have a better understanding of what you're experiencing?" She wore her best listening face as she kept her gaze focused on me.

"Sometimes, from out of nowhere, I'm terrified that I'm going to physically hurt her, and I don't even know why. I get scared to even pick her up because I don't trust myself." I writhed my hands together on my lap. "I'm terrified I'll drop her or throw her into the wall. Even though I don't want to. I really don't. I just have these terrible images of me doing it. Like actual little movie clips that play in my brain. Twice I've hidden her in the closet while it's happening to keep her safe. That's how bad it freaked me out. It felt like the only way that I could protect her from getting hurt." I looked away. I couldn't have her peering at me with her therapist eyes, seeing right into my soul while I talked about this.

"Your experience sounds very frightening, and I can understand why you're concerned."

"Do you know what I did after I called you and left you a voicemail that night?" I didn't wait for her to answer because of course she didn't. Nobody did. "The next morning, I made a sign for the fridge that said *If you feel like you're going to snap—put her down! Call someone. Lock the door if you have to.* I taped it right next to the bottle schedule along with the mental health crisis line. If you've got to write a note like that, then something is definitely wrong."

"I understand how overwhelming this must be." Her face melted in genuine sadness and concern. "But I do want to point out that you've made very positive choices in handling what you're going through. Calling me was a great idea. So was putting up that note and finding a list of resources to call if you're feeling distressed and overwhelmed."

"I'm *obsessed* with keeping bad things from happening to her. Like, cannot stop. But what if I'm the bad thing? What if I'm who she needs protecting from?" My voice cracked, and suddenly, without warning, the tears that had always been frozen inside of me were rolling down my cheeks.

Maura leaned over and placed her hand on my forearm. She spoke softly. "You are *not* the bad thing."

"But you don't know me like you think you do, or you wouldn't say that." She had no idea what I'd seen or the things I'd done. Maybe if we'd had more time in therapy, I would've gotten to all the pieces of my story, but it was too late now. "Whatever messed-up trait turned Cerena into a terrible person clearly exists in me, and that's why I'm so scared." At the end of the day, it really was that simple. I never wanted to be like her. But could I outrun my genes?

"That is a very real and valid fear, but I want you to hear me when I say this, okay?" She paused to make sure I was present with her and paying attention to what she had to say next. "Bad parents don't ever stop to consider or wonder if they've done something wrong or made a mistake in their behavior toward their children. Truly narcissistic parents—which your mother sounds like she was—only see themselves as victims. They don't apologize or take responsibility. You know the other thing they never do?" She gave me a pointed look. "Wonder if they're a bad parent. The fact that you stop to question whether or not you are says a whole lot about your character. And you know what I think?"

I felt like I was going to cry again. "What?"

Maura's voice was low and careful. "Becky, you're not a bad mom. You're an overwhelmed one. That's a very different thing."

"I'm SO tired. I feel like I'm one crisis or loud noise away from breaking in half." I pressed the heels of my hands into my eyes. Right before our session, I left Janie crying on the living room floor while I went into the bathroom and screamed into a towel.

She leaned forward. "Can I make a suggestion?" I nodded, but barely. "You need someone with you. Not forever. Only right now. Just until you catch your breath again. Is there anyone you love and trust enough to call to come stay with you for a while?"

I started to shake my head no—I didn't have any family, and I couldn't tell my friends about Janie—but I stopped halfway. Someone flickered in the back of my mind. The memory of him was never far away. Always there, lurking in the shadows.

"Maybe," I said slowly. "There's this one guy, Orion. He's not perfect, but he's . . . safe. We grew up together."

I hadn't called him in years even though I had his number memorized by heart. I checked his social media sometimes just to make sure he was okay. I trusted him more than anyone else in the world. But I couldn't reach out to him. That was too dangerous.

Maura's voice got even softer. "You know I don't like to tell you what to do, but please, call him, Becky. Do it today if you can. Just ask him to show up. Let someone help you hold this weight for a while."

I bit the inside of my cheek. My hands shook.

"Okay," I whispered. "I'll call him."

We hadn't spoken to each other since we were seventeen. It was too risky. But he was the one person I could call who'd drop everything and come running to help me—he'd already done it once.

HIM

(NOW)

It'd taken three days, but Vega finally got in touch with Charity's therapist, and she'd provided him with the residence listed on Charity's paperwork in less than ten minutes, even though it violated all sorts of HIPAA guidelines. He pulled up in front of a beat-up yellow duplex on Hawthorne Street. He knocked on the weather-warped front door. A dog barked from somewhere inside. After a long pause, the door cracked open just enough for a single brown eye to appear.

"I'm looking for Charity Greene," Vega said, holding up his badge.

"Please, I don't want any trouble," the woman behind the door said instantly. The chain pulled tight between the frame and door. "I haven't done anything wrong."

"I know." He looked at her reassuringly and softened his tone. "I'm not here for that. I'm investigating a case from some years ago involving a foster home. You were listed as a former resident."

She hesitated. Her eyes darted around nervously before she undid the chain and opened the door fully. Charity was older now—mid-twenties, maybe—but she still carried the posture of someone who was used to being smaller than the world around her. Hunched over like she was trying to hide inside herself. She wore a hoodie despite the heat. Her hands trembled. Dark bags circled her eyes.

"Which foster home?" she asked, even though he could tell she already knew.

"The Millers. In Waldorf?"

Her jaw clenched. "I figured. I saw the news. Did they identify the body?"

"We're still waiting on identification." That's what Vega told her. It's what they told all the public and the press, but CSU had identified the remains as Earl Miller. At least the first ones. They'd discovered another gravesite today. Looked like more than one set of remains. Nobody knew about that yet, though. He'd just gotten the call from Santos on his way here. "I was hoping you'd talk to me about your time at the Millers'."

"I don't know what I can tell you that wasn't already in the reports. I told that social worker everything years ago, when they interviewed me the first time." The dog hadn't stopped barking behind her. Vega did his best to ignore it.

"I've read the reports," he said. "They don't say much other than you were removed from the Millers. I'd love to know why."

Charity stared past him for a long moment like she was calculating the risks of speaking with him. After a few more beats passed, she opened the screen door and stepped aside, motioning him into the house.

"Five minutes," she said. "That's all you get because I need to get ready for work, and I can't be late."

"Thank you," he said quickly before she could change her mind.

Charity's living room was small and overly neat, like she was ready for a surprise inspection at any moment or was planning to put her home on the market. The furniture was mismatched, like it had all come from different garage sales, but it was just as clean as the rest of the place. A TV hung perfectly straight on the wall.

Charity sat on the far end of the couch with her knees together and her hands clenched on her lap. Vega took a seat across from her and pulled out his notebook, but he didn't open it yet. "I'm not here to talk about anything you're not ready for."

"It's okay. I said I'd answer your questions, so just ask." Her voice was flat and controlled. He recognized it—the survivor tone of measured detachment.

"You were placed at the Miller foster home in 2007. You were there about nine months. Is that right?" he asked.

She nodded.

"What was that like?" He opened his notebook and pulled the pen out of his shirt pocket. "Again, only what you're comfortable sharing with me. I know this is difficult to discuss."

She nodded her appreciation. "That place was awful. They took way too many kids and packed us in there like cattle. They rationed all our food. Made us work all day even when we had school. It was kind of like being in prison or the army. The only good thing about being there was that I lost weight." She gave a bitter laugh.

"There are notes in the CPS records that say you were removed after a 'series of emotional disturbances.' Can you tell me anything more about that?" he asked.

She snorted softly. "Is that what they called it?"

"Can you tell me what that means from your side?"

She looked down at her hands and tugged at a loose string on her shirtsleeve. She twisted it around her finger while she spoke, never lifting her eyes. "It means I tried to slit my wrists with a pencil sharpener blade during lights-out."

Vega let the silence stretch between them. Detectives used some of the same techniques as psychologists. Most people found silence uncomfortable and automatically started talking to fill up the space. Charity was no different. She was uneasy within seconds.

"They sent me to the hospital when they found me, and the Millers told them that I was unstable, which obviously I was, because who slices their wrists when they're stable?" She snorted again. "But it wasn't the way they made it sound. The caseworker said that I had PTSD from my biological mom and couldn't adjust to being in group foster care, but that's not what was going on . . ." Her words drifted off along with her stare.

"What was going on?" Vega prompted after a few more seconds had passed and she'd lapsed into silence again.

She folded her arms tighter, crossing them against her chest like armor. "I was a kid being raped in the middle of the night, and nobody did a goddamn thing about it."

"Did you tell anyone back then?"

"Tell?" Fury lit her face. "The last time I told someone that I was being sexually abused, I got taken out of my home and sent to live with the Millers, so no. I didn't tell anyone this time." She glared at him. Her situation made him just as angry.

Vega wished, like he had hundreds of times, that there was more he could do to fix the broken system of child welfare, but there wasn't. He already did everything he could, including apologizing to Charity even though he couldn't make it right. "I'm so sorry you went through that."

She shrugged. "Whatever. It wasn't just me. Earl messed with lots of us. He knew exactly who to pick. The quiet kids. Sleepwalkers. The ones who wouldn't talk. He started with this boy, Orion. Then me." Charity laughed again, dry and bitter. "I told Helen once. Right after I'd gotten out of the hospital for slitting my wrists. She said she was sorry and she'd make sure he stopped. The next week I was moved to a group home three counties over. Never heard from her again."

Vega didn't speak for a long time. He just sat there, listening to the dog bark in the other room and the creak of Charity's seat every time she shifted. She kept her arms crossed like she was holding herself together. She wasn't unstable. She'd been failed by the system in every way.

He stood slowly and stuck his hand out to her, struggling to control his emotions. "I know you have to get to work, and I can't thank you enough for taking the time to speak with me." He cleared his throat. "I'm so sorry for what happened to you, and I promise that I'm going to do my very best to bring you justice."

He was a man of his word. He'd do it for her and every other kid in her position.

NINE

"No! Noooo!" Janie screamed, kicking and flailing her arms against me. I jerked my arm back so I wouldn't cut her with the electric razor in my hand. It's not like I wanted to shave all her hair off, but the lice hadn't left us any other choice. I'd tried the shampoo twice and they kept coming back. Nibbling away at our scalps. Dropping their eggs in our strands, especially hers. For some reason, they preferred her to me. Maybe they had a thing for toddlers.

"Quit it!" I yelled, trying to hold on to her with one arm. She flung her head back and her skull cracked into my nose. "Ow!" I immediately brought my hands to my face—letting go of her—as blood gushed out of my nostrils.

She scurried forward and pressed herself flat against the wall like I was going to come at her, but I was seeing stars. If I moved, I might pass out. She glared at me from her position, breathing hard. Nostrils flaring in and out. Fists clenched at her side. She'd been unmanageable since the moment she started walking.

"You think I like this any better than you do?!" I glared right back at her as I grabbed a shirt from the floor and brought it to my nose. The shirt smelled dirty, and I was probably going to get some weird staph infection on top of the lice. I'd known what was happening the minute I felt that weird prickling on my scalp. I couldn't count the number of times I had lice as a kid. It's not like I wasn't going to have to go through exactly what she was going through if they came back in my hair.

The nurse used to come around in elementary school wearing latex gloves and go through every student's hair. I was mortified and always tried to get away because I knew they were going to find something in my hair. If it wasn't bugs, it was days-old crust, because washing your hair with only water when you didn't have any soap or shampoo could only do so much. Either way, it was humiliating. At least her infestation was private. Nobody was going to know about it except us.

Janie still didn't leave the house. I'd tried introducing her to the outside world, but I couldn't control her out there. She took off and ran away from me if I let go of her hand. But the problem was, she hated having her hands held, so every time I tried, it was a huge fight. She'd bite me. Kick me. Even spit. Her favorite thing to do was turn her body into a loose, floppy noodle. It was impossible to get her to do anything then.

The last time I took her to the park, she got away from me, darted across the street, and almost got hit by a car. So now her world consisted of these four walls, a small bathroom, and a closet again. Just like when she was a baby. I couldn't wrap my brain around the fact that we'd been living this way for over a year. Going on two. How was that possible?

Maura left me another message today. She asked when I was going to come back to therapy, and it'd bummed me out for the rest of the day because I really missed her. Even with the reduced rate, there was no way I could afford therapy with her anymore, even though I would've loved to see her again. But it'd been so many months since our last session. She still called every few weeks to check on me, though.

"Come here, Janie," I ordered once my nose stopped bleeding, but she just stared at me like she was daring me to grab her again. She hated being told what to do. "I said come here." I tried to keep my voice calm, but it was impossible. She looked completely ridiculous, and I had to do something to fix it. There was a bald strip down the center of her head with puffs of pale blond curls on each side.

My nose throbbed. The headache was already pounding behind my eyes. I took a breath—sharp and quick—then lunged at her and wrapped my arms around her. Janie screamed. She kicked and flailed, pounding her fists against my chest.

"No! No no no no no!" she shrieked.

I hauled her to the kitchen chair by the sink, refusing to let go. The chair. She knew what it meant.

She twisted in my grip. Her face red with rage. Legs thrashing. She jerked her head back, trying to headbutt me again.

"I'm sorry," I muttered breathlessly. "I can't leave you looking like this, and you won't sit still. We wouldn't have to do this if you'd just cooperate."

I shoved her into the seat, bracing her with my body as I grabbed the belts still looped on the backrest from last time. What else was I supposed to do? I didn't do it to hurt her. Just long enough to get through what needed doing. Sometimes it was changing her clothes. Other times it was to get her to eat or to clean one of the injuries she'd gotten from hurting herself.

You couldn't reason with her. You couldn't reach her.

I didn't want to have to resort to this, but it was the only thing that worked.

"All you have to do is sit still and we can get this done," I said as she struggled against the restraints, violently shaking her head back and forth. "Janie! Don't move so I can do this," I ordered.

But my words didn't touch her. They never did.

I pushed her head against the chair with my forearm and pressed the razor to her head with my other hand. I whipped my way back and forth across her head as quickly as possible. She screamed the entire time like the razor was cutting her scalp. All the neighbors had to hear.

She gasped when I finished, and I quickly untied the belts. She sprang up from the chair and shoved it at me. I quickly dodged it, letting it smack into the sink. Janie scurried to the other side of the living room and glowered at me with her hands on her hips.

She stood against the wall that was gleaming white when we moved in. Now it was marked with her scribbled crayon drawings. Holes kicked through the bottom from other fits she'd thrown. She looked sick. Like one of those kids on the St. Jude's commercials. Her skin was so pale, it was practically translucent. You could see her thin blue veins. Her sunken-in eyes were accentuated without hair. Bags underneath even more pronounced. Fading bruises from smashing her head around on the wooden floor when she was mad because her diaper was wet and I didn't move fast enough to change it.

Still.

None of this was okay. I needed to be a better mother. I shouldn't have to tie my daughter up in order to control her. Maybe if Cerena had been any kind of mother to me at all, I might not be so awful at this or in this position. I walked over to the center of the living room and picked up my phone from the coffee table. Orion's number was still pulled up from earlier today. Every time Maura left me a message, she made me think of him because he was the last thing we spoke about. I'd never called him even though I'd promised her that I would. My thumb hovered over his name like it'd done so many times before.

God, I couldn't believe I was even thinking about calling him. It'd been almost a decade since we'd spoken. We were just kids back then. Traumatized and desperate, with no one but each other. The only way to make sure our past stayed a secret was to never speak to each other again. But I'd never expected Janie. I'd never expected this—a secret pregnancy that had become a secret child, cutting me off from the rest of the world. One that sent me into a dark hole that I didn't know how to dig my way out of.

I'm starting to suspect that her fits are more than just being in the terrible-twos stage of development. I've tried everything the parenting books suggest, and none of it works. She still hates being told what to do no matter what, and her fits are completely unpredictable. Sometimes she just has them for absolutely no reason.

But then I think—what if it's me?

Maybe I was never supposed to have a kid. I was supposed to be the responsible adult, but I could barely care for us. Yesterday, the landlord served us with an eviction notice, and I've never felt more like Cerena in my life. I cried all afternoon. I haven't worked in months, and I have no money. I breastfeed Janie just so that she doesn't starve. It's really bleak.

I need help. Like, real help.

Orion will understand. He always did. We were broken in the same ways, and he never judged me. Not once. But what if calling him opens the door we swore to keep shut? And what if he hasn't changed—if he's worse? What am I inviting into our life?

But if I didn't call . . . I didn't know how much longer I could do this alone. I had no one else. I quickly tapped the call button before I talked myself out of it.

(THEN)

"I hate it here!" I screamed at Cerena as she slammed the front door in my face during the middle of our argument.

She whipped it back open immediately. Her nose within inches of mine as she spat, "Then you should've thought of that before you turned everyone against me!" She shoved me hard, and I fell backward into the entryway before I had a chance to respond.

"Don't you dare fucking leave this house!" she yelled as she slammed the door again.

Her angry footsteps pounded away as she cussed underneath her breath, violently ripping me to shreds with her words. Fury surged through me. Then, the sound of the lobby door crashing closed behind her as she stormed out. Good. I hope she disappears forever.

I hate her. More than any other moment in our history. How was she possibly going to make this about me? But of course, she was. That's exactly who she is. She could never take responsibility for anything. She's always the victim.

As if she wasn't the one who seduced Mr. Parker and destroyed his entire family, getting us run out of town. Like she hadn't just pulled the exact same scam she did in every place we've ever lived from as far back as I can remember. I watched it happen that day at church. The moment she picked him out in the third row on Palm Sunday. Four seats in. Him and his two daughters. His beautiful wife, Madeline.

Church was one of Cerena's favorite places to prey. Because the thing about Cerena is that she's actually quite predictable. At least to me. I've been studying her since I can remember, and she's a well-rehearsed script. I know all her lines. Every move.

She found a pool of victims when she brought me to my first preschool. She's been using me to get men to notice her and feel sorry for her ever since. Forever playing the single-mom card. But most women aren't that stupid, and I could see that, especially now that I am a teenager. They put an end to that kind of shit with her almost immediately, and I admired them for it. Sending her a lawn service to cut the grass. The list of handymen in the area to fix the back door. Numbers to the plumber and electrician. Some of them on magnets to put on the refrigerator. The referrals all came with cards that, even though they said various versions of *Thinking of you*, might as well have said *Keep your hands off my fucking husband.*

I didn't blame them.

Mr. Parker was her hardest target yet. For a while, she even fooled me, and I'd caught on to her tricks SO long ago. But for once, I thought she was into him. Like, *really* into him. Everyone was capable of falling in love, and maybe after all her tricks and scheming, she was finally ready to settle down.

I can't believe I'd actually been excited about it, but she'd never worked so hard to get someone to notice her before or spent so much time with them once they had. She even went to work as his receptionist in a dental office for nine months. A job that included cleaning the patient bathrooms. That's the reason I thought she was serious about him. She'd never gone to those lengths for anyone before. And scrubbing a toilet? Please. She was definitely in love.

Then, at the beginning of the year, my high school held a fundraiser for Mr. Parker and his family. That's when I discovered his wife had stage IV colon cancer. My jaw dropped in the hallway when I spotted the flyer. His wife was literally dying, and my mother was trying to steal him away from her.

"How can you do something like that?" I asked her when I got home that afternoon, horrified. It's all I'd been able to think about the rest of the day. I didn't know it was possible for a human being to be that awful. She had no redeeming qualities. I'd searched for years and come up empty handed. When I was little, I made them up. But I wasn't a little girl anymore, and this was despicable. She disgusted me.

"It's my biggest challenge yet." That's what she said, and I wanted to slap her. I dug my fingernails into the palm of my hand to keep myself from saying a word. Erased the judgment from my face.

She had no shame. Once she got him to leave his wife and children, she flaunted him in front of everyone, like she always did. She wore the men she stole like they were designer purses. She took great joy in other people's reactions. She loved the high she got from being the prettiest and most threatening woman in the room. Everybody was talking about the affair.

Then, last month, Mr. Parker's wife drove her car straight into a tree, leaving him and their two young daughters behind.

I came home to find my mom watching the news clip of it over and over again on her phone. The newscasters kept saying how a distraught wife with cancer found out her husband was having an affair and took her own life. There was a glint in my mom's eye every time they said it. A tiny smile turning up the corners of her mouth.

"I can't believe you," I said. Just when I thought she'd gone as low as she could possibly go, she sank to a new level of depravity.

"What do you mean?" she asked, feigning innocence. She could easily fool others with her charm, but she couldn't fool me. Not anymore.

"You know exactly what I'm talking about. Don't you even feel the least bit guilty?"

My mom laughed and batted her long dark eyelashes at me. Sprayed herself in perfume. Expensive Chanel No. 5 from Mr. Parker, so out of place in our run-down double-wide. "Are you kidding me? Do you know how dreadful it must be to run around feeling guilty all the time? Like, I can't even imagine. Guilt is such an absolute waste of time."

If there were any pieces of our invisible umbilical cord left, she'd just severed them completely. She's a monster, and she's not my mother. To mark the occasion and to be sure I never forgot—I stopped calling her Mom and started calling her by her first name. She didn't deserve the title, so I stripped her of it.

Cerena.

That's who she is to me now, and she got us chased out of Eau Claire. This is all her fault. The women in the Midwest despise a home-wrecker more than anything else, and she'd just imploded an entire family. Devastated them beyond repair. She didn't mind the hate from jealousy. That fueled her. But she ran from their scorn.

And this time?

Everybody hated her. The entire town. We couldn't go anywhere without dirty looks. Nobody talked to me either. It was the one place I'd ever remotely fit in, and she'd ruined it for me. People threw things at us in the grocery store. Refused to serve us in restaurants. They taped signs on my locker at school. Mostly one word: **MURDERER**. Like I'd done anything wrong. I'd known it was over then. Once people started looking down their noses at her—and let me tell you, that happens once you've stolen a husband from his dying wife—she was done. She couldn't tolerate other people's disdain, especially people she thought she was better than.

As soon as she felt it, we were out. On to the next rural town in the middle of cornfields. We roamed through the tri-states—Minnesota, Iowa, and Wisconsin. I don't even know what this town is called. It doesn't really even matter, though, because they're all basically the same. Most of them filled with families that have been there for generations. The quintessential rural Midwest. Bowling leagues and softball teams. Church every Sunday. One high school. Conservative, traditional values, where the dad was the breadwinner and the mom was the homemaker. All still very 1950s vibes.

But nobody cared. They lived there because they liked it that way. The patriarchal structure. The simplicity of life. They refer to those kinds of towns as places where everyone knows everybody else, and they don't say it just because it's cute. It's true—people really do. They raise their kids in the same schools they'd gone to themselves. Some people never left. They'd never even been out of the state. We couldn't have been more outsiders. We might as well have had a scarlet letter tattooed on our foreheads every time we rolled in to one.

This place isn't any different. It will only be a matter of time before she finds her next victim. She acts like people are robots. That they turned off when she wasn't interacting with them. Nobody is real to her. That's why it's so easy to hurt them.

But she's done hurting me.

TEN

Knock. Knock.

I froze in the kitchen. My hands trembled over the sink. A single overhead light cast shadows on the walls behind me. I couldn't believe he was actually here. I quickly glanced at Janie on the cracked vinyl couch, where she'd been curled into a ball for the last fifteen minutes, napping. She never slept during the day, but she was running a fever, so today was an exception. The timing couldn't have been more perfect.

I slowly walked toward the door. Each step deliberate. I didn't need to check the peephole because I already knew who was standing on the other side. I still couldn't believe this was happening. I took a deep breath, hoping I hadn't made a mistake, and slowly opened the door.

Orion.

He was taller than I remembered. He stood with a green duffel bag slung over one shoulder. Midnight-black curls framed his chiseled face. Dark-brown eyes rimmed in thick lashes. A scruffy layer of facial hair.

"Hey," he said softly.

"Hi," I replied just as quietly. Barely above a whisper.

And then we just stood there. Frozen. Each one taking in the other. The first time seeing each other after so many years had passed.

After a few more beats, we stepped inside. The apartment smelled like sour milk and sweat. I watched as Orion took in the space. The broken toys scattered in the living room. The formula-stained bottles lined up like dirty soldiers on the coffee table. A space heater buzzing too loudly in the corner. Dirty dishes piled high in the sink and lining the counters. Overflowing trash by the door. He dropped his bag and slowly turned to me.

"You weren't kidding," he said.

"I told you it was bad." I never would've called him if it wasn't. I crossed my arms tight on my chest. Defiant and ashamed all at once. "You didn't come for the decor."

"No. I came because you called." He gazed at me. Our eyes locked.

Everything inside me stilled. My body remembered him before my mind caught up. The way his shoulders used to make me feel safe. The curve of his mouth, that one dimple that only showed up when he let his guard down. I haven't thought about kissing anyone in years—not really—but suddenly the memory was there, in full color and unreserved.

God, no. Not now.

Janie stirred on the couch, breaking the spell of the moment. We both looked toward her and away from each other.

"Is she okay?" he asked. Concern etched all over his face.

"She just has a fever. I gave her some Tylenol earlier." I didn't tell him that I'd stolen it from the grocery store because I had literally zero dollars to my name. I'd searched the entire parking lot for dropped change before I left. I'd found seven cents.

"You need help," he said, as if it wasn't obvious.

"I know." A lump of emotions rose in my throat. Seeing him made me want to collapse into his arms just like I used to. He was the only person who could ever make me feel better.

Orion stayed standing near the door with his hands in his jean pockets, like he hadn't decided if he was staying or just catching his breath. The duffel bag sagged by his feet.

I swallowed hard. My mouth was dry. "I didn't tell you everything."

He looked up slowly and brushed his curls off his face. "I figured."

"It's not just that I don't have any money or food. Or the fact I had to leave college. Those things are bad, but that's not even what worries me the most. It's Janie . . ." I took a deep breath. "She's not like other kids. She doesn't talk much—barely at all—but she understands things, even though she pretends like she doesn't, and she's always watching. Not like a toddler watches their mom. It's different. Like she's studying me. I can't explain it."

He raised an eyebrow but said nothing. Just the quiet whir of the space heater behind him. So I continued trying to explain what she was like and why it was so concerning.

"She does things on purpose too, like she's messing with me, and I know how weird that sounds, but she does, I swear. She moves stuff and breaks things that she knows I need. She loves hiding food. One time I woke up and every knife in the kitchen was in the bathtub. She was standing over them, just grinning. It gave me the creeps."

Orion's expression darkened. His arms dropped to his sides. "Have you taken her to see a doctor?"

I shook my head. "I told you on the phone—nobody besides my old therapist knows she exists."

He gave me a quizzical look, like he was trying to gauge whether I was the same person he used to know when we were kids or if I'd turned into someone else. I knew him well enough to know that he was also assessing my mental state. Rightfully so. I would've done the same thing in his position.

"I'm scared they'll take her away from me if I say anything. And besides, no one would believe me anyway. But I swear, she really pretends not to hear me, and I can't physically force her to do anything or she bites me. She's even started spitting at me. I tried telling my old therapist what was happening, and she said it was normal stress. She's the one that suggested I call you."

He stepped closer and lowered his voice. "I'm glad you called me, Becks. I think about you all the time and wonder how you're doing."

"I think about you too." I swallowed hard.

He lifted up my chin with his fingers and reached for my hand just like he used to. "I can tell you're scared."

I nodded, barely able to speak. "I am."

But I couldn't even articulate my fears. It was just this unrelenting sense of foreboding that something terrible was going to happen. That I'd made the wrong choice, and it was all linked to Janie. Or that it was the karmic lesson returning to settle its debt for what we did all those years ago.

"I just—" My voice cracked. "I need someone else to see it. To see *her*. To tell me I'm not crazy. Or maybe that I am. Either way, I can't do this alone anymore."

A rustling.

We both turned.

Janie sat up on the couch, quiet and slow. Her face flushed as she turned toward Orion. Her hair stuck out in damp tufts all over her head. She blinked once. Twice. Then locked eyes with him.

She didn't say a word.

Didn't smile.

Just looked at him with an unreadable expression. But her eyes—they sharpened and focused. Like she'd just realized something important. Then, she did the strangest thing. She pulled the edge of the blanket up to her chin like a curtain and grinned.

Not a toddler grin. It wasn't sleepy or innocent.

It was a grin that was too knowing. One entirely too old.

Like she knew something we didn't.

ELEVEN

It'd been three weeks since Orion moved in. Three weeks since I'd exhaled for the first time in over a year. The apartment still smelled like old formula, but felt so much less like despair. There were groceries in the fridge—actual food, not just stale crackers and milk nearing expiration. The trash didn't overflow. Dishes didn't sit for days. The landlord had agreed to a thirty-day extension on the rent.

We hadn't really discussed Orion moving in. It was pretty much just understood that he would, since he'd used all the money he'd saved from his job working as a night security person in Dallas to buy a bus ticket here and get us caught up on the bills. I couldn't just kick him to the streets and tell him to find a place to stay after he'd done all that. He'd already filled out applications all over the city for similar security positions.

"As soon as I get a job, you have to go back to school," he said as we munched on the ramen noodles we'd just made. He liked the chicken seasoning. Same as me. Some things hadn't changed.

I shook my head, slurping the noodles into my mouth. "I'm not sure. I think it might just be better for me to find a job too. I'd like to save up enough money so I can get us out of here and into a better place. This mold can't be good for us. Maybe I'll wait and just go back to college once she starts kindergarten." I pointed to where Janie sat cross-legged on the floor, tearing paper into strips. It was one of her favorite activities. She rarely played with her toys, but she liked ripping things up, and she'd spend hours on a notebook. Sorting her strips into piles. It was weird, but I didn't mind as long as it kept her busy.

"You're so close, Becks. One semester. Maybe two and you'd be done? Please don't throw it away. Not after you've worked so hard." He placed his hand on my knee. A small gesture, but his touch seared through me like heat. We didn't touch often. An unspoken boundary until now.

He was my one. My only one before the one-night stand at the bar. He couldn't say the same for me, but he'd always sworn I was special. How many more girls had there been since me? I desperately wanted to ask, but we didn't talk about those things. Not yet, anyway.

"I'll work while you go to school. Just let me help you." His eyes were soft and pleading.

I wanted to believe it was that simple. That we could just share the household load and I could stop drowning. But it wasn't fair to ask him to continue helping me once I was on my feet again. He had his own life. I couldn't expect him to just give all that up and help me raise Janie.

"I can't ask you to do all that," I said, shaking my head.

"I didn't say that you were. I want to do it. And Becks, I know that it's bad. You're in trouble—real trouble. You can't keep doing all of this alone. It's too much for one person." I looked down, refusing to meet his eyes.

Even after all this time had passed, he still knew me better than anyone else. He'd been abandoned in a gas station bathroom when he was three. Left there like luggage someone forgot to claim, with a note taped to his chest. And somehow, after all that, he'd turned into the most loyal person I'd ever known. He'd shepherded me through my first time in a foster home. That's how we met.

"There's also . . ." I tilted my head down at Janie, trying to keep her from picking up on the fact that I was talking about her. "And *that's* too much."

"She's just adjusting. Give her time," he said, knowing exactly what I was referencing.

Things were slowly improving around the house, but Janie grew more and more difficult every day. She wasn't a fan of Orion and was extremely threatened by his presence. I couldn't help but feel guilty. How else was a child supposed to react when they'd lived their first two—almost three—years in isolation? She'd only ever known me, and she wasn't interested in sharing me with another person.

It started small. Spilling her milk every time Orion handed it to her. Screaming the second he picked her up, then going completely silent the moment I returned. She threw his truck keys into the trash can in the kitchen all the time. She hid his clothes. Last week I caught her pouring salt into his coffee.

But that didn't stop Orion. He kept trying to connect with her despite her resistance and the way she treated him. He would play blocks with her. And she'd line them up, perfectly spaced. Then, when he reached to help her, she'd shove the whole stack off the table and scream like she'd been hit. Sometimes she threw the blocks at him.

If I left the room or the apartment, she'd throw herself on the floor in a huge tantrum. Screaming, kicking, hitting herself. One time she bit her arm hard enough to leave teeth marks. Then, when I rushed in, she pointed at him and said one word:

"Badboy."

That was the first time my stomach truly dropped. Where was she learning all this? All of it was so deliberate and calculated too. At least it seemed that way to me.

"What two-year-old acts like this?" I whispered to Orion that night after she'd finally fallen asleep. I'd insisted on him sleeping on the couch. I'd made up a pallet on the floor next to Janie.

"It's okay. She's going to be fine. I already told you—she just needs time. She sees me as a threat. That's all. As soon as that shifts, we'll be the best of friends. Promise."

HIM

(NOW)

Vega rushed back to the precinct after the text from Santos. The hallway buzzed with phones and printers and the steady churn of incoming cases and not enough staff. Santos was already waiting at Vega's desk with a fresh stack of files in her hands and a look on her face that said she hadn't eaten lunch.

"They pulled two more sets of remains from the site this morning," she said without preamble. "One of them was less than five feet tall."

Vega stopped mid-step.

"A child?" he asked, horrified. It would be the third set of remains this week. So far, CSU had discovered four bodies. The media had started referring to the possibility of a serial killer in the news after someone let it leak. The community was officially freaking out.

"Looks like it. CSU says it's an early adolescent based on femur length, but there's no ID yet. Dental impressions are in progress, but you know those take forever. And get this—they weren't buried with the other two. This one was found on a completely different side of the property. Not the same decomposition rate."

"So different times. Different events." He nodded, thinking out loud.

"Likely." Santos dropped the files onto his desk. "This isn't one bad night or a few incidents. It's a pattern of behavior probably over a period of years." Vega sat and leaned forward. His elbows on his knees as she pulled out a yellow legal pad. "I've been sorting through all the reports flagged as AWOL from the Miller home between '02 and '09. It's a hot mess—bad documentation, incomplete transfers, no follow-ups. Some of these kids weren't even reported missing for months."

Vega rubbed a hand over his jaw. "I noticed the same pattern. Start cross-referencing them against the unidentified remains list. See who drops out of the system with no trace."

"We're not looking for who killed Earl anymore." Santos tapped her pen. "We're building a list of children that nobody ever came for. How sad."

Vega didn't reply. He didn't need to.

The Millers' farm was a graveyard filled with ghosts, and nobody wanted to talk about them. Helen lived with her younger sister in upstate Michigan, and she refused all their phone calls. Wouldn't even come to the door when they'd showed up at her house. Her sister simply said, "Earl ran off with a younger woman years ago. Now leave her alone." The Miller kids had confirmed the story, but they weren't any more willing to talk to Vega or Santos than their mother.

The detectives both knew the former foster kids were the key.

Santos reached into the folder and handed him a single page. "Here's one that jumped out at me that you might want to take a look at, because she was living there right around the time Earl went missing. Those are the ones I'm focusing on now, by the way. She's only an eight-month placement, so probably just a temporary placement, but still. Good timing. Age sixteen. She was transferred from a different foster home due to behavioral issues, but those notes are vague. It looks like she reported abuse to her social worker multiple times, but there are no official incident reports or follow-ups after she left."

He looked down at the name:

Soledad Carter.

There was only one photo attached—black and white with low resolution. She wasn't angry or scared. Just skeptical. A young girl with a head full of tight braids who looked like she saw everything and said nothing. That's the face that she wore.

Vega frowned. "Where did she go after she left the Millers?"

Santos flipped to the next sheet. "That's the thing. She didn't. There's no placement record after Miller. She's one that just disappears."

"No report?"

"None."

Vega stared at the photo again, feeling something tighten in his gut. "Let's find her and see what she has to say."

TWELVE

I hated watching Orion suffer. He tried to hide it. All his worries. The lack of money as the weeks grew into months without getting hired. He worked as a day laborer whenever he could or other odd gigs that he found on job boards. Those paid cash but only lasted a few days. That was the only thing keeping us afloat. He couldn't find anything permanent.

His unemployment wasn't from his lack of effort, though. He applied for every job he could find that he was even remotely qualified for and even some that he wasn't, but the endings were all the same. Eventually, everyone ghosted him. A few places called for interviews, and then nothing. One sales manager told him they were "looking for someone more presentable." That gutted him. He didn't say it, but I saw the way he looked at his worn and tattered boots when he got home. Like they were the reason everything was falling apart. I knew exactly how he felt. I'd seen the look hundreds of times.

He'd used his last ten dollars to buy a cheap six-pack of beer that night, and I hadn't said a word about it. He deserved the escape. If I didn't hate the taste of beer, I would've joined him, but I couldn't stomach it.

I could feel the stress settling into the apartment again. He did too. We both snapped easier. The lightheartedness and giddiness we'd experienced after seeing each other again after so many years had been replaced with the stark reality of what we were up against. Poverty was like that—a joy stealer. The space heater blew out last week, so now we were freezing in addition to being stressed out of our minds.

But that wasn't even the biggest problem—six days ago, Janie stopped eating.

Just stopped.

No warning. No fever. No complaint. She just clamped her mouth shut last Thursday morning, and that was it. She hasn't eaten anything since. Barely even drank any water.

I've tried everything. Applesauce, crackers, even her favorite banana yogurt that's only ever a special treat because it's so expensive. I pulled out the old bottle I'd stashed in the back of the cabinet and tried feeding her like a baby, cradling her against my chest like I used to.

Still nothing. Not one bite.

"She'll eat when she's hungry," Orion said that first morning at breakfast with complete confidence. "Won't you, Janie?" He gave her a huge encouraging smile. She scowled back at him.

But he'd changed his mind and his tone after two days passed and she was still refusing to eat anything. "Maybe you should take her to the doctor? Just to be safe?"

I knew what would happen if I took her to the hospital or urgent care. A two-year-old with bruises from falling down and violent tantrums, plus a mysterious aversion to food? That wasn't going to go over well with anyone. And there were no medical records of her on file. No evidence that she even existed. There would be so many questions. Forms. Visits. Probably CPS. I couldn't let CPS get involved. No way. Not after what they'd done to me. They'd done the same thing to Orion, so he understood.

We had to figure this out on our own. We didn't have any other choice.

I disappeared in a rabbit hole of Reddit boards, searching for answers. Researching what methods parents of kids with food refusal had tried to get their children to eat. There were so many different ideas and suggestions—making the food into fun shapes, using colorful plates, being over the top with praise and rewards—but none of the strategies worked any better than all the other things I'd tried. Most of them said that the behavior was attention motivated and you should ignore it, but you couldn't ignore a child that didn't eat for more than four days. That was too dangerous.

By day five without food and barely any water, I was absolutely desperate and paralyzed with worry. I knelt in front of her, tears running down my face, and resorted to begging.

"Please, Janie. Just eat something. For Mommy. Please. Can you do that?" I crouched in front of her. I was so afraid she was going to die if she didn't eat. Or that her system would shut down in some irrevocable way that would have lasting effects on her health.

She looked at me, her big blue eyes glassy and blank, and whispered, "Tell him go bye-bye." She pointed to Orion.

It took me a full five seconds to register what she meant. That's why she was doing this? To get Orion to leave? There was no way. I placed my fingers under her chin and lifted her head. "What did you say, Janie? Tell Mommy what you said again."

But she acted like she didn't hear me. She went back to tearing paper, pretending like I hadn't spoken.

"I think she said something about going bye-bye," Orion piped up from behind me.

"Oh." I laughed. "Maybe she's finally ready to leave the apartment." But I'd heard her the first time. I couldn't believe the level of sophisticated manipulation behind her actions, but I didn't want to tell him what she said because it would hurt his feelings after he'd worked so hard to bond with her.

It did, however, spark a new plan.

Maybe it really was time for Janie to leave the house again.

My strategy was to get as much delicious and yummy food as possible, and then create a buffet for her that she wouldn't be able to refuse. Who could say no to rocky road ice cream or chocolate chip cookies? A greasy hamburger or fried chicken. I wasn't sure exactly what she liked because we only ever bought essentials and whatever was cheapest, but we'd try it all until we found something that did the trick.

The three of us piled into Orion's beat-up Chevy truck and drove to the grocery store. Janie sat between us, wide eyed and staring out the window as she took it all in. Neither Orion nor I acknowledged what we were about to do, but we both knew what would happen once we got to the grocery store. We were old pros at stealing food. That's how we survived as kids in foster care, and we smiled knowingly to each other as we pulled into the parking lot. We would've loved to have a truck when we were younger.

We sat in the parking lot and waited until the store was nearly empty—past midnight on a Tuesday night, when even the tired moms had gone home. The fluorescent lights hummed overhead as we walked through the doors, harsh and too bright, making the bags under my eyes feel like bruises.

Orion pushed the cart. I walked beside him, pretending we were just another exhausted couple with a cranky toddler and not two broke criminals about to steal their next meal. Janie sat in the cart, bundled in her thrift-store jacket, with her chapped lips, taking everything in with amazement like she was at Disneyland for the first time.

She wasn't the only one who hadn't eaten. We hadn't eaten all day either. I was just as starved. All the food made me swoon.

"What do you think will entice her to eat?" Orion whispered.

I thought fast. I didn't really know since she'd never had the opportunity. "Peaches. Mac and cheese. Anything shaped like an animal. Get those little smiley-face fries. Those look like they're candy. She might like those."

"Okay." He turned into the frozen food aisle. "Then we're throwing her a damn feast." He handed me a reusable shopping bag we'd brought to look legit. I slipped it over my arm and started slowly packing it—one item at a time, like I was comparing prices or ingredients. A box of spiral mac. Canned peaches. Chicken nuggets shaped like stars. A loaf of bread.

It all came back to me that quickly. You had to move like someone with choices who wasn't doing anything wrong. Orion moved too, casually loading a few items into the cart, then slipping others into the lining of his jacket, one pocket at a time. Crackers. A jar of peanut butter. A block of cheese.

"Meat or no meat?" he asked under his breath.

"Lunchables," I whispered. "If they have them. She likes to stack things."

We rounded the last aisle. Paper towels and toiletries. Janie reached out her hand as we passed a stack of pink cupcakes. Store-brand and probably stale. But her fingers curled toward them.

"Do it," Orion said as soon as he noticed.

I grabbed them and slid them into the bag. Then, we pulled Janie out of the cart and left it in the cleaning-supplies aisle. We headed to the front of the store and slipped out the sliding glass doors without the alarm going off, just like we used to. No one looked twice. We held back the urge to sprint to the truck, walking fast. We piled in, giddy and excited.

Back at the apartment, we got to work as soon as we arrived. We laid everything out on the counter like a holiday spread. A chipped plate for each item. A cleanish spoon. Two sippy cups. One red candle Orion found in the back of the cupboard.

Janie sat in the middle of the kitchen floor like a queen. Silent and solemnly watching us as we worked. Orion turned on the radio, and we sang and danced as we added the final finishing touches. He twirled me around by the stove when the song got to our favorite part. I laughed happily. The water boiled over in the pot, and he raced to turn the heat down on the burner.

Suddenly, Janie stood and walked up behind him. At first, I thought she was going to hug him as she reached out her arms, and for a second, my heart melted. But then, before I knew what was happening, she grabbed his calf and sank her teeth into it.

"Aah!" he yelled, dropping the spoon and burning himself on the stove. He let out another scream. I hurried over to them. Janie still had her teeth in his leg. I grabbed her by the shoulders from behind, but she wouldn't let go.

"Janie! Stop it! No!" I yanked her off, pulling her back as she finally released her hold. Orion dashed to the sink, immediately turning on the water and putting his burned arm underneath the faucet.

Janie stood and grinned at me like she was proud of herself for hurting him.

"You can't act this way!" I shrieked. "Time-out!"

I grabbed her arm and dragged her down the hallway kicking and screaming, but I didn't care. She couldn't keep controlling the house like this. She had to learn a lesson. I hadn't put her in the closet since I used to hide her in there to go to class, but she needed to know how serious this offense was. I was done playing around.

I opened the closet door and pushed her inside. "You cannot hurt other people—do you understand me?" I stabbed my finger into her chest. "That is NOT okay. I want you to sit in here, and think about what you did just now. You're on time-out."

She stared up at me. Her blue eyes wide and wondering. I'd never flipped out like this before, but she'd pushed me over the edge and she knew it. Her lower lip trembled like she was going to cry, and I quickly shut the door before I lost my nerve. She needed to learn a lesson, and I didn't know any other way to teach her.

I hurried back over to Orion, who was still in the kitchen. "I'm so sorry she did that. Are you okay?"

He was wrapping his burned arm with ice and a dish towel at the sink. "I'm fine." But he wasn't fine. He grimaced as he spoke. His calf was swollen from her bite. She'd broken through the skin in multiple places. He'd probably get some nasty infection. All the life had been sucked out of the room that quick.

"What are we going to do?" I asked.

I didn't expect an answer, and he didn't have one to give. We sat there in silence while we listened to her rage in the closet. Thrashing. Kicking. Breaking things. Her tortured screams like she was being physically hurt. What would the neighbors think? I felt her pain in my own body. Orion sensed it even though he was the one who was really hurt.

"Come on." He took me by the hand and led me over to the couch to try to calm me down just as she gave up her fight and her screams cut off mid-wail. That's how it always went. As fast as her fits came, they were gone just as quick. Most of the time, I just waited them out and did my best to keep her from hurting herself. I took a seat as he went over to the closet. He gave me a knowing look, and I nodded back. He opened the door.

Janie came out, sucking on her thumb and quiet as a mouse. She kept her head down as she climbed on to my lap without saying a word and nuzzled her face into my neck like nothing had happened.

Everything forgiven and forgotten.

Or so I thought.

THIRTEEN

I almost killed her. I really almost killed her. Oh my god.

It'd been four days since we started putting Janie in the closet for time-outs, and so far, it'd been working to get her to eat. We hated doing it, but she'd left us no other choice. She had to eat. What happened in there today?

"Please wake up, baby!" I cried, holding Janie's body against mine as I raced through the glass doors and into the lobby of the emergency room. Banging on the plexiglass to get the receptionist's attention.

The young woman sitting behind the desk startled and looked up. "Can I help you?"

"Can you help me?! Yes, obviously I need help! You don't see my daughter?" I shrieked, frantically looking around for a doctor. Someone. Anyone to actually help me.

"Okay, ma'am, yes. I understand. Can you tell me your name?"

"Name? You want my name? My daughter's dying! This is an emergency!" I smashed myself up against the glass. "Please, somebody help us! She needs a doctor!"

"Ma'am, I understand that you're upset, but I need you to calm down. This is for her safety. I have to check you into our system first. All you have to do is give me her name and birth date, so I can put something on her wrist really quick. Making sure nobody can grab her and steal her while she's here. Somebody's coming right now to help you." Her voice was calm and steady. Meanwhile, Janie's body flopped lifeless in my arms. I kept shaking her, hoping she'd snap out of it.

"Beatrice—Becky Watson. Hers is Janie."

"Date of birth?"

"March twenty-fourth, 2019."

She quickly printed out a wristband and slapped it on Janie's wrist just as a male nurse wearing a mask came around the other side of the glass and ushered us through the double doors behind him.

"Is she conscious?" he asked, scanning her body up and down. Opening her eyelids and shining a small penlight in her eyes while I held her in my arms, walking fast beside him.

"No," I said, trying to keep the hysteria out of my voice because everyone was staring at us now, as he ushered us into another room.

This was bad. Like really, *really* bad. I almost killed my daughter.

But she hit me with a hammer while I was sleeping. I argued with myself while a different nurse wrapped a blood pressure cuff around Janie's forearm and the first guy stuck a thermometer on her temple.

She hit me. What kind of a toddler did that? I held her listless body against mine. My head still throbbed. It hadn't stopped in the three days since she'd done it. A big egg protruded out of my temple. Discolored bruises all around it. I probably had a concussion. What if they asked about the injury? I looked like I'd been hit with a bat. It certainly felt like it when it happened.

"How did she get these bruises on her face?" the nurse wearing the green scrubs asked, while the male nurse took Janie from me and placed her onto the small hospital bed. He immediately started a rig for an IV.

"She fell and hit her head on the coffee table. She's really clumsy," I said, but I knew how it sounded. I also knew how Janie looked. Her peach fuzz hair was growing back in weird patches. She was only wearing a diaper, and it was totally soiled. That's all she'd been in when I put her in the closet for a time-out, and I didn't think to throw on any of her other clothes or change her diaper before I left. Once Orion and I knew she was in trouble, we'd raced here as fast as we could. I wish he was with me, but there was already going to be so many questions about Janie, and we couldn't risk them connecting our past, especially not on paper.

The nurses glanced at each other while they slipped a small white gown over Janie's head and placed the heart monitor on her pointer finger. Janie looked even tinier lying on the hospital bed. She still hadn't moved. Not even when they poked her with the needle to run her IV.

"My name is Denise, and we're going to take Janie back with us because her vitals aren't good, but we need you to give all of her information to the charge nurse up front that you saw in registration," Denise said as they unlocked the wheels on the hospital bed.

"I don't think I want to leave her. I—" But it was too late. They were already whisking Janie away, pushing her through another set of double doors down the opposite hallway.

I turned around. A group of nurses sat huddled around the receptionist area, whispering and motioning in my direction. I walked toward them since they were clearly waiting for me, but I didn't want to talk to anyone, especially not to answer a bunch of questions. I knew that I stank. How I looked. Just as dirty and disheveled as Janie. But it was laundry or eat. I could feel their judgment radiating off them and toward me.

This was it. There would be no more secrets.

The secret was out.

I had a baby.

One that was over two years old.

Was that even still considered a baby? I didn't know.

A woman with an iPad stepped forward from the group and stuck out her hand. "I'm Ramona. Let's move over there to that other conference room so we have some privacy, and you can tell me what happened to Janie," she said, motioning to the doors on the other side of the waiting room.

I hadn't thought this part through. Other than the fact that Orion couldn't come inside the hospital with me. The only thing we wanted to do was make sure we hadn't killed Janie. I never considered what I was going to do when I got here and had to explain what happened to her. How was I going to do that?

"Can I use the restroom first?" I asked, moving my body uncomfortably like I suddenly had to pee. Really, I needed time to get my story together. Calm myself down.

She nodded. "Sure, just use the one in the lobby. It's unlocked."

"Thanks. Be back in a second," I said, hurrying toward it.

It'd been chaos in the apartment since Janie hit me with the hammer. After her first time-out in the closet, she came into the living room afterward like everything was fine. We'd all gone to sleep that night completely exhausted but certain the crisis was over. At least for the moment.

The pain had hit like lightning. Hot.

I woke up to a crack and a wet warmth running down the side of my face. Disoriented. Gasping. I rolled over and saw Janie. Standing perfectly still next to the couch. Orion's small hammer clenched in her hand. Her expression wasn't angry. It wasn't confused. It was blank.

She watched me the way someone watches a spider crawl across the ceiling. Detached and curious.

Orion was already on his knees beside me. His eyes wide and wild.

"Oh my god! What happened? Becks? Are you okay?" He crouched next to the couch as I tried to sit up. But raising my head sent my world spinning, leaving me incredibly nauseous.

Janie just stood there, silent. Staring and watching us.

I brought my hand to my head. There was blood in my hair. The pain behind my left eye already blooming and exploding.

"She hit me," I whispered to Orion while I locked eyes with Janie. Horror and disbelief fought for first place inside of me.

Orion slowly turned around to face Janie.

She dropped the hammer at her feet. The sound echoed, sharp and final.

Orion was furious with her, and our home had turned into a battle of wills between those two. Earlier this afternoon, he put her in the closet for a time-out after she kicked him in the shins. It was the only form of punishment she responded to, so we kept doing it. I figured it was better than tying her up to the kitchen chair. We didn't mean to leave her in the closet for that long. We really didn't. We were just *so* tired, and we'd accidentally fallen asleep on the couch.

I woke to pitch black in the apartment. I threw Orion's arm off me and sat up. That's when I remembered the time-out and raced to the closet. I whipped open the door to find Janie curled up in the fetal position and passed out in the corner. Her back to the wall. In a puddle of her own pee and vomit.

"Janie!" I screamed, scooping her off the floor and shaking her. Her head just rolled around loosely on her neck. Eyes stayed closed. Her small body lifeless and floppy. "Janie! Wake up! Knock it off. This isn't okay."

She was faking it. She had to be faking. Being dramatic. But her skin looked funny. Her breathing shallow and hollow. A white circle around her lips. Orion burst in behind me and scooped her up, carrying her into the living room. He lay her flat on her back on the wooden floor and put his face up to hers.

"Is she breathing? Please tell me she's breathing." I shoved him off her and hovered over her body, listening closely to make sure she was still breathing. It looked like her chest was still moving, but I couldn't tell for sure.

I slapped her. Hard. Straight across the face. Her eyelids fluttered open for a brief second. Her eyeballs rolled back in her head. Nothing but whites. She couldn't fake that.

That's when I'd thrown her over my shoulder and we raced to the emergency room.

My pink hand mark on her cheek stood out against her pale skin. I hadn't thought about that part. It was so obviously a hand mark. They were going to think I abused her. I wasn't an abuser. I only hit her to try to rouse her and see if she was faking it. I couldn't waste money on an unnecessary emergency room trip, but they didn't know that.

My eyes scanned the waiting room as I waited for whoever was using the bathroom to finish. Had they called the police? Is that what all the nurses were whispering about? They were going to arrest me. I could feel it. I quickly used the bathroom and hurried back to where they were all waiting for me, my heart in my throat.

The chubby-cheeked one with the red glasses made her way toward me. A grim expression on her face.

"Are you her sole guardian?" she asked with her glasses perched on her nose, peering down at me.

There was something about the way she said it that let me know I was in trouble. My fears weren't unfounded. "You mean does she have a father?"

"Yes, or another legal guardian besides yourself?"

I shook my head.

"Is there someone else you can call? Another family member?"

"I don't understand. Did something happen to Janie? Is she okay?" I frantically looked behind her, but the doors were closed. The hallway was empty. I knew I shouldn't have let them take her from me. I should've put my foot down when I walked in and demanded to stay with her.

The woman motioned to the security officer standing behind her, and he took a step closer to us. I wasn't fully panicked until I saw her do that. "Janie's fine. She's still with our team of doctors. It's just that when we see injuries like the ones that we see on Janie, we're automatically required to contact our child services department in the hospital. They might determine that there needs to be an investigation and the child isn't safe to return home. If that's the case, oftentimes they'll let the child go with another family member or legal guardian."

"What do you mean, injuries like you see on Janie?" I asked, feigning innocence, but I knew exactly which injuries she was talking about. It wasn't my fault that Janie got hurt in our power struggles. They had no idea how strong she was. She might be tiny, but she could fight. Sometimes she liked to hit herself too. But they didn't know that either.

"There are marks on her wrists consistent with child abuse. Bruises on her buttocks. Lots of older scars from previous injuries, especially on her torso. She's severely malnourished." Her voice was hard. She hated me and thought I was a terrible mother. But she didn't know Janie. She didn't understand our situation.

Do you have any kids? Do they spit at you? How about hurt you when you fall asleep? Janie left us no other choice. Not after what she'd done to me with the hammer.

But I looked in her eyes and knew I couldn't say any of that. Nobody would believe that my toddler tried to hurt me. I sounded crazy. Looked even crazier. Even I knew that, especially in my dirty and worn clothes. I was fully aware of the way all this looked to them. I could see the judgment and disdain in her eyes.

My head spun. What was I going to do? What if they took her from me? What would happen to her? The questions tumbled so fast. One right on top of the other. Were they going to charge me with child abuse? Was that a felony? I couldn't go to jail or lose Janie.

In a fit of desperation, I blurted out, "I want to call my grandma."

(THEN)

I hate this new apartment as much as I knew I would from the very first night we got here. I miss the trailer court, which is so funny because I used to HATE it. That's how much I've grown up. It really is true. What they say. How you just grow up overnight. I don't even know when it happened. I couldn't stand the trailer courts when I was little. Next to being homeless and sleeping in cars, they were the worst. Anytime we got an actual apartment, I was ecstatic. There are certain things they can't shut off in apartments during the winter in Minnesota. Like heat. So even if we didn't pay the heating bill, we didn't freeze. But as I've gotten older, I've grown to love the trailer courts.

At least there I didn't have to pretend to be a regular kid, like I do at school. All the kids in the trailer court were just like me. They all knew what it was like to be hungry and scared. Left alone for days. Joshlyn stayed with me whenever her stepdad was drinking because he liked to crawl into her bed after he'd had a couple beers. She couldn't stay when Cerena was home because Cerena hated having my friends in the house, but I kept Joshlyn safe whenever I could. Same with Rachel. She came to my house last month after her mom's boyfriend knocked her mom out, and she needed to call 911. Their phone got cut off last month, so they'd been using ours whenever they needed to make calls. That was fine, seeing as we used their cable.

What were Joshlyn and Rachel going to do now? I didn't even get to say goodbye to them.

I wanted Cerena to be drunk or an addict. Like so many of the other moms in the trailer court. That left me for days to go on crack binges. Or was out drinking and hooking up with men to pay the rent. But she didn't. Somehow the fact that Cerena was sober when she did everything made it so much worse than everyone else's parents.

It meant I missed out on the honeymoon periods too. You know, how they abandoned their kids when they were using, but they were the most attentive parents when they were sober? That part. The wonderful stage where they're so eager to make up for all the time they've lost, the birthday parties they've missed or never thrown at all, and the hundreds of promises they didn't keep. It wasn't like their parents didn't beat them. They did. Kyle's dad gave him black eyes on a regular basis, but he bought him brand-new Jordans afterward. I didn't get any of that.

We all rode the bus to the last stop on the outskirts of town. The Thunderbird Motel. That's where we all got on and off.

Mostly, we didn't talk to each other at school, though. Nobody wanted to be associated with the fact that you lived in the trailer park behind the Thunderbird. No one. So, we pretended we didn't know each other at school. All of us in our different friend groups, just trying to survive.

Cerena was just plain old-fashioned mean. We didn't have to be there. She didn't suffer from any addiction or alcohol affliction. Her selfish and terrible decisions were made from a sober and clean mind. That was worse. At least for me. But she didn't care.

Cerena doesn't care about anyone but herself. That's the problem. It took me a long time to figure that out. You can't fathom that kind of rejection as a child. It's too cruel. Totally incomprehensible that the woman who carried you inside her womb for nine months and pushed you out of her body—who shared your DNA—didn't want you.

But she doesn't.

I missed the trailer court tonight. So much. I'd never had such close friends, and now that I'd experienced how that felt, I didn't know what I was going to do without them. Cerena ruined all of that for me, though. Everyone at school hates me. How could they not? I have zero friends. Even the girl with her daddy in prison had friends, but I was a pariah.

I took a deep breath and tried to settle down. I'd get through this. I always did. I just had to focus on school. Getting good grades was the most important thing to me, anyway. Not making friends. Because I was going to do whatever it took to get out of this hellhole. To not be like Cerena.

That was the key to getting out—an education. Then, a good job. Maybe if I study hard enough, I can be a doctor.

FOURTEEN

I watched Lillian from the hospital bed, where I lay with Janie tucked underneath my arm. Janie was hooked up to an IV, pumping fluids and medicine into her system. She got really agitated after they took x-rays, so they'd given her something to sleep too. I'm not sure what it was, but it knocked her out and she's been sleeping ever since. I wish they'd give me some of whatever it was to take home with me.

I didn't regret calling Lillian.

Lillian Beaumont.

That's my grandmother.

She even sounds rich.

Lillian had taken over the situation from the moment she got on the phone. It'd taken three wrong numbers before I got the right one, and I'd spilled out the details as fast as I could.

"Let me speak with the emergency room doctor," she demanded as soon as I'd finished, and I gladly gave her permission to discuss Janie's case with the doctors so I didn't have to.

They surrounded her now—the entire team—speaking in hushed whispers. The doctors. Nurses. The receptionist who'd checked me in. Most importantly, the police officer and social worker who'd arrived this morning. They were officially opening a child abuse investigation on me.

I couldn't stop staring at Lillian, stunned. Tall and sinewy, with the kind of figure people drank in with their eyes, she'd breezed into the emergency room three hours ago. It'd taken her almost sixteen hours to get here because she came from Florida. But she'd gotten on a plane the minute we hung up the phone. She was sparkling and fluttered her hands when she talked, like an actual fairy godmother that was here to save the day. She was even more beautiful than Cerena. Long, luscious, flowing locks. High cheekbones. Pouty lips. A tiny mole-like birthmark on her right cheek. She'd shocked me into silence when she walked into our hospital room, partly with her beauty, but also the fact that she'd actually come.

"Oh, my baby, my precious darling. We've been looking everywhere for you," Lillian cried as soon as the curtain was pulled back. She raced over to the bed. "I'm so sorry. So, *so* sorry. I can't imagine all that you've been through. Come here. Let me get a good look at you! My grandbaby." She cupped my face in her hands and peered into my eyes. A softened version of my mother's twisted face. No lines. Her skin was so smooth and bright. She was so clean. Smelled like rich people. "You're so precious. So beautiful, my darling. Do you know how long we've been looking for you?" She covered my face with kisses.

"I think they're going to take my baby or charge me with a crime," I whispered to her as she was squeezing my cheeks and showering me with kisses, exclaiming over how much time she'd spent looking for me. "I don't want to go to jail for child abuse, and I can't lose Janie. She's all I have in this world."

Lillian brushed my hair off my face and leaned in even closer. Almost like we were going to kiss. "Don't you worry about anything, darling. Your grandmother is here, and I'm going to take care of you." She pinched my cheeks again and gave me another huge smile. I'd never seen someone so happy to see me, and it felt weird. A bit disorienting.

I've barely had a moment to say or do anything since she arrived. She took over immediately, and it's been that way ever since. I didn't mind at all, though. It was a welcome relief. The one I'd desperately been searching for since the moment I gave birth. Even more so than Orion, because she had the money and power to make things better, and so far, she'd been making good on all her promises.

I've never seen anything like it. It was unbelievable the way she commanded a room. What would've happened if I'd called her all those years ago? Back in high school when I'd first looked her up on the school's computers in the library. It'd been easy to find her because the one thing Cerena told the truth about was her last name and that she'd come from money. That narrowed down the pool, especially with social media. It hadn't taken me long to locate Lillian. The biggest surprise was that she was in Florida. I hadn't expected Cerena to grow up in the South. I'd always just assumed she was from the Midwest. There'd never been a hint of a Southern accent in Cerena's voice. Not like there was in Lillian's.

After I found Lillian and my grandfather, I stalked their social media and anything else I could find on them for months. I'd always wanted to locate my family. Partly just to see if what Cerena said about them was true. It was when I was living alone in the shed that I finally got the courage to look them up. The shed had been fine in the late summer and early fall, but as the seasons crept into colder and colder temperatures, I started worrying about the winter and what I'd do once it got so cold that being outside at night would kill you with the below-freezing temperatures.

I started my background search with Cerena. I'd half expected her identity to be fake and was surprised to discover that it wasn't. She was who she said she was, so it was easy to find her parents, especially when Cerena had been featured in so many local newspapers and media outlets for her ballet performances. She'd won lots of awards. I watched all the old clips of her on the local evening news. Twirling and spinning. Standing on her tiptoes. I read through all the newspaper articles too. Looked at all the pictures. Her smiling wide in mirrored dance studios.

Black leotard. Pointed toes. Hair slicked back in a tight bun on top of her head. Shiny, bright lipstick on her lips. Rail thin.

I'd toyed with calling my grandmother back then. I'd even written her number down. Especially as the temperatures dropped. But the fact that all the stuff Cerena said about her past was true made me wonder if all the bad parts about her childhood were too. Like how Lillian put her on really strict diets to make her lose weight and gave her enemas. How she made her practice even when she was sick or injured. Making her dance with a stress fracture for an entire month once. But that wasn't the worst of it. According to Cerena, she'd wake her up in the middle of the night and make her perform all sorts of bizarre tasks. Like washing her feet and making her kneel on uncooked pasta the entire time. She had to ask permission to use the bathroom, and she was only allowed to go on a particular schedule. Lillian's favorite torture method was to have Cerena perform manual labor until she collapsed from sheer exhaustion. Ridiculous things like making her stay awake and dig a hole in the backyard for seven hours straight. No breaks. No water.

In the end, that's why I chose not to reach out to her. It was too big of a risk, and I didn't want to trade one bad situation for another. At least Cerena's evil was predictable. The evil I knew was better than the one I didn't. But it looked like I might've been wrong. What would've happened if I'd called Lillian all those years ago? Could she have saved my life? Prevented all this? I might have been able to go through college the regular way. There were so many other possibilities that her presence and her money would've afforded me.

It didn't matter. She was here now.

The doctor was stumbling all over his words. He did that every time he tried to talk to her. Cerena used to trip men up with her beauty too, but this was on an entirely different level. Lillian was intoxicating. Part of it was also her voice. It was just so soothing. Like a cup of hot chamomile tea.

I couldn't help but laugh as I watched her work her magic. No wonder Cerena hated her so much. She couldn't stand anyone being prettier than her. It's why she kept me ugly when I was a little girl. She wasn't like the typical narcissistic parent who saw me as an extension of herself—she saw me as her direct competition, and she did everything in her power to make sure I never had an opportunity to steal any of her spotlight. She loved making me hideous.

Once, I had this cute pink T-shirt with little rainbows all over it. I can't even remember how I got it into the house. I think one of her boyfriends gave it to me, which is probably the only reason she let me keep it. Anyway, we were checking out at the grocery store and the cashier took an interest in me for some reason that day.

"Oh my gosh. Aren't you the absolute cutest thing that ever did live," she gushed in a completely over-the-top voice. "That shirt is perfect on you. It makes your eyes nearly sparkle. Brings out your precious little dimples too." She'd leaned across the scanner to pinch my cheeks, and Cerena had quickly jerked me out of the woman's reach.

Cerena gave her a nasty glare and pushed the grocery cart forward to the end of the checkout counter. She stared at the woman so hard without saying another word. The cashier practically shrank from her silent rage. She fumbled with all our groceries as she ran them across the conveyor belt. My insides were liquid gold. I couldn't keep the smile off my face.

I thought Cerena had defended me. For once in my life, she'd stood up for me. She'd pulled me away from an overbearing woman so that she couldn't touch me. That's what I assumed her annoyance and irritation were about. Why she glared at the woman and treated her with such disdain until we left the store.

Two days later, I caught Cerena cutting up my T-shirt with scissors in the kitchen. She sliced it into pieces, then threw it in the trash. All with a big smile on her face. When I asked her about it, she said the shirt got ruined in the wash. A stupid lie, since she never even did my laundry. I'd been washing my own clothes since I was eight, when we were lucky enough to afford detergent.

That's why I couldn't have anything pretty. Didn't dare even wear makeup in the house. I hid it in my backpack and put it on at school. Not that I wore all that much anyway. Just eyeliner, a little mascara, and a dab of ChapStick. Sometimes concealer when I had a bad pimple. That was it. You could barely even tell I had anything on most days, but I made sure to wipe it off my face before I ever stepped foot back home after school.

Cerena would've never been able to share the spotlight with anyone else, but I was so grateful for Lillian. She could have the spotlight. She could have anything she wanted as long as she helped me out of this.

HIM

(NOW)

Soledad lived above a pawnshop on the east side of Chicago. Her apartment smelled like Chinese takeout and fabric softener. Vega had to duck under a drying rack full of baby clothes just to get through the doorway. She had three kids under six—all boys.

A toddler napped in the next room, and another boy was strapped to her chest in a navy blue baby wrap. Soledad kept her voice low, perched on the couch with her legs crossed. Vega let her settle while Santos leaned against the wall, ready to quietly take notes. They'd discussed that he'd take the lead on the way over.

"Thanks for being willing to talk," Vega said, opening the conversation before any of the kids woke up and derailed it. He knew how children were—he had three of his own at home. Except his were all girls.

Soledad folded her hands on her lap. Her nails were bitten to the quick. "I said I'd try."

"You lived at the Miller residence starting in 2007 for about eight months?" he asked, not wasting any of their precious time.

"Eight months, four days," she said, clearly without having to think about her response.

That kind of precision usually meant trauma. Vega had learned that the hard way. He and Santos listened as she described what it was like living with the Millers. She relayed the same stories they heard from everyone else they'd interviewed so far—lots of kids with not enough resources to feed them, overworked and underfed, working long hours, and, of course, Earl. All roads led back there.

"I hated that house. Evil was in the air from the moment you walked in the door. You could just feel it. You couldn't even breathe in there after dark. Everything felt like it was caving in. You just waited for the floorboards to creak—that's when you knew he was coming for you," Soledad explained.

"Earl?" Santos asked like they needed confirmation.

She nodded once. "Always Earl. I don't know how he chose who to mess with at night. Sometimes he came for me. Other times he didn't. But he always came for someone. He couldn't keep his hands off us. Disgusting pervert." She grimaced.

"Did anyone ever fight back?" Vega asked.

"In the beginning, everyone tried, but that didn't last long because Earl had a gun. He made sure you knew it, and he also made sure you knew it never left his side. No one was trying to die over that shit."

"Were you there the night Earl disappeared?"

She raked her hands on her arms. Both covered in spiral tattoos weaving elaborate sleeves up to her shoulders. Her eyes darted all over the room like she was suddenly nervous. "I'm not sure when he disappeared, but I was there the night of the fight," she finally said.

Vega glanced at Santos out of the corner of his eye. This was the break they'd been waiting for. Why it'd been so important for them to find someone who'd been in that house during the period of time that Earl went missing. This was the first they'd heard of a fight.

"Can you take us through what you remember?" Santos asked delicately from her spot against the wall. She still hadn't moved.

Soledad blinked slowly. Long thick eyelashes. Probably fake. "It was raining. Not hard—just enough that you could hear it hit the roof. I don't know why I remember that, but I do. So random." She laughed nervously. "Anyway, Brock had been messing with everybody all day. He was always trying to pick fights, but that day, he was way worse than usual."

"Brock?" Vega's interest was immediately piqued. They'd been planning to ask her about Kyle Wallace. The forensic team had found another grave next to Earl's, except this one was missing a body. The cadaver dogs had sniffed it out. It'd been recently dug up, and they suspected someone had moved the body. Fortunately, there was a driver's license left behind. A sixteen-year-old boy: Kyle Wallace. CSU found strands of hair in the dirt on scraps from the fabric of a blanket and were running the samples as they spoke.

Nobody had ever mentioned anyone named Brock before, and Vega hadn't seen anything about him in any of the reports.

"The bully of the house." Soledad's expression flickered. "He terrorized everyone."

"How so?"

"He made us miserable every chance that he got. He'd corner kids and scream in their faces. Steal clothes. Food. He picked fights constantly for no reason. He thought he ran the place. He kept a stash of Skittles under his mattress and made the little kids 'pay rent' to use the bathroom. Oh, and he hated Orion."

"Any idea why?"

"Because Orion was the only one that stood up to him. He didn't take his shit. Most of us stayed quiet to survive, but Orion didn't. For whatever reason, he refused to back down. Not just from Brock, but from anyone. The two of them were always fighting. I think it was an alpha male thing, you know what I mean?" The baby stirred on her chest, and she quickly jostled him back to sleep. "Anyways, that day, they'd literally been fighting since the morning, and when I asked Orion about it, he kept saying Brock was acting weird and he didn't like how he was sneaking around."

"Was he?" Santos's turn to ask questions.

Soledad hesitated. "I don't know. Maybe? Brock had this way of going silent when he was thinking. You'd find him staring into space like he was plotting something, so who knows." She shrugged.

"Go on," Santos prompted.

"So that night . . . Earl didn't do his rounds . . ." Soledad shifted uncomfortably in her seat and stared at the floor.

"You mean his usual walk through the rooms?" It was a good thing Santos was the one asking questions, now that they'd shifted into sexual abuse territory. People automatically trusted her more because she was a female, and it made it easier for them to share. Soledad was no different.

"Yeah. At ten thirty. Like clockwork every single night. He was the one who put us to bed, and he always told Helen it was to make sure we weren't sneaking snacks or cell phones into our rooms, but we all knew why he was really there. So did she. That's when he picked who he was gonna mess with later that night." Soledad leaned forward and peered at the detectives. "But he didn't come that night. No one saw him. Brock was pissed and storming around the house. He said Earl promised him something. A new pair of shoes or something, but I don't really know what he was so upset about. I was just trying to stay out of his way. We all were. The thing I remember most was how Brock kept going out into the shed in the backyard all night."

Santos raised her eyebrows. "The shed?"

"Where they kept the tools and Earl's stuff. Nobody was allowed in Earl's shed."

"What happened next?"

Soledad's voice dropped. "It was past lights-out and I'd just fallen asleep, when suddenly I heard all this yelling outside. Multiple voices, but it only lasted for a few seconds. I thought it was over, but then the yelling moved into the house. That's when it got really loud. I could tell it was Earl. He was the one doing most of the screaming. There was all this crashing around like people were fighting, and then a huge bang. Like someone fell. Or maybe hit the door?"

Vega stepped forward. "Did you look?"

"No. I was too scared." She twisted her hands on her lap. "I remember holding my breath and waiting to see if anyone else was going to say or do anything. But nobody did anything. It was just quiet. So still . . . Eventually, I got up enough courage to get out of bed, and that's when I ran across the hall to Orion's room, but he wasn't in his bed. Neither was Brock. Everyone in their room was gone. I didn't know what to do, so I just ran back to my room and hid in my bed until morning." She let out a deep sigh. "We never saw Earl again."

"Did anyone ask questions or talk about it?"

She laughed. "Hell no. We were all just glad he was gone."

Vega's phone kept buzzing against his leg. He glanced down. Multiple texts from Santos. He quickly looked at the most recent:

Kyle was never at the Millers. He's not in the system.

The remains of a teenager from the community and not in foster care like all the others? That cracked the case wide open. Was it possible they were looking at a serial killer, like the media kept suggesting? Used to thinking on his feet, Vega pivoted quickly.

"Did anyone report Earl missing?" he asked.

Soledad laughed bitterly. "You think anyone cared? We were all *so* happy that he was gone. Even Helen was relieved, I think. She was the one that created the story. She just sat us down at dinner a few nights later and said, 'Earl ran off with another woman.' None of us questioned it. We just felt like we won the lottery."

"What about a boy named Kyle Wallace? Was he ever at the Millers'?"

She shook her head. "Never heard of him."

PART TWO:
The Middle

FIFTEEN

Embarrassment flooded me along with the rancid smell as soon as we entered the studio. Orion hadn't been back since we'd left for the hospital, and our leftover dinner sat spoiled on the coffee table along with the dirty diapers in the corner. The faint scent of Janie's vomit wafted out from the closet. Cleaning up had been the last thing on our minds when we dashed out the door. It'd only been a few days, but it already felt like another lifetime ago.

I wanted to sneak out from the hospital last night and tell Orion goodbye, but he didn't think it was a good idea. I'd been calling him from the phone in Janie's room ever since they'd admitted us, and he was thrilled about Lillian coming to help us. But we both agreed we didn't know if we could trust her with our secrets yet, and until we did, we couldn't take the chance of her asking too many questions and finding out about our past.

"I'm going to miss you so much," I whispered into the phone right after sunset, when Lillian had gone out to get a cup of coffee for herself and a Diet Coke for me.

"I'm going to miss you too," he said, his voice heavy. The sound of traffic in the background. He was already on the road. I couldn't help but smile. He'd made up his mind before the call. "You just let me when it's time to come back, and you know I'll drop whatever I'm doing to get there."

Where was he now? I missed him already, but I was used to missing him. We'd spent more time missing each other in our lives than we'd had together.

The doctors had kept Janie for another night at the hospital, and Lillian hadn't left my side. They'd hooked Janie up to machines monitoring her vitals, oxygen saturation, and heart rhythm, and Lillian sat in the most uncomfortable chair next to her and didn't complain once. It had felt so weird having her there with me. Even stranger having her here in our home.

She immediately went into get-shit-done mode and started bustling around the apartment, talking to herself and making notes in her phone. She commanded the situation in the same way that she'd commanded the hospital. Just like then, I didn't mind at all, other than the fact that I was so ashamed of the place and thinking of how she must be judging us.

I set Janie down, and her eyes slowly fluttered open as she stretched. She'd been asleep the moment we got in Lillian's rental car to leave the hospital. Lillian had even gotten her a car seat. Something I'd never even considered. That's how you knew she'd been a mother before.

Janie stood next to me, swaying side to side and sucking on her thumb while she eyed Lillian's every move. She'd done the same thing at the hospital. I was mesmerized by Lillian too. She was so clean and bright, she practically sparkled.

What was it about rich people that made them seem so much brighter than the rest of us? Her teeth were perfect and gleaming white too. Another obvious sign of wealth. Nobody poor ever had good teeth. When you started being able to take care of your teeth, that's when you knew you'd officially reached another income bracket.

I didn't know what Janie was thinking as she stared at Lillian, but I was in disbelief that Lillian had produced Cerena. Not only was I shocked when she answered the phone and that she showed up at the hospital, but I was equally stunned at how opposite she was from what I'd expected.

She was just so *nice*. The kind of nice that came from the eyes. That's how you knew it wasn't fake. Her eyes didn't look anything like Cerena's. Maybe that's why. Cerena's eyes matched Janie's—pale, translucent blue. Lillian's were a golden brown.

I couldn't imagine Lillian's pupils getting big like Cerena's. Cerena's eyes were almost always wide and dilated. Not from drugs, but from psychopathy. Lillian's eyes were dreamy and soft. They reminded me of melted chocolate.

Look at me. I shook my head. The tiniest bit of love showered on me, and I was already turning into a sap.

But it was impossible not to. Besides Orion, nobody's ever paid attention to me or cared about anything I was doing, especially not a parental figure. Never cooked me a meal or asked about my day. Done anything for me. That's all Lillian's been doing since the moment she showed up at the hospital. She keeps running out to get me food. Picking up my Diet Coke. Reaching to help with Janie the moment she makes a peep. She's constantly trying to anticipate what I need. It's amazing.

Janie already looked like she'd gained weight just from the fluids they'd pumped into her over the last thirty-six hours. Her skin was full of color. Pink cheeks. Rounder and not nearly as sunken in now. I hadn't realized how terrible she looked until I started seeing her through everyone else's eyes. She looked rough. So did I.

Janie was as cautious with Lillian as she was with her. Like they were both circling the other and sniffing each other out. Up until four days ago, Janie had never seen another person in our home besides Orion. Janie's eyes had been opened to an entirely different world. It was hard to wrap my brain around how wild this experience must feel to her. I swear half the reason she'd been so subdued is because she's overstimulated.

My world has been rocked too. I exist as a mom now, officially. So officially that a woman from social services was going to pay us a visit within the next seventy-two hours. That's what they told us when we left the hospital today. What would the social worker do when she saw our apartment?

"I'm sorry," I said, hanging my head in shame. "I'm not usually this messy. I'm actually a huge neat freak most of the time, but you'd never know it by looking at this place. It's so gross. I know. Like, who lives this way, right?" I tried to laugh, but it sounded totally forced and phony. She had to pick up on it, even though we were still basically strangers to each other. "It's just—I have no financial support, and I can't work to make things better because I don't have anyone to take care of Janie. I had one of my friends here for a little while, and he was helping me out, but he's really struggling too . . ." I stared at the floor. I preferred our conversations at the hospital, with all the lights turned down. It felt less embarrassing when she couldn't see me.

I walked Janie over to the other side of the room and set her down by her toys. The ones I bought at the dollar store with the last of my financial aid check a year ago. The same ones she never touched other than to break them or throw them at me. That was the only game she played with them—chuck them at Mommy. "Anyway, I never planned on having Janie. I didn't even know I was pregnant. So, I went from not knowing I was pregnant to giving birth overnight. I—"

She cut me off. "You don't mean you *really* didn't know you were pregnant?"

I nodded and smiled. "No, that's exactly what I mean. I had no clue. When I went into labor, I thought I had the worst constipation of my life. It never occurred to me for one second that I was about to give birth."

She brought her hand up to her mouth. Eyes wide in disbelief. "My goodness. What did you do?"

"The only thing I could do—I pushed her out in the toilet." I laughed.

"All by yourself?" Her voice was incredulous. Filled with awe. She hadn't moved from her spot. Janie's eyes were as big as Lillian's, and she was intently listening to me too, in a way she never had before. I couldn't tell if she was actually listening or just mimicking Lillian. I'd never thought to tell Janie her birth story. Did she understand what I was talking about?

I shrugged sheepishly. "I didn't really have any other choice. It all happened so fast. There wasn't any time to plan or even think. All of a sudden, she was just here, and I've been keeping her a secret ever since."

She balked and pointed at Janie standing in the center of the room. "You've been keeping her a secret? What do you mean? How long? I don't . . ." She moved her head, like that would make it all make sense.

"Up until the hospital, nobody knew she existed other than a couple students who heard her crying, but besides that, nobody besides my friend has ever seen her. That's the first time she's been out in the public eye."

"But you said she's two years old?"

"She is." I looked away again. What did she think of me now? This was the part I'd been afraid of telling her, but there was no way to keep it from her any longer.

"I can't believe it. This is so unreal." She was still shaking her head. "So, you didn't know that you were pregnant, and then once you had your baby, you kept her a secret?" I nodded, trying to settle the disbelief in her eyes. It was an incredible story. I wouldn't have believed it, either, if it wasn't mine. "How come?"

"I don't know anymore. That's the strangest part." I wished I had a better answer for her. "In the beginning, I didn't say anything because I was in denial and shock. And for a while, I thought I was going to give her up, but the more time that went on, I just never could. So, then I ended up keeping her, but I didn't really know what to do with her . . . things have gotten so out of control." That's how I phrased it to her. Still stuck in formal language, skirting intimacy. "I've really been struggling. I got put on academic probation and I was going to fail, so I took a medical leave of absence for a year to keep it off my transcript. But I swear, I've never been like this in my entire life. I'm always so responsible. I get amazing grades. How do you think I got into college? Everything changed once I had Janie. Everything. I just . . . I just . . ."

I stumbled to find words to explain myself and rationalize my choices. I wanted to show her I wasn't a person who lived in this filth. I was so much better than this.

She strutted over to me and put her hands on my shoulders. Her gaze deep and penetrating as she spoke. "That's all nonsense, sweet baby girl. Don't you even worry about it for one second. I've been a mama too, so I know exactly what it's like. Being a parent is one of the hardest jobs in the world, and you're practically still a baby yourself," she said in such a kind voice it almost made me want to cry. Same feeling I would get in therapy with Maura. Just like then, the urge quickly disappeared. "And you're a single mama too? With nobody to help you? I had a good husband and a whole entire family to help me out after I had your mama, and I still felt like I was drowning. Messing everything up with my baby." She tilted her head to the side and gave me the most compassionate look before shaking her head. Tears welled in her eyes. "You need to give yourself a break, child. Do you hear me? You don't need to keep doing things by yourself anymore either. You've got family now, and that's exactly what I'm here for from now on. To take care of you, and her." She pointed to Janie, still listening just as intently to our conversation. "You understand?"

I nodded at her. Totally mesmerized in the same way I'd been for the last couple of days. It was amazing how quickly your entire world could change. Just like that, without warning. I didn't know where we went next or what happened, but she was right—I had family. And not just any kind of family. One that wanted to fight for me.

Lillian pulled her phone back out of her Louis Vuitton purse. The huge rock on her hand sparkled as she typed away. Her phone case as glittery as the jewelry adorning her body. "First thing we're going to do is get someone in here to clean everything up and fix those walls." She turned up her nose at the mention of them, but I didn't even feel bad because she was right. They were disgusting. "One of those cleaning companies will be able to whip this place into shape in no time. Don't you even worry about it." She pointed to a spot in the corner of the room. The most uncluttered spot. Books lay stacked against the wall. Those were my most prized possessions. The collection I'd started in fourth grade and carried with me ever since. As many as I could keep. My two favorites—*Go Ask Alice* and *Are You There God? It's Me, Margaret*—sometimes felt like my two closest friends. "You have a seat over there and just rest with the baby. I'm going to gather up all these clothes and take them to the laundromat. Do you have one in the building?"

I shook my head at her. "You don't have to do all that. Really, I can just—"

She interrupted, waving her hand at me. "Nonsense. I've been wanting to take care of you since I found out I had a grandbaby. I can barely wait to spoil you rotten. This is only the beginning. You just wait and see." She glanced at Janie, and Janie eyed her right back, but she looked sleepy again even though she'd only been awake for a few minutes. Like this brief excursion had tuckered her out. The doctors said that was normal. That it'd take her body a while to recover from the dehydration.

So far, Lillian hasn't even asked me what happened, for us to wind up in the hospital. It wasn't all that hard to figure out why social services had gotten involved once you looked at Janie. She certainly looked like a battered child, and who would believe me if I told them I was the victim? All Lillian kept saying was that they'd been looking for me for years. She hadn't asked about Cerena either. What'd that mean?

I couldn't make sense of any of this, and I was dying to talk to Orion about it. I stared at Lillian while she bustled around the apartment. Cerena had despised her. She avoided talking about her. But when she did, it was with such venomous hate. Could she really have that much hate for her mother just because she was so beautiful and kind? Was it possible she'd made us live the way we did and cut me off from my family simply because she couldn't stand to be around another beautiful woman? Especially one that was so amazing and that other people loved?

Sadly, I didn't think it was that far fetched an idea.

SIXTEEN

The transformation in the apartment was unbelievable. Absolutely stunning. It didn't even look like the same place. It looked straight out of an interior design magazine or one of those lifestyle vlogs on Instagram. The entire place was spotless. I wished Orion was here to see it, but he was probably back to his life in Texas by now.

The cleaning crew had come in with trash bags, disinfectant, and a team of people clothed in hazmat gear. They'd carried everything out and tossed it into dumpsters in the back of the unit. Completely gutted the place. Even the furniture. Not like we had much besides the sagging mattress on the ground and the abandoned couch I'd grabbed off the side of the road. Our valuables fit into a box, and they were mostly just books and important documents.

I'd stood there in the sparkling-clean space, holding the box and feeling like I did every time Cerena's antics had led to another move. It was impossible not to feel like a loser when everything you owned fit into a single box. Back then, it was a trash bag. That's how I transported all my belongings from place to place.

The floors had barely finished drying when a truck from the Ashley furniture store pulled up in front of the building. I'd watched in amazement as they unloaded a brand-new futon and carried it into my building. But that wasn't all they had. The entire truck was full of other furniture pieces for them to unload as well—dressers, a coffee table, chairs, and shelves. Quickly followed by the order from Target that arrived next, with towels so soft and fluffy, they might as well have been from the Four Seasons. There were boxes of diapers. Wipes. Lillian had thought of everything to furnish the apartment. It looked like an entirely different place. Our former selves were gone. Completely erased like the markings on the wall.

For the first time ever, I officially had a fresh start, and I owed it all to Lillian. I'd turned to her then—the tears that had been frozen in lumps for so many years finally received their sweet release down my cheeks.

"Thank you," I tried to say, but I was crying too hard to form words. She reached for me, and I fell into her arms. No one had ever held me while I cried, and that only made me sob harder.

We've been sitting here awkwardly on the couch ever since I stopped crying. Would Lillian stay here with us tonight? The new futon was nice, but it was still only a full-size bed when you laid it out flat. I didn't know if I could sleep with her that close to me. It'd felt good to cry in her arms, but it'd left me feeling vulnerable and exposed. I wasn't ready for another step of intimacy so quickly, and sleeping practically on top of each other definitely fit that bill. Would she get offended if I pulled out the blankets and made a pallet for myself on the floor next to it?

Her voice interrupted my thoughts. "I wanted you to have a TV, but it's not being delivered until tomorrow. They could've delivered it today, but they couldn't put it up, and I don't know about you, girl, but I sure don't know how to install a TV on a wall, so I told them we'd wait for delivery until the technician could install it too."

"It's fine! Don't worry about it. You've already done so much. I can't thank you enough. Really." I couldn't count the number of times I'd already thanked her, but it still felt insufficient. Not after everything she'd done for me and Janie.

Maybe she would stay in Champaign for a while and not go back to Florida. My grandfather was dead. That's one of the things she told me about last night. We had an entire lifetime to get caught up on. He died of a heart attack two years ago. A widow-maker. That's what she called it, and that's exactly what it made her. She kept saying how lonely she'd been since then. Cerena was their only child, so I was their only grandchild. Was she lonely enough to move in with a granddaughter she barely knew? I loved what she'd done for the apartment. I was so grateful for all her help.

I wondered what Maura would've said if I asked her about it. I missed seeing her. She had such an impact on my life in such a short time.

What would we call Lillian if she stayed around? Grandma? That seemed so weird. She didn't look like any grandmother I'd ever met. She could've passed for being younger than Cerena. I was sticking with *Lillian* until she told me different. She didn't look like someone who wanted to be called Grandma anyway.

"Are you hungry?" I asked like I knew how to cook anything she'd put in my cupboards. She'd stocked the kitchenette as thoroughly as she'd stocked the closet with supplies. It'd never been so full.

She shook her head and gave me a kind smile. "Thanks so much, but do you think the two of y'all will be good here for the rest of the night by yourselves? I'm so exhausted from everything that happened today, and I'm sure you are too." She stretched and yawned dramatically to emphasize her point as she stood up. I stood next to her, doing the same, breathing a huge sigh of relief.

"I'm tired too. It'll feel good not to sleep in a hospital chair tonight," I said.

"Right? You poor things." She pointed at the closet outside of the bathroom. "Remember they put all the new sheets and blankets in there."

I nodded. I wouldn't forget any of the nice things she'd brought into the house today. I couldn't wait to take a shower and use the new lavender-scented shampoo. Put on a couple of those eye patches after I got out. She'd thought of everything. I almost started crying again, but I held back the tears.

Lillian walked over to where Janie sat in the middle of the floor, surrounded by all her new toys. The green caterpillar. Blocks. Puzzles. So many different books. Even if Janie wasn't excited about reading them, I sure was. There were new markers, in all these bright colors. Fresh coloring books and notebooks. So many things to play with, she had to eventually find something she liked.

Lillian crouched down on the floor in front of her. Flashed one of her melt-your-insides smiles. "Janie, sweetie, your grandma is going to head back to her hotel, so that I get some sleep because I'm really tired. I want you to go to bed like a good girl for your mama tonight so she can get some rest too. Can you do that for me? Can you do that for your grandma?"

Janie stared back at her blankly, like she wasn't comprehending what Lillian was saying. She barely blinked. I knew the stare well. It didn't keep Lillian from trying to talk to her, though.

"I don't look like a grandma, do I?" She shook her head playfully. "I don't sound like one either. I think we're going to have to come up with something different for me, don't you think?" Janie gave her a tiny smile, and Lillian grinned back. "How about Lala? What do you think about that? Do you like it?"

Janie's smile grew, and she nodded her head. Lillian didn't press her luck. She turned back to me. "I guess that settles it then."

"I like it," I said quickly, like I was completing the family vote. "Lala fits you way better than Grandma. I wasn't trying to call you that either."

Lillian straightened and got up from the floor. Her hip popped as she did, sending us squealing with laughter at the irony of the timing. Lillian wiped the tears from underneath her eyes once we'd finally stopped giggling. "Oh my god, that was too funny."

I nodded back at her. I couldn't remember the last time I'd laughed that hard, and it felt so good.

"I have a room at a small bed-and-breakfast in Waldorf. I'm booked through tomorrow, but if you'd like, I wouldn't mind extending my stay a bit longer so that we could get to know each other more. Plus, I thought it might be a good idea to have me here when that social worker comes sniffing around again. But only if you're up for it. Absolutely no pressure." She held her hands up as if to emphasize that she meant it.

"I'd love it if you stayed! I can't tell you how grateful I am for everything you've done today. You didn't have to do any of it. Really. Thank you!"

"Of course!" She threw her arm around my shoulders and squeezed. "I already told you—I've been waiting to take care of you forever."

(THEN)

I stood on my tiptoes, trying to see out the tiny window in the aluminum shed. It wasn't really a window. Just a square piece of plexiglass cut into the door, but at least the shed wasn't completely enclosed. I drilled two small holes in each of the side walls to give myself peepholes there too. Clematis has overgrown the entire back part of the shed and serves as good camouflage, so I left that side alone and didn't worry about an opening. Nobody's coming through that way, and even if they tried, I'd hear them before they could get to me.

I've got a shovel propped up in front of the door as a barricade and to use as a weapon if someone busts through. I don't know what kind of critters might come crawling around in the dark, so I'm prepared for those too. There's bug spray next to my pallet on the floor. I've got a knife hidden underneath my pillow. Another one in a bucket by the front door. That's as safe as I was going to get out here alone in the woods, so I'd just have to see what happened and hope for the best.

I finally did it! I'm on my own. Sometimes I still can't believe it, even though it's been almost two weeks since I left.

I'd spent months plotting and planning how I was going to run away. Ever since Cerena made Mr. Parker's wife drive herself into a tree, I knew I couldn't stay with her a second longer. No way. I couldn't have that kind of energy around me. But I really wanted to do everything the right way. Be successful and live a better life so I never turned out like Cerena or had to see her face again.

I was going to finish school. Period. I wasn't going to get on drugs to cope either, and I certainly wasn't going to sell my body. That was a great big no for me.

I was obsessive. I made charts. Drew maps. Created endless lists. Laid out the pros and cons of each place. Then, I spotted this old storage shed when I took the long way home from school on Valentine's Day and knew I'd found the perfect place to live.

The shed was tucked behind the trees in the fields behind the middle school, on the other side of Houston's Pond. You could barely see it from the road, and if I hadn't really been looking, I would've missed it. It was just over a mile past my high school, which was exactly what I needed. Not having plumbing or electricity was going to be the biggest problem, and if I got desperate or in any kind of real trouble, being so close meant I could run to the school.

It took weeks to clean it. I could've finished quicker, but I had to lug everything back and forth from my apartment to the shed. I was close to my school, but I was four miles from the apartment and had to walk. Thankfully, Cerena was gone, but her comings and goings were always completely unpredictable, so I never stopped being paranoid about getting busted the entire time. She would've thrown a fit that I was taking *her* cleaning supplies out of the house.

I cleared a pathway to the front door, just enough so I could get in and out easily. But mostly I kept the shed hidden. Left all the brush thick. The trees were overgrown around it. I didn't want anyone to know someone lived there. Being undetected was key.

The following weekend, I hauled all my blankets and things over once it was all cleaned up. I was an expert at creating pallets on the floor, and I set mine up in the back corner of the shed, splitting up the living space. Half of it was the bedroom part, and the other half my makeshift kitchen and supply area. It actually looked kind of cute.

One of my friends at school gave me their family's portable camping grill. All I really needed was a way to boil water. I could live off cup noodles and oatmeal for days. I've got some nuts and fruit that I stole from the grocery store. I wished for the thousandth time that I had the EBT card or number and didn't have to steal, but Cerena kept the card when it came in the mail, even though I was the one who'd filled out the application.

For the most part, things were actually going well.

The night I decided to finally take the plunge and leave Cerena's house, it was completely spur of the moment. After all those months of obsessive planning and preparation—when it actually happened, it was effortless, as if a switch had just gone off in my brain that said it was time to go.

I'd just poured the last can of kidney beans into the boiling water and covered the pot. Besides that, I had black olives left to eat in the refrigerator and not even the good ones. The picked-over mushy ones that I'd already passed over in the first three rounds. Eighteen saltine crackers and a moldy banana that I found underneath the couch. I still wasn't sure if I was going to eat the banana. If it was worth the food poisoning risk.

I leaned against the counter, bleary eyed and worn out. I hadn't slept at all last night because Cerena decided to bring some random guy home. Prior to that, she'd been gone for almost two weeks again. She could've brought home groceries or toilet paper, but instead she brought him. I could never decide which was worse—her being gone on her excursions or her coming back.

Most of the time she came back by herself and crashed out for days, but there were rare occasions like the night before when she brought a man with her. The men she brought home were a totally different type than the ones she had affairs with and stole from their wives. These guys tended to be losers. No money. No wife and no family. Usually no job. She brought them in like stray animals let in from outside, but instead of domesticating them and taking care of them, she abused them more. Making them wait on her like a servant while she said the vilest things to them, and they just took it.

She'd left with him this morning. She'd never even checked to see if I was there. Not when she brought him home last night and not when they headed back out today. That's how it was with Cerena. The world centered around her.

I wanted stability and routine. To graduate. Eat. A real life. One where I felt safe. And I was old enough to give myself those things now. I didn't have to do any of this with her anymore, and everything at the shed was already set up. What was I waiting on?

They say it takes domestic violence victims seven times on average before they leave their abusers. But then, once you're done—you're just done. When you've really crossed over, there's no going back, and that was me. I was sick of being hungry. Dirty. Tired and abused. People treated their pets better than Cerena treated me, and I was officially over it.

That's when I'd turned off the stove and headed upstairs to get the rest of my stuff.

I've never looked back.

HIM

(NOW)

The Wallace house sat low and wide on a quiet street. The vinyl siding was dull, and the gutters sagged from too many winters. The neighbor's sprinklers kicked on right as Vega and Santos walked up the cracked sidewalk to their front door. Wind chimes jangled on a bent hook hanging on the porch.

Mrs. Therese Wallace opened the screen door before they even knocked. She'd clearly been waiting on their arrival. Probably watching them from the big bay window overlooking the street. She was in a red housecoat. Her mascara smudged underneath her eyes like she hadn't slept in years. She wore the weight of grief on her face.

"Detectives Vega and Santos?" she asked before they even introduced themselves.

"Yes, ma'am," Vega said, flashing her a smile along with his badge. Santos and Mrs. Wallace had spoken on the phone earlier this week to arrange the meeting. "Thanks for meeting with us today."

"Absolutely." She responded eagerly like she couldn't wait to talk about her son. She stepped aside, motioning them into the house.

The air was stale with the faint smell of old carpet and reheated coffee. Photos lined the wall of the stairway: Kyle as a toddler, with birthday cake frosting smeared all over his face. Kyle in an orange soccer uniform. Marching in a Halloween parade dressed as Spider-Man. So many school portraits with forced smiles and bad haircuts. No other children marked their walls. He was probably an only child, which only made it worse and that much harder on his parents.

"I knew this day would come," Mrs. Wallace said as she led them into the living room. "I just didn't think it would take this long. My husband, Walt, is on the road, or he'd be with us too. He drives truck." She motioned to the couch. "Please sit. Can I get you coffee? Tea? Anything to drink?"

"I'm fine, thank you, ma'am," Vega said, taking a seat on the upholstered couch next to Santos as she declined a beverage too. Mrs. Wallace sat across from them. Nervously perched on the edge of the faded leather recliner.

"You filed a missing persons report on him in 2008?" Santos asked as she pointed to the mantel that was covered with more pictures of Kyle. A cross hung above the fireplace.

"I did, but it's been a ridiculous runaround with the police department since the very beginning. Nobody would even take the missing persons report for the first two days after he disappeared. They kept saying he'd probably just run off for a while, and they had to wait forty-eight hours. That teenagers did it all the time. But I know my boy and he never would've done anything like that. He loved sleeping in his own bed at night. Didn't matter how late it was, he'd come home." Her voice tightened. Hitched like she was about to cry. "That other detective that I spoke with on the phone said you had his driver's license. Can I see it?"

Vega pulled a small evidence photo in a plastic bag from the file folder in his leather bag and handed it to her. Ragged edges. Soil. A cracked driver's license half embedded in the dirt. It was faded, but the name was legible:

Wallace, Kyle A.
DOB: 02/02/1992

Mrs. Wallace stared at it like she was seeing a ghost. Her hands trembled. The tears she'd held inside up until this point flowed down her cheeks. She took short, jerky breaths. Vega hated this part of the job.

"That was found at one of the gravesites on the Miller property," he said, repeating what Santos had already explained to her over the phone, but he wanted to keep her grounded. "The fourth one so far. There's likely more. However, this one was different. The dogs sniffed out the site, but it was empty and clearly dug up recently." He handed her another picture. This time the one of the burial site—mounds of unearthed dirt, a deep hole surrounded by loose soil, and the perimeter dotted with CSU tape and yellow evidence flags sticking out of the ground.

"They still haven't found any bones?" she whispered.

"No. Just that." He pointed at the picture of the driver's license and gave her another few beats to process before jumping in with more questions. "We suspect someone moved the body."

"Kyle didn't run away. I always said that. I knew when they started pulling those bodies off that property that my baby was going to be one of them. He was all mixed up with that Orion boy, and he stayed there. I never liked their relationship. Not one bit. I told that to the officer that took the missing persons report, but I bet that's not in there, is it?"

Vega shook his head, even though it was, but he wanted to hear her version of events.

"Him and Orion got close. And I'm not going to lie—I didn't want them getting to be friends to begin with, so I always discouraged their friendship. Did everything in my power to prevent it." She shook her head in frustration. "But you know how teenagers are. I tried keeping them away from each other, but I just never could. I'm sorry, because

I'm probably not supposed to say that, but it's the truth." She sniffled, clutching both evidence photographs against her chest like she was hugging Kyle.

"What was it that you didn't like about their relationship?" Santos asked.

"Orion was in a foster home, and nine times out of ten, those are bad kids." She put her hand over her mouth. "I'm sorry. I'm just saying all sorts of things that you're not supposed to say these days. I know we shouldn't label children as bad, but you know what? Some of them just are, especially the ones that come from horrible homes. And that's why those kids are in places like the Millers' to begin with, right? Because they've got terrible parents or they've done something awful. So, you know what? I'm not going to apologize about not wanting my boy to hang out with those kinds of children, especially if one of them did something to hurt him." She was barely keeping it together. Just moments away from tears.

"How did the two of them become friends?" Vega jumped in, trying to keep her focused.

"They worked together at the Dairy Queen. They never would've met otherwise because they didn't go to the same school." She pulled a Kleenex out of the pocket of her housecoat and blew her nose. "I'm sorry. This never gets easier."

"You told my partner that sometimes Orion would get in trouble, so the Millers would ground him and you wouldn't see him for weeks at a time?" Vega asked, doing his best to be sensitive to her feelings while still getting the information he needed.

Mrs. Wallace nodded.

"You also said Orion would write Kyle letters when he was grounded? Do you by chance still have them?" he asked, suspecting she did, since the rest of the house was a shrine to him. She nodded again. He couldn't believe his good fortune. "Can I see them?"

She disappeared down the hall.

"This is perfect," Santos said with a smile. Vega nodded his agreement and gave her a thumbs-up.

Within seconds, Mrs. Wallace returned with a Nike shoebox like it'd already been out and easily accessible. The box was tied with a purple ribbon. She handed it to him.

"Can I keep these pictures?" she asked, referring to the evidence photos he'd given her moments ago.

"I'm sorry, but I can't let you do that. They're confidential and we can't have them leaked to the public," he said as he took the box from her along with the photos.

He set the box on his lap and untied the string. There were yellowed envelopes inside filled with letters written on lined notebook paper. Most of them were in sloppy, juvenile handwriting. Some just doodles. Vega skimmed through all of them quickly in case this was his only chance to review them. One caught his eye immediately:

That new kid Brock is always watching me. If he touches my stuff again, I'll beat his freak ass.

Vega leaned forward. "Do you know anything about Brock? Was your son friends with him too?"

"I never heard anything about Brock besides what Orion said about him in those letters. Kyle definitely didn't hang out with him." She pointed at the box. "If you read through the letters, you'll see Orion always called Brock a freak. He couldn't stand that kid. Said he was always watching him and that it gave him the creeps. He really hated the place, and I can't blame him. It sounded awful. In one of those letters, he describes how there were bugs in his cereal that morning." She wrinkled her nose and frowned at them. "Can't imagine why I didn't want Kyle hanging around anyone that was associated with that place."

“I understand,” Santos said. “Do you mind if we keep these for now?” She pointed to the box of letters on Vega’s lap.

“Sure, if it helps with bringing him home.” Mrs. Wallace’s eyes welled with tears again. She reached over and grabbed his knee. “Just please bring my baby home, Detective.”

SEVENTEEN

The social worker, Gloria, was a completely different person than the woman from the child services department at the hospital. She'd had a frown on her face from the moment I opened the door, and it hadn't left the entire time she'd been inside. It didn't matter how much Lillian pranced around in front of her, pointing things out and smiling. Gloria wasn't impressed. Her face still wore a permanent scowl.

"Just you and your daughter, Janie, live here, correct?" Gloria asked, eyeing the studio like there were other people who were going to suddenly appear from the hallway.

"Yes, just us. This is home sweet home." I motioned around me. The studio was bigger than most of the homes I'd grown up in. Four hundred and fifty square feet was a huge step up from a closet or an aluminum shed in the woods, but I didn't say that to her.

"Isn't it such an adorable place?" Lillian gushed, grabbing Gloria's arm and pulling her into the center of the living room. "Don't you just love what she's done with it? The way she's absolutely maximized every inch of space? Those curtains?" She pointed to the drapes she'd picked out and had delivered. "So beautiful. I can't believe the eye she has for interior design. She definitely doesn't get it from me, that's for sure."

Lillian turned around and flashed me a huge grin followed by a barely perceptible wink. I smiled at Gloria and tried to contain Janie as she squirmed against me, trying to wiggle herself free. She didn't want to be held, but I wanted Gloria to see everything clean and in order before Janie tore everything apart, which was exactly what she'd do if I put her down. She'd toss all the new throw pillows off the couch. Pull out the blankets from the basket next to the couch and throw them on the floor. While you were cleaning that up, she'd race across the living room to the set of brand-new dressers and toss everything inside out. We'd barely put everything together and tucked it all away again before Gloria arrived.

"Does Janie have a bedroom?" she asked like it wasn't obvious this was a studio apartment. The only other rooms were the tiny bathroom and the closet next to the kitchenette. I shook my head. "Where does she sleep? Do the two of you cosleep?"

Lillian jumped in before I had a chance to speak. "Janie has the greatest Pack 'n Play. I can't believe how comfortable those things have gotten over the years. They've changed so much since I had my daughter." She pointed to the closet where the Pack 'n Play was neatly folded next to Janie's new high chair. All Lillian's Target purchases. "And she loves it. She goes in there just to play and hang out even when it's not time for her nap or to go to sleep at night. It's like her own private little space. I have some of the cutest pictures. Would you like to see them?" Lillian pulled her phone out of her purse and started scrolling through it.

Gloria shook her head, dismissing her quickly. "No, no, that's fine."

What would Lillian have done if she said yes? There weren't any pictures on her phone of Janie in the Pack 'n Play. We'd only just gotten it at the beginning of the week, and so far, every time we put her in it, she climbed out even though it wasn't supposed to be possible. The makers had underestimated Janie, though. She was an excellent climber and could get herself out of almost anything. I'd gone to sleep with her in the Pack 'n Play that first night back from the hospital in our redecorated place, thinking we'd solved all the problems and I'd finally get a good night's sleep, but I woke up around two o'clock in the morning with Janie sticking her finger up my nostril. She jammed it in there hard, and I woke up screaming. Instant flashbacks to the hammer.

Janie kicked against me, but I held her tighter and tried to keep the grin on my face. I couldn't risk putting her down, because what if I had to discipline her in front of Gloria? I had no control over Janie. She didn't listen to anything I told her to do, and I didn't want Gloria seeing that. Janie might suddenly decide she wanted something, and nothing turned her into a tyrant faster than telling her no. Janie went ballistic if she didn't get what she wanted. Things had to go her way or there was hell to pay.

I shifted her to my left side. She grunted and scowled at me. She pointed to the ground. I shook my head. She grunted again. Louder this time. I squeezed her body against mine before she could lurch out of my arms.

Gloria looked down at the iPad in her hand, obviously reading something. "It says here that the hospital staff noticed Janie doesn't talk. That she's primarily nonverbal. Is that correct?"

"She talks," I said. Why was everyone suddenly so obsessed with Janie talking? She didn't call me Mommy yet, but she screamed no all the time. She told me to get rid of Orion. That had been a full sentence.

"She's just real shy," Lillian jumped in again. "You should hear her get to babbling the moment we're alone and other people aren't around. She practically doesn't shut up then." She gave Janie a pointed stare and batted her eyelashes. "Don't you, Janie girl? You've got all kinds of words to say when you're comfortable and not around strangers."

Janie nodded her head back at Lillian as if to say yes. She nodded her head like she'd understood Lillian, maintaining eye contact the entire time. As if they were having a two-sided conversation. It took everything in me to keep a straight face because I didn't want Gloria to notice my shock.

Gloria nodded at us and then proceeded to walk back through the room again, scribbling notes into her iPad. What could she possibly be writing about? Our place looked incredible. Like different people lived here than the ones who went to the hospital less than a week ago. Was it that easy? Could we just step through an imaginary door and into another life where we lived like these people? The kind of people that had candles burning on their coffee table and fresh flowers on the counter? In a vase, of all things.

"Do you mind if I look in your refrigerator?" Gloria asked.

"Feel free," I said, pointing at it in the center of the kitchenette like there was any other refrigerator we were talking about. I couldn't believe our good fortune. Less than four days ago, the same refrigerator would've been empty except for the ice in the bottom compartment and a few old condiments on top. Now it was packed with food. Lillian had even bought organic fruit. I'd never had organic fruit in my life. And there was goat milk. She thought it might help with Janie's allergies and we could start trying that warmed up in a bottle to help her sleep at night.

Maybe if Janie started eating more food, we could finally quit breastfeeding. I'd been so embarrassed to tell Lillian that I still was. I'd managed to hide it from her at the hospital, but I had to explain why Janie had practically ripped my shirt off me the first night when we all sat down on the futon together after my emotional meltdown. Janie had reached into my shirt and grabbed my left boob like it was hers.

"How long have you lived here?" Gloria asked, even though I'd answered the same question at the hospital to the other social workers.

"Almost two years." In some ways it seemed like the months had gone by so fast, and in other ways, time had never moved slower.

"Are you aware of the diaper bank at St. Thomas?" she asked next.

I shook my head at the same time Lillian asked, "Why would you ask something like that?"

Her tone had a distinct bite to it, but it didn't faze Gloria in the least. "Because the hospital noticed Janie had lots of sores and infections on her legs and buttocks consistent with being in soiled diapers for a long period of time. Sometimes people leave their children in diapers because they can't afford diapers, and St. Thomas gives out boxes of free diapers to families that might need them, every Tuesday afternoon."

"Oh, Becky doesn't need any assistance from the government. She's got lots of family behind her helping her out." Lillian dismissed her quickly. Meanwhile, I would've said *Thank you so much, and absolutely yes—we'll be there every Tuesday.*

Diapers were ridiculously expensive. Over twenty dollars a box, and that was for the cheap generic kind. It's not like you could just get the diapers either. You needed wipes too. For a while, I tried just using a washcloth, but it was too rough on Janie's skin. It gave her rashes and made her break out.

Hearing Lillian call us family felt so good. What would it be like to have family support? To have someone to call if something broke down or I needed money for textbooks. I always marveled at the other kids in college whose wealthy parents or grandparents paid their rent or bought them houses to live in while they went to school. Gave them cars to drive. Weekly allowances on their debit cards. I never understood how any of them didn't get straight As when the only thing they had to focus on was school. Did Lillian really plan on continuing to help out, or was she just saying that so I didn't look bad in front of Gloria?

Gloria's back was to me so I couldn't see her face as she snooped around the kitchenette, opening every single cupboard and drawer, but I'm sure she was impressed. I couldn't imagine she'd do another home visit today where she'd find organic strawberries and goat milk in their refrigerator.

I'd never believed in God. Not once. Never even considered the proposition because the idea of some higher power watching over me and taking care of things was ridiculous. But this? What was happening now? I'd clearly been saved from whatever fate would've happened with the police and social services if Lillian hadn't come. My life had been spared and set on a different path. That was a true redemption story, and I didn't know how I'd gotten so lucky.

Maybe that's how it went. You had enough bad things happen in your life that eventually the universe had no choice except to tip things in the other direction. Or maybe . . . one day you wake up and you have a real-life fairy godmother that's come to save you, and you get your happily ever after. Either option worked for me.

EIGHTEEN

Janie's colorful toys lay splayed out around us while we formed a semicircle on the rug. Janie handed Lillian one of the red blocks to put on the stack.

"Lala," Janie said with a grin.

Lillian beamed and clapped just like she did whenever Janie said it. It was Janie's latest thing, and she knew it sent Lillian over the moon every time. Janie loved Lillian's attention, and she'd blossomed into a little girl I barely recognized in the weeks since Lillian arrived. Neither of us acknowledged the fact that Janie still hadn't called me Mom. She'd gone from being so possessive of me that she didn't want Orion living with us to Lillian being her favorite person.

"Lala loves her little baby Janie," Lillian said, rubbing her nose against Janie's nose, making Janie squeal with delight. Janie loved bunny kisses. It was one of her favorite games to play with Lillian, but she turned her face away whenever I tried the same.

Her rejection hurt, but I was glad Janie had found someone else she liked and connected with besides me. It made me feel less terrible about my parenting mistakes when there was someone else there to correct and counterbalance them. I liked sharing the burden of responsibility with another person for how Janie turned out.

Lillian and I still hadn't talked about Cerena. It'd been almost a month since she showed up at the hospital, and we had yet to even mention her name. It was hard to believe it'd been that long already. We'd talked about so many different things and other parts of our histories. She'd gone on and on about how much time she'd spent looking for me while managing never to work in the fact that I came from her daughter, and obviously, she couldn't have searched for me without looking up Cerena too. How else would she have found me? I didn't know how Lillian felt, but I was dying to know what she had to say about Cerena. Lillian's version of events and who she was. Didn't Lillian want to know the same about what Cerena had said about her?

Over the next few days, I found myself watching and waiting for an easy way to slip Cerena into the conversation. It was much harder than I expected, because even though we'd never acknowledged that we wouldn't talk about her, we'd somehow become skilled in avoiding the topic. We spoke in ways that made it difficult to work her name in. Finally, I just gave up trying.

"Do you want to talk about Cerena?" I blurted out the following night over dinner. We'd just ordered pizza and sat down in front of the TV while Janie was cuddled up on her pink beanbag chair in the corner, devouring her uninterrupted hour of *Peppa Pig*.

She paused midbite. "Well, I noticed she wasn't here . . ."

"No, she's definitely not here and hasn't been for a while." I laughed nervously. "We haven't been in touch for years."

"There's so much that I want to know about you." Lillian put her plate of pizza back down on the coffee table and turned toward me. "Absolutely everything, I can promise you that. But I know that we just met, and I want to be respectful of your privacy." She reached over and gave my knee a squeeze. "We're so new to each other. That's why I don't ask. Not because I don't care."

"I feel the same way . . ." I couldn't make eye contact with her when she was looking into my face so kindly, especially when I knew my next question. "What was my mom like when she was growing up?"

"Honey, I'll tell you this. I loved your mama so much. Still do. She was my one and only baby. Your pawpaw and me were beyond ecstatic when we found out I was pregnant. I was so afraid to do anything while I was pregnant because I was terrified of losing her. I've never been so careful. The day she was born is still the greatest day of my life. We were absolutely beside ourselves with joy." Her eyes shone with a combination of pride and love, wet with tears. "Your mother was absolutely perfect. Like this tiny little porcelain doll. Your pawpaw was immediately in love with her too. Absolutely *obsessed*. You should've seen him." Her voice wavered with emotion. The pain of losing him obviously still so fresh. "He was one of the good guys, and I wish you could've met him. He would be so happy right now that I found you, and that we're sitting here having this conversation. He wanted to find y'all as much as I did. He never gave up looking." She sighed again. Taking a moment to silently remember him and then another moment to collect her emotions enough to continue. "Our entire lives revolved around Cerena. Those years were so magical. Being a mother was everything that I've ever wanted."

I listened in awe as she talked, describing how Cerena had been so naturally talented and gifted at ballet since the moment she could walk. How she'd twirled around the kitchen on her tiptoes like she'd been destined for pointe since the beginning. Lillian made her sound like a dancing savant. She went on to describe their summer beach trips and other holiday traditions. The way Cerena made sure to leave out cookies for Rudolph along with the ones for Santa. She showed me pictures of the Mother's Day cards Cerena had colored for her. How Cerena loved mangoes and hated cucumbers.

Her stories about my grandfather were just as fascinating. Cerena never talked about him. I didn't tell that to Lillian because I didn't want to hurt her feelings, but Cerena never mentioned her father. Not once. I'd always assumed it was because he'd done something awful. Somebody had to have messed her up, and he was the most likely culprit, so I figured there was a pretty good chance he was a bad guy.

None of that fit with Lillian's descriptions, though. According to her, Cerena's dad was her hero. He doted on her from the moment she was born. Lillian showed me pictures of him in a rocking chair with Cerena doing the baby scrunch on his bare chest. She shared others of him braiding Cerena's hair before her dance recitals and of them cuddled next to each other on the couch, watching their favorite cartoons on Saturday mornings. The matching pajamas the family all wore at Christmas as they huddled around the tree. Cerena beamed and smiled in every single picture. She looked so happy and content.

Had Cerena loved her father, and that's why she never talked about him? Was it too painful? Trying to imagine Cerena caring about anyone other than herself was difficult to do. Every time I'd found a shred of goodness or humanity in her, I'd been fooled, and I wasn't sure this time was any different. Except Lillian was her mother, so maybe she had insight into Cerena that I didn't.

Lillian knew a Cerena I'd never met and never would, but surprisingly, Lillian's descriptions about Cerena's childhood matched Cerena's descriptions too, especially the dance parts. The only difference in their versions was that Cerena made it sound like she was dancing and competing because Lillian wanted her to be a star. She made Lillian sound like one of those overbearing mothers who was vicariously living through their child. But Lillian's version was that all the performances and practices had been Cerena's choice.

"She begged us to go to Idyllwild Arts Academy when she was fifteen. Your pawpaw was so against it. He'd never imagined such a thing. Sending a teenage girl off to a school thousands of miles away when we had some of the best schools around for her to go to. And you have to understand, darling—it was a different time back then.

People didn't just send their kids off to private schools like they do nowadays. But I could see how much she wanted it, and one thing about your mother was that she was relentless. If she had her mind set on something, she wouldn't let it go. She was convinced she wanted to be a professional dancer, and Idyllwild was the only path for her to get there. She broke me down after a while, so I fought for her to go even though the thought of only seeing her on the weekends and holidays was absolutely unbearable. I'll regret that decision for as long as I live." Tears filled her eyes again.

"Is that where she met my dad?" I asked with my emotions in my throat. It's the only piece of the story Cerena had let slip.

She nodded. "She fell *hard* for that boy. Head over heels for him in the way that you only fall for your first love, you know what I mean?"

"For sure," I said, instantly remembering Orion.

"He was one of the janitors at her school. He was seventeen, and he worked there with his daddy, cleaning the bathrooms and scrubbing the floors at night because he got kicked out of high school in tenth grade. He'd already been in trouble with the law once. He was such a loser, but of course, all Cerena saw was a bad boy, and she was smitten. I should've put her on birth control before she left, and I'll be kicking myself that I didn't forever." She quickly realized what she'd said and the implications for me, putting her hand over her mouth as soon as she made the connection. "Oh my—I didn't . . . I was just . . . I was just . . ."

I laughed and threw my arm around her shoulders, giving her a quick side hug. "It's okay. I'm not offended. I get it."

She let out a nervous laugh. She still hadn't asked me where Cerena was. Did she know? Had she looked her up? It'd been over three years since I'd googled her. Maybe there was something new.

"Did you know her?" Lillian asked, just as tentatively as I'd asked about Cerena.

"Yes, I grew up with her until I went into the system as a teenager," I said softly, testing the waters. Not sure how much of the history was necessary.

"System?" She put her hand over her heart like it'd shocked her. "You mean like jail? You were in jail?"

I shook my head. "The child welfare system. So, I stayed in a foster home once and was on my own a lot."

"Oh my goodness. Sweetie, I'm so sorry. That must've been so terrible. What happened?" She looked at me with such kind and pleading eyes. Nobody had ever asked with such sincerity before, and she deserved to know the truth. After all, Cerena was her daughter. Even if she'd started out good—somewhere along the way—she'd gone bad. Lillian deserved to know that.

(THEN)

The police officer stood behind the social worker's huge aluminum desk—the same kind they had in the principal's office at my last school. This one was cluttered with so many papers and client files that I didn't know how she kept anything straight. She put the phone on speaker while she spoke with my mother.

"Becky? You have Becky?" Cerena asked after she'd answered the phone and the woman introduced herself as one of the social workers from Waldorf County. It'd been over four months since I'd been living in the shed, and our first contact. Cerena had never come looking for me. Her voice instantly made the food sour in my stomach, like it'd gone bad.

"Yes, we do, ma'am. We do," Monique, the social worker, said, nodding at me while she spoke to her. Giving me that encouraging it's-going-to-be-okay smile she'd been giving me ever since they brought me over from that other shelter in the white van. Tinted-black windows. How could they think it wasn't weird that they were transporting juveniles in a white van? Had they run thorough background checks on all the drivers?

"What'd she do this time?" Cerena asked, like I'd had run-ins with the police before, which probably made Monique doubt everything I'd just told her about never being in any kind of trouble.

But just the sound of Cerena's voice, and I was immediately three years old again. Curled up in the corner of the closet with her sneering at me, looking like a demon. Growling and barking. She said words, I'm sure. But I was three, and in my memory, she's a rabid dog about to bite my face off.

Once, she yelled at me so bad I peed my pants. Then, she beat the shit out of me for peeing my pants.

"You filthy, foul-smelling child." She waved her hand in my face. "Go shower and then get away from me. I don't want to see your ugly face for the rest of the night."

I'd scurried away. Scrubbed my skin until it was raw and then crawled into the wooden chest in the bedroom. The one we'd gotten from Goodwill for seven dollars. I pulled the top over my head like it was a coffin, crossed my arms on my chest like a vampire, and played dead. How do you measure time when you're three? I could've stayed in there for hours. It might've been days.

All I know is that never once did Cerena come looking for me.

So, I shouldn't have been surprised when she told the social worker she didn't want me to come home.

"Becky's been arrested for shoplifting and assault on a police officer. We need you to come down to the station so that we can issue her a citation and you can pick her up," Monique said solemnly while the officer behind her glared down at me. She was the partner to the other officer that I'd supposedly assaulted.

I didn't assault a police officer. That was being way too dramatic. We fell together when he was chasing me on the sidewalk. I could've easily been the one to land wrong and break my wrist, but it just so happened to be him.

I steal out of necessity. Not because I'm a criminal. Do I get a rush out of it sometimes? Yes, but that's beside the point. Your adrenaline shoots through the roof the moment you take that first step outside the door, but I wouldn't steal if I didn't have to.

And what I'd stolen that day?

Tampons and Midol because I had the worst period of my life that week and no money. I was dying from my cramps, and there was no way I could just stuff paper towels in my underwear at school like I could at home. I might've skipped school if I hadn't had a Spanish final that day. That's how bad it was.

If it hadn't been period things that I'd shoved down my pants, I might not have tried so hard to get away. I probably would've just offered up whatever I'd stolen to the undercover officer right away when he grabbed me. It wasn't just that I was about to get caught shoplifting, it was because I was embarrassed to show the man I'd shoved tampons down my pants. How mortifying.

The only reason he'd charged me with assault on a police officer was because he was so embarrassed about falling and the fact that the entire store watched it happen. That's why he wanted to assert his authority and make me pay by tagging on a more serious offense.

I'd begged the police officer not to call Cerena while we were at the police station, so he didn't, but the moment that other lady came down from social services—the one whose booty was as big as his belly—and stepped into the room, him having any kind of say was over. I enjoyed watching her treat him like an idiot, and I would've gotten an even bigger kick out of it if the ass-chewing wasn't over calling my parent or a guardian. Apparently, he should've called them the moment I got arrested.

"How about your daddy? Can we call him?" Monique asked me when I first flipped out about calling Cerena.

I hung my head. My cheeks burned in shame. Being raised white trash was like dirt you could never wash off your face. It felt like a disease. These people. My stupid, terrible parents.

Cerena refused to talk about my father no matter how drunk or angry she was. He was off limits. I didn't even know his first name even though we shared the same last one, which never made any sense, seeing as she hated him so much. She referred to him as my sperm donor.

The only meager piece of information that she'd leaked was that her pregnancy was the reason she'd gotten kicked out of her house and cut off from her family.

She railed on and on about how she was never going to be like her mother. She made her sound like a terrible person. She'd tell me all about her in a witchy voice like Cruella de Vil from *101 Dalmatians*. It was the only time she ever used voices in her stories. That's the reason I loved talking about my grandmother.

Lillian was a big part of the reason Cerena was the way that she was. A fuck-you to everything they'd bred her to be. That's why she took such great delight in stealing husbands and destroying families.

But I didn't know any of that when I was little. I spent my childhood thinking I had a mom that hated me. And if I ever doubted that fact, the conversation with Monique that afternoon confirmed it.

Cerena took a few seconds to think about Monique's request before responding. "You know what? If Becky thinks she's got it so bad at home, then why don't you just keep her? That'll teach her a lesson. Probably help her appreciate exactly what she has."

"Ma'am, you realize that if you don't come down here to the station so we can release her into your care, we're going to have to take her to an emergency foster home?" She lowered her voice when she said it, as if that would lessen the impact. As if I weren't standing right there next to her desk.

"Absolutely," Cerena said without hesitation. "Take her there and let her live somewhere else. See how she likes it."

Click.

The line went dead, and Monique sat holding the phone, looking like she was going to burst into tears for me at any second.

Who feeds their own child to the wolves? But that's exactly what Cerena did. She served me up on a silver platter to teach me a lesson.

NINETEEN

I was astounded by how easily it'd been for Lillian and me to slip into a routine. It was like we'd known each other forever, even though it'd only been a few months. We were just so in sync together. I guess that's how it was when you were family.

Lillian was still staying at the small bed-and-breakfast in Waldorf, twelve miles away. After the first awkward night, we'd accepted that even though we spent the days together, we'd retreat to our private worlds at the end of them. Nighttime was our alone time. She probably needed the space away from us as much as I needed the time by myself. She was probably used to staying in much nicer places, but she never complained, and I appreciated that about her. There was so much I appreciated her for. She'd changed my life.

Beginning with making social services go away. After Gloria's initial visit, they'd disappeared and left us alone. How could they not after seeing our stunning apartment with its high-level interior design and our Oscar-worthy performance? There was a part of that whole interaction that had felt so much like Cerena, but there was one huge difference—Lillian was still on my team after the social worker left. She'd turned around and high-fived me after she shut the door behind Gloria. Given me the biggest grin, and all I could do was smile right back at her.

I'd been so nervous that Lillian would leave after Gloria signed off on the report officially closing the case, but she hadn't. I was too nervous to ask when she would. I loved our new life and our routines. I didn't want any of it to end.

Lillian came over in the morning and helped with breakfast and Janie while I showered and got ready for school. At first, we were like two strangers orbiting the same space—polite and cautious with each other. But as the days passed, a rhythm settled between us, and now it was like a perfectly choreographed routine. Lillian always brewed coffee as soon as she got here, and I'd shuffle into the kitchen still half asleep to grab the first cup before getting into the shower. Sometimes she made me toast before I headed out the door.

I spent my days at the library, studying and trying to get caught up. I hadn't planned on going back to school, but once Lillian showed up and took over the day-to-day tasks with Janie, a space opened up that I hadn't realized I needed. It wasn't easy—I was on academic probation and my scholarship hung by a thread—but I walked back onto campus and started auditing classes. I sat in the back of the classroom and kept my head down while I scribbled notes. It felt so good to be back there. I always loved being a student.

Everything would've been perfect if it wasn't for Janie. She was still giving me trouble. Even though social services had backed off and nobody was meddling in our life anymore, Janie's issues hadn't gone away. There was a reason I'd locked her up in the closet, and even though I hadn't gotten into legal trouble over it, I hadn't forgotten that she'd hit me on the head with a hammer to punish me for putting her in time-out.

Lillian and I hadn't talked about what brought me and Janie into the hospital that day either. She avoided discussions about the precipitating incident as much as she avoided talking about kicking Cerena out of their family home and cutting her off. I understood not wanting to talk about Cerena because it was probably so painful and complicated for her, but I wasn't sure why she avoided talking about how Janie and I ended up in the hospital.

The thing about it was, the moment Lala left, Janie became a different person. It eerily reminded me of Cerena. She had the exact same switch, and could flip in an instant. Even Lillian had commented on that part. How much Janie reminded her of Cerena.

"She's so much like Cerena, it's scary." That's what she said at dinner last night after Janie had just tapped out a song with her silverware on the plate. Lillian meant it as a compliment, but she didn't know Janie's other side.

More and more, Janie was beginning to act like a regular two—almost three—year-old. She was talking. Engaged and interactive. She could recite all her ABC's and knew a bunch of her colors. When Lala was around, you could tell her to get her shoes or put her toys away, and she understood the requests. She'd respond accordingly. She was polite and well mannered with Lillian. Really tried hard to please her and understand what she wanted of her. She was always on her absolute best behavior.

With me?

It was like she knew nothing and had zero skills. She was back to pretending like she didn't hear me. Most of the time, she wouldn't even acknowledge that I'd spoken.

But I didn't say anything to Lillian about it, and I wasn't going to, no matter what happened. She seemed just as happy and content as I was as we settled into our routines and continued getting to know each other. I didn't want to ruin things. Everything had turned around since she showed up, and now that I had her, I didn't want to lose her. I wanted her to stay for as long as she possibly could. Forever, if she wanted to.

(THEN)

A woman from the social services office drove me here—to this house in the middle of nowhere—without saying a word and dropped me off like I was a package. They signed for me and everything. At least the emergency foster parents didn't take my backpack. It was mortifying when the officers went through it down at the police station, but thankfully they hadn't taken anything, and they gave it back to me when I left. All my important documents, including my birth certificate, are in this bag. In a few years, I'm going to need it if I ever want to get an ID.

All my things in the shed are probably going to be gone by the time I get back. Completely ransacked and ruined by bored kids who might stumble upon it. I never knew each day when I left my little makeshift home to walk to school if it'd be there when I got back or what condition it'd be in. I've already had to start over twice.

The woman in charge of the house, Helen, handed me a blanket and a pillow. She and her husband, Earl, had nine kids staying here. "You'll sleep in the last room on the right." Her voice was practically a grunt as she pointed down the hallway.

I glanced at the kitchen on my left. She'd already told me that the cupboards were padlocked, and all the food was rationed. Apparently, this place wasn't going to be all that different from home.

I took a deep breath and pushed open the bedroom door. I read all the rules in the foster care pamphlet Monique gave me while we were waiting for that other woman to bring me here, and these people obviously didn't care about the rules. Every kid was supposed to have their own bed and dresser, but we were stacked four kids deep to a room—a set of bunk beds on each side, one dresser in the middle of the room for all of us to share.

The floor creaked as I walked over to the open bed on the right-hand side of the room and climbed up to the top, even though I'd much rather be on the bottom bunk. I didn't like the ceiling being so close to my head. It made me claustrophobic. I set my backpack on the side of my pillow. I wasn't letting it out of my sight. I wasn't changing my clothes either. Not like I had pajamas to change into anyway, but still. I was keeping all this on. Even my socks. I turned down the gray army blanket and crawled underneath it, pulling it up to my chin. It was rough and scratchy, making everything itch.

Bodies breathed all around me. I'd never been in a room with so many people at night. I've never even been on a sleepover, for the same reason Cerena tried to keep me away from my friends. She was too afraid I might spill all our secrets if I got far enough away from the clutches of her control. It felt so strange, sleeping with others in the same room. How did people do this?

Are they awake? Do they know I'm here? There's no way I'm going to get any sleep tonight. Not with three strangers in the same room within feet of me. How am I ever going to be able to do that, even after I know who they are?

I'm used to sleeping alone. How do you share this kind of space with another person? The more I thought about it, the more I panicked. I can't stay here. My heart races. Squeezes in my chest. It felt like I was having a heart attack. I couldn't breathe. I knew it was just the panic surging through me, but it sure felt real. My shirt felt like it was choking me. Everything was choking me.

Relax.

It's not like they've got you in handcuffs. They aren't the police.

Helen is at least fifty pounds overweight. It'd probably been years since she'd done more than a fast walk. If it actually came down to running, there's no way she'd catch me if I took off. How far away from town was I? It was so hard to judge, and my head had been spinning too fast to pay all that much attention on the way here. Nothing but farms and fields for miles. Endless stretches of green between gravel roads. I remembered seeing a creek once we passed the water tower on Seventh Street. If I made it to the creek, I could follow that all the way down to Samson's pasture. Sleep in those barns behind the grain bins. I'd done it before. I could figure out my next steps from there.

What would happen if I went to school tomorrow? Would someone from social services show up there? Would Helen? Or maybe nobody would even notice or care that I was gone. That was a possibility too. I didn't know how any of this worked. I just didn't want to get in any more trouble than I was already in.

Suddenly, the kid below me let out a huge snore. I heard the sounds of him rustling around the bed, trying to get comfortable. Someone on the other side of the room coughed. Let out a small fart. I pulled my shirt up over my nose the moment the smell hit. The place already smelled like feet.

Yuck. How disgusting.

I couldn't live like this, especially when I hadn't done anything wrong. Stealing a box of tampons because I was on my period didn't warrant being locked up with these weirdo kids in whatever kind of kid factory this was. I didn't want to stay long enough to figure that part out. I sat up in bed. They couldn't make me stay here. I wasn't a prisoner. I scooted to the edge of the bed and slid my legs over the side, trying to be as quiet as possible.

Shit.

I didn't have any shoes. They'd made me take my shoes off at the door when I got here. I put them next to all the tennis shoes and boots lined against the wall. The entire place smelled like a farm. Even inside.

My shoes were in the mudroom all the way across the house, and I'd probably wake someone up if I tried to sneak over there.

This was all Cerena's fault. I fumed. It's not like she even had to keep me once she picked me up from the police station. She could've come, gotten me, and then dropped me off a block away. She wouldn't have even had to bring me home. Did she know they were bringing me to this place?

Probably not.

She didn't know anything about child services or foster care. She'd grown up rich. Not poor, like she'd made us. But even if she had? She probably would've said the same thing. That woman might've birthed me, but she didn't care about me. Not even a little.

I was just going to have to figure out a way to do this on my own. Like always.

I eyed the room. There was a small window above the dresser. I crept over to it. Tiptoeing and trying not to breathe. I slowly pulled open the dresser drawers until I found the one with socks. I put a pair on over my own. It would make me clumsy and slow, but at least it would protect my feet for a while until I could figure out what to do about shoes.

The dresser creaked just like the floor as I climbed on top of it. I stopped for a minute, waiting to see if any of my movements or sounds woke the other kids. Nobody stirred. Were they actually sleeping or just faking it? Didn't matter. I grabbed the window and pulled it up. An alarm blared, making me jump. I almost fell off the dresser.

All three kids sat straight up in their beds, but nobody moved in my direction. Three sets of glowing eyes stared at me in the dark.

I didn't have time to think. I hurtled myself out the window, toppling onto the grass with a thump. I quickly jumped up and bolted across the yard. Right around the corner of the house and into the barrel of a shotgun. I froze. Put my hands up in the air.

Earl—at least I think it was Earl, I'd never seen him before—pointed the shotgun at me. Straight at my chest. He took another step toward me. "Where do you think you're going, little missy?"

Well, that was one way to keep us here.

I swallowed hard, keeping my arms in the air, and shrugged. "I don't know. I must've been sleepwalking. I'm so sorry."

HIM

(NOW)

It'd taken them two days, but they'd finally found someone that knew Orion from his time in Waldorf and stayed friends with him afterward. Santos had worked tirelessly trying to find a connection, and she'd finally succeeded. Orion was the primary suspect in their investigation, especially since one set of remains had officially been identified as Brock Tapp. What were the chances Orion was connected to two murders without playing a part?

Slim to none.

All hands were on deck to find him, and until then, they were focusing on any other connections to him that might give them additional leads, like Tawny Reed. One of the other detectives discovered a connection between Orion and Tawny when they were teenagers at another group home.

They met Tawny at a rehab halfway house in Marion, Iowa. A clean facility with peeling inspirational posters and a cafeteria kitchen. All the walls inside were painted institutional white. Tawny had agreed to speak with them on the condition that it wasn't in a precinct, so they'd made the four-hour drive down to see her. It gave them something to do while they waited to hear more about Orion.

Tawny led them to a small meeting room off the main lobby of the facility. Aluminum folding chairs surrounded a small table. She had thick hair pulled back in a bun and wore a T-shirt that read **I USED TO BE A HOT WIFE. NOW I'M JUST A HOT MESS.**

"We really appreciate you meeting with us today," Santos said, shaking her hand. "We'll make this as quick and as painless as possible. We know you have a lot on your plate."

Tawny staying out of prison for ten years for selling meth was contingent on her successful completion of rehab and staying sober. They didn't want to cause any stress that would jeopardize her newfound sobriety. Her probation officer said she'd been working really hard and had thirty-two days clean.

"Thanks for talking about Orion." Vega echoed Santos's gratitude. "Anything you can tell us about him would be super helpful."

"Well, I haven't actually seen him in a while," she said, whipping her blond hair out of the bun and twisting it around her fingers while she talked. "Not since he moved down south a few years back. I think it's been a few years. Maybe more. He went to Texas. But I hear maybe he's back? Anyways, we still message sometimes. On holidays or birthdays usually."

"You two were close?" Santos asked.

She shrugged, throwing her hair back up in the bun she'd just taken down seconds ago and twisting it on top of her head all over again. "I wouldn't say we were exactly close, but we were friends. Mostly because we met in foster care, and that pretty much bonds you for life. Not at the Millers', though. We met right after he left there. In a group home."

"What was he like?" Santos shifted in her seat. The folding chair squeaked when she moved.

"He wasn't aggressive and loud like a lot of them other boys. He kept to himself and didn't talk much, but he was . . . kind, I guess? In his own way. He just didn't let many people get close to him. But once you did? He was super loyal. He was that type of person, you know."

"Did he ever talk about the Millers?" Vega asked next. Everyone was familiar with the case because it'd been all over the news. Earl's face was plastered everywhere, so Tawny knew exactly why he was asking.

She hesitated. "Not very often. Other than to say he hated it there, but everyone hated getting placed at the Millers' back in the day." She chomped her gum while she talked. "We all knew what went down there, though. It's not like it was any big secret. I only got sent there once, and I'll tell you what—I made them think I was crazy just to get myself kicked out of that place as fast as possible. The psych ward was better than there, so that should tell you how bad it was." She pulled her hoodie around her neck, hiding an attempt scar. At least that's what it looked like.

Vega jotted that down. "Did he ever mention any other kids there? Any names?"

"He had a girlfriend that he'd been in the house with . . ." She wrinkled her face while she thought. Stared up at the popcorn ceiling. "Bee . . . or Becca? Something like that. I don't remember her name. It's been too many years and I've done way too many drugs since then." She gave them a silly grin, revealing rotted and chipped front teeth. "He was really into her, though. I remember that. She came around sometimes. Seemed nice. Pretty sure she went to our school."

"What about Brock?" Santos asked.

"Brock. Of course." Tawny shook her head. Snapped her gum.

That's the real reason they were here. They all knew that.

"That kid was a nightmare. A real bully. He picked on all the younger ones, but he also had a special beef with Orion. The two of them were always fighting. And not just at the Millers'. They kept fighting even after Orion left there and we'd all see each other at school. He called Orion some kind of racial slur in the cafeteria once, so Orion threw a trash can at his head. They both got detention for it. Orion was only ever really responding to what Brock did to him because, for whatever reason, Brock *hated* Orion."

"What's the worst thing he did?"

"Besides calling him names and humiliating him every chance he got?" Tawny lowered her head like she felt Orion's shame. "He accused Orion of being gay. Said he was the 'favorite' at the Miller house. He even started rumors that Orion and Earl were doing it by choice. You know how boys get when they're scared—they get cruel. Brock was vicious."

That definitely sounded to Vega like a good reason to want to hurt someone. Out of the corner of his eye, he caught Santos thinking the same thing.

"Did Orion ever talk about what happened to Brock?" she asked, reading his mind.

"Are you kidding me?" Tawny laughed. "Everyone talked about what happened with Brock. He was famous for what everyone assumed he did to Earl. Even though Brock was a huge asshole and everyone hated him, he became a total legend. For months, that's all anyone talked about, even the regular kids at school. There were all these stories about what Brock had done with Earl's body and who'd helped him hide it. Some of them were so wild. You never knew which one was true or not. And then when Brock went missing? We all just figured he ran away, so that he didn't get caught." She shook her head. "I still can't believe he's been dead all these years. Just laying out there, rotting in the dirt all this time."

Vega watched her closely. "Did Orion have a temper?"

Tawny shifted in her seat and immediately looked uncomfortable. "Yeah . . . sometimes, but you have to understand, it was only because he was always on guard because of everything he'd been through. He snapped easy. Hated being touched. Hated loud noises too. He'd flinch if someone came up behind him. I don't think he even realized he was doing it, and then when he did go off on someone? You could tell he was really embarrassed and mortified afterward."

"Was he ever violent?" Santos asked.

She looked down at her hands. "There were always rumors . . . and there was one ex . . ." She gave it another few beats before definitively deciding to tell them. "It was a girl he dated a couple years ago. Back when we still saw each other and lived close. I don't know all the details, but I heard that the cops got called once or twice. I asked him about it, and he said it was mutual. Like they both pushed each other around." She seemed even more uncomfortable. "I think that's when he moved down south for a while. Probably to get away from all that."

"Were you ever concerned for your safety?" Vega asked.

She shook her head. "No, but I also never dated the guy."

"And what about since then?"

"Like I said, we don't talk much now and I haven't seen him in forever. Last I heard he was somewhere around Champaign and back to working security night jobs."

"When was your last contact?" Vega's phone buzzed in his pocket. Hopefully with good news about the case.

"Not since a few months ago. He sent me a pic with him and a little girl. He said she wasn't his and that he was helping a friend, which made sense because the girl looked pretty sick."

Vega frowned. "Little girl?"

"Yeah. She had curly blond hair. Looked wild. He said she was a handful." Tawny smiled for half a second. Santos caught it too. "I asked if he was okay. He said he was trying to be."

"Anything else you can think of that might help us?" Santos asked.

Tawny shrugged, glancing at the clock. She jiggled her knees. She'd clearly had enough. Reached her limit. Vega stood and pulled out his card. He was ready to go too. He was itching to look at his phone and get back to the office.

"Thanks so much for your time, and if you think of anything, please call me." He left his card on the table, and they stepped back out into the heavy afternoon air.

Vega climbed back into the car and flipped open his notepad. The margins were full of names and notes. Bodies not yet identified. Potential suspects. Connections.

He drew a circle around one name:

ORION ELLIS

Then he underlined it twice.

(THEN)

I called Cerena every single day from the phone in the hallway at school. We didn't have a phone at the Millers'. They had one in their bedroom, but their bedroom door was locked with a dead bolt, and they were the only ones who could get in it. The foster kids were only allowed to go back and forth between the Millers' and school. Our every move was monitored like we were prisoners, which meant we had to check in and out of the office every day.

"Please, Mom, please, just let me come home. I'm so sorry. It won't happen again," I begged, almost in tears. I hadn't cried in front of her or called her *Mom* in years, but I didn't know how much longer I was going to be able to keep everything inside.

Living with the Millers was an absolute nightmare. Worse than I could've imagined or predicted. The entire place smelled like chicken shit. It didn't matter that you washed—four-minute showers before the water turned cold. You could scrub all you wanted, but you couldn't wash the smell off you. That's what happened when you were raising hundreds of chickens. Their coops lining the warehouse in the back.

That wasn't the worst part, though. Earl was a disgusting pedophile. It'd only taken a few nights in their home to figure out the real reason they only took in teenagers as foster kids.

"Oh, now you want to come home? Life with me doesn't seem so bad now, does it?" She laughed. She was enjoying this way too much.

That's the only reason she took my phone calls every day. My misery brought her incredible delight, but I didn't care. I just wanted to come home and regroup. I needed another plan because I couldn't stay here.

Earl came in our bedroom at night. I'd heard him messing with the other kids. First, with this new kid, Orion, on the bunk underneath me. I was hoping it was just him. Like he was just Earl's prized pet. The one he'd picked special. I'd overheard Earl telling him that. I felt so sorry for Orion, obviously, but it meant the rest of us were safe if Earl was only interested in him.

Except he wasn't.

A few weeks ago, we heard the familiar sound of the door cracking open and his shuffle across the floor. The smell of beer and sweat filled the room. Instead of going left into Orion's bed, he crossed to the other side of the room and climbed up the bunk to Charity. While Earl struggled to hoist his way up to her, Orion let out a deep sigh of relief underneath me. Orion never made a sound when Earl messed with him, but Charity whimpered the moment he touched her, and it wasn't long before she was crying, telling him no and begging him not to touch her.

I fumed, clenching my fists against me, and fighting the urge to jump out of the bed and onto his back, to pummel him and throw him off her. Why were we all just lying here doing nothing? There were three of us, and we could attack him. Easily overpower him. But then I quickly realized we needed a plan once we got him off. What would we do then? It's not like we could tie him up. If we ran away, he'd just shoot us. The other kids already knew that. They'd been through this before. That's why nobody was moving or doing anything.

I grabbed my pillow and smashed it over my head to drown out the sounds of Charity's cries. I did everything in my power to cancel them out, but it was impossible. Was it only a matter of time before he came after me?

I was terrified.

I'd grabbed Soledad's arm in the bathroom when we were brushing our teeth the next morning and whispered, "Did you hear Earl get into Charity's bed last night?" Of course she heard. Everyone heard. It was impossible not to. But we'd barely spoken since I'd gotten to the Millers', and I didn't know how else to start the conversation.

She just kept brushing her teeth. Didn't even look at me. "He comes into all our beds," she said, spitting her mouth full of toothpaste into the sink. "We all get a turn with daddy Earl."

"Are you serious?" I asked as she confirmed my worst fear. How did social services jerk kids out of their homes and put them in one where they got molested by a dirty old man? What kind of a system was that?

Soledad nodded at me like *Duh*. I'd always thought if I told the social workers the truth about Cerena that they'd put me in a safe place with a loving family, but I'd been too afraid of how she'd punish me once she had me in her clutches again if I ever did something like that, so I hadn't. Now I was grateful I never did.

"That's so awful. He can't do that to us. We have to do something. Tell somebody. Who can we tell?" I grabbed her arm again. "What about Helen?"

She burst out laughing. "You think anybody cares what happens to *us*? You know how many times I've told my social worker that Earl is into kids?" She shook her head at me. "You're definitely new around here. And Helen?" She shook her head again. "Do you know why they started getting foster kids in the first place?" She looked around to make sure nobody else was listening. "Because they have three kids of their own and she did it as a way to keep Earl off them. It was her way of satisfying his sick need and keeping her own kids safe." She shrugged nonchalantly like she hadn't just told me the most disturbing thing on the planet. "At least that's what Ebony told me before she left, and she stayed here almost three years. Almost made the record. Everyone thought she was going to get adopted by the Millers, but they put her back into the system at seventeen." She leaned in closer. This time she was the one to whisper. "Rumor has it, Ebony left because he got her pregnant. They shipped her off to one of those group homes for teenage mothers. They might want to put us on birth control if they're going to keep letting him screw us."

That was the day I started calling Cerena from school during lunch, and I haven't stopped since. I didn't care that school was the only place I got a decent meal. I spent all thirty-six minutes of my lunch period cycling through the phone line and begging Cerena in a way I'd never pleaded with her about anything in my life.

Obviously, I wasn't just going to let him touch me. I was going to fight back. At least try to stop him. Except he was a big man. I'd seen his muscles. He might have a belly protruding over his pants, but his biceps still curled like the football player he'd been in high school. I'd do anything to keep him off me. Even live with Cerena again, if it meant never being one of his victims.

I knew how to manage her abuse. She might beat me to death. Starve me until I couldn't stand. But she'd never rob me of my innocence the same way that Earl would if he got ahold of me.

"Please, Cerena. Please, just let me come home. I'll do anything."

"Anything?" she asked, finally with that telltale break in her voice that I'd been waiting and desperate for.

"Yes," I said quickly, before she had a chance to change her mind. "Anything. I promise. Just please let me come home."

TWENTY

Janie whipped off her diaper. She squatted like a dog and stared me straight in the eye while she dropped a huge turd in the middle of the living room.

"Stop doing that!" I yelled. "Just go in the toilet!"

She stuck her tongue out at me and walked away, kicking the toys at her feet that I'd just told her to pick up seconds ago. Her behavior made me furious. She never did this with Lillian. Lillian had gone downstairs to get our pizza, and of course, Janie acted out immediately. She always did.

She loved destroying the apartment when we were alone. She kicked holes in the walls. Took her markers and scribbled all over them. She'd stabbed the futon with a fork twice.

Janie was still an angel for Lillian and a nightmare for me. She did everything Lillian asked of her. She was polite. Sweet. Well mannered. She followed all Lillian's instructions, and she was composed and respectful while she did it. Not for me.

She and Lillian had such structured routines around eating and sleeping. Ones Janie adhered to flawlessly. After they had lunch, Janie went potty, they read a story together sitting on the futon with one of her stuffed animals, and Lillian laid her down in the Pack 'n Play after they finished. She slept for ninety minutes, like clockwork. But when it came time for me to put her to bed at night, she refused. Fought me every step of the way. Kicking, screaming, and throwing her body around. Once she bit my finger so hard, I thought she was going to bite it off.

Her behavior change wasn't just when Lillian left anymore, though. That was only when it was the most dramatic. She was starting to treat me poorly in front of Lillian too. I liked it better when she kept her acting-out a secret.

"Janie, stop!" Lillian said whenever Janie crossed a line. Like last night when she tried to headbutt me for taking away her iPad at dinner.

"Janie, honey, use your words like you do with Lala," Lillian had said when Janie went into full meltdown mode on the floor after she'd been called out. Lying on her back, kicking and screaming.

Janie had stopped mid-fit—just like that—and sat straight up. She glared at me from her position on the floor. "I hate you."

That was her latest thing to say to me—*I hate you.* Like she was already a teenager, and I'd somehow ruined her life. She said it to me in private all the time, but it was the first time she'd said it in front of Lillian. I'd been immediately mortified.

"Stop that! Don't say mean things like that to your mother," Lillian said as soon as it'd come out of her mouth. "Now, you go on and apologize to her right now."

Janie had stuck her tongue out at me instead. Same as she did just now.

Lillian had let out an exasperated sigh. "She becomes such a different kid around you. I'm sure it's her way of getting your attention because she misses you so much from being gone all day. Toddlers do that, you know. They just want any kind of attention they can get. They don't care if it's positive or negative," she'd said in a fake cheery voice. I'd never met someone so upbeat, and I wasn't going to lie—there were times it was a bit much and tonight was one of them.

"Exactly," I'd said, forcing a smile into my own voice.

Attention was the last thing Janie wanted from me. She was perfectly content for me to leave her alone. And then, once Lillian left, it was her personal mission to torture me. I think it was for all the times I'd left her in the closet when she was a baby and drugged her on Tylenol. Like somehow, in her subconscious, she remembered I'd done it. Or . . . there was also a teeny, tiny voice inside of me that couldn't help wondering if she was like Cerena. But I always refused to let myself go there. Kids couldn't be born bad.

"Here's what I've been thinking," Lillian said, coming back into the apartment and carrying the pizza over to me. She set it on the coffee table. One thing about Lillian was that she was super maternal and a little miss homemaker, but she was also a huge fan of ordering out.

She walked back into the kitchenette and grabbed paper plates from the cupboard. She avoided dirtying dishes at all costs. "I was thinking today while you were at school that maybe it might be time for me to head back to Florida." She paused, glancing at me out of the corner of her eye to see how I was going to react to her news. I kept my face blank and waited for her to continue. There was more. I could tell. "The other thing I was thinking that might not be so bad, is how you would feel about me taking Janie with me . . ."

"Taking Janie with you? You want to take Janie?"

"Well, I mean, not forever, obviously." She gave a nervous laugh, then looked away. "Just for a while. I know how much it helps you while I take care of her when you're at school, and I was just thinking, if she was with me while you were finishing up college, it would make things so much easier on you."

I still couldn't wrap my brain around what she was saying. She wanted Janie? Was that why she'd come? All this time, she'd been so excited about me. So I thought. Had she just been loving on me and being so wonderful to me because she wanted Janie? It felt like she'd slapped me. She must've seen the surprise and hurt on my face.

"Of course, it's no worries at all, or hard feelings. If it's something you're not comfortable with, then I totally understand. I'll just go home by myself and let the two of y'all get back to living your own lives." She turned around so that I couldn't see her face. "I'm sure you're sick of me being all up in your space anyway."

Florida was so far. Like, at least a thousand miles away far. It might as well be another country. I'd never be able to afford to visit her. Would she fly us out? Come back after she'd left? Was this it? Suddenly, nothing felt stable.

Everything came to a screeching halt. And without warning, it wasn't Lillian's face in front of me but Cerena's. Telling me all the stories and reasons that she hated her mother.

"You think I'm cruel?" Cerena had tossed her head back and laughed. "Do you know how long my mother made me work out every single day? Twelve to fourteen hours at least. It didn't matter if I had torn muscles or the flu. A stress fracture. Oh no. We still practiced. Once I danced with a broken foot for an entire month. On pointe! If I complained? I practiced longer. You're lucky I just let you lay around down here and be lazy. You never would've survived my childhood."

That's what she said to me after I'd been in the basement for three days. She'd knocked over my pee bucket when she came down the stairs, and she'd gone ballistic. Like I'd set it up there for her to trip on or something. She talked about me being locked up in the basement like she was doing me a favor. She never tired of telling me how much worse it could get. How good I actually had it.

"You think you have it bad?" she'd practically hissed in my ear. Sometimes, when I was little, I pretended she got possessed by the devil when she was angry. Most of the time she was a snake. Because of the way her voice sounded. The venom in her words.

And as I stared at Lillian, her face the transposed image of Cerena, I wondered if she was an even bigger snake than her daughter. Maybe she was the one who'd taught her everything she knew, and I'd been wrong all along. Was that possible? Could love have made me that blind?

(THEN)

I've never been so grateful to see Cerena's face a day in my life. I was so happy that I almost hugged her when she picked me up from school that afternoon in a blue Honda Civic. And I would have if I didn't hate her so much.

She was still in the same two-bedroom apartment that she'd been in when I left nine months ago. I felt like I'd lived a million different lifetimes since then, but by the looks of things, she'd just been standing still. Everything was a mess.

"Things are going to be different around here if you're planning on staying with me from now on," she said with her hands on her hips. Her face serious and all business. "I can't have you living here, treating me and acting the way you were before. You understand me?"

My insides burned with anger, but I forced a smile on my face and kept my voice steady. "Of course, I understand. I promise to treat you with the respect you deserve."

What she deserved was to be the one sentenced to live at the Millers' and sleep in a bunk every night petrified that gross Earl was going to crawl into her bed at any second. The same guy with the gun he pulled on you whenever someone tried to leave. Apparently, I wasn't the only one who tried to run away. Running away on the first night or at some point during your stay was a rite of passage in the Miller household. Everyone did it.

"The first thing that's got to change is that you're too old to be living here for free. It's time you stopped being so lazy and started doing things around the house instead of having your head stuck in a book all the time." She took a long drag of her cigarette, and I held my breath as she blew the smoke out in rings.

Was she serious right now? She couldn't be serious right now. But she was. I could tell by her face. She really believed her lies. Everything she was saying. I would never understand her twisted and distorted version of reality.

She walked through the living room. It was filthy. Probably hadn't been cleaned since I left. Grimy windows still covered by the same nicotine-stained lace curtains. Walmart bags stuffed with trash. Fruit flies hovering around plates of leftover fried chicken on the coffee table, surrounded by dirty cups. The TV barely hanging from the wall. Who knows if she'd even been here. Had she ever even wondered where I'd gone?

God, I hated that I cared.

"This room is a mess, and the first thing you can do is start by picking it all up. I want this entire place spotless by the time I get back in the morning. And don't touch my room." She reached toward the coffee table and grabbed another cigarette out of the pack. She tucked it behind her ear.

I was allergic to the smoke. It gave me asthma, but she didn't care. Instant regret flooded me.

Stop. This is better than Earl, I reminded myself.

And it's temporary. I was only here long enough to regroup. To come up with a different plan. Orion promised to help me. He's been in the system a long time, and he knows all about something called emancipation, where teenagers can basically divorce their parents. He's the only good thing that came out of the Millers', and I'm so glad we get to still see each other at school, even though I'm not living there anymore. He kissed me goodbye when I left today.

I wanted to stay at my same high school until I graduated, but I might not have that choice anymore. Maybe it was time to think about leaving and going far away. So far that they'd never be able to catch me or find me. I just had to stay focused.

"I'll get on it right now," I said, sounding every part the servant. Same as I'd sounded at the Millers'. Same as every second I'd lived here before.

But I could do this. It's easy to do hard things when that's all you've ever known.

TWENTY-ONE

Lillian's rejection hit hard.

Why didn't she want me? She could easily take both me and Janie with her to Florida and help us start over there. Truly a new beginning. It'd probably be easier to do in her own city because she already had a huge house and tons of family to help. Plenty of resources. We could all live together until we were on our feet again. It wouldn't be hard for me to get into another school and have all my credits transferred there. But Lillian didn't want me.

She only wanted Janie.

She'd never been interested in me. Just like in foster care—nobody ever wants the big kids. They only want the babies. Would she have come when I called her if I hadn't told her about Janie? That was one of the first things I said when I called from the hospital—"I have a baby and they're going to take her away from me. Please help." I'd been so desperate. Had she used my desperation? Set out to get Janie from the beginning?

I was furious. Not to mention blindsided.

Why bother giving me love if she only planned on taking it away? If she wanted Janie, all she would've had to do was show up on that first day at the hospital and ask. We could've at least had a discussion about it. Maybe even worked something out where she had a form of partial custody. There were so many other options. She didn't have to pretend to care about me or ingratiate herself into my life in such a life-altering way. That wasn't fair.

For all I knew, she planned on taking Janie to Florida and I'd never see her again. If that's what she'd planned on doing all along, then she shouldn't have made me care about her. This just felt cruel. But she wasn't saying anything about it, so I wasn't either. She arrived the next morning, acting like it'd never happened. She hasn't brought it up again.

We acted like it hadn't changed things, but it was impossible not to feel the shift. The air felt heavy with unspoken words and questions. Our interactions were stilted and held back. She quit touching me. Her physical affection gone, just like that. Everything cold. An instant chill in the air around her.

I didn't know what we were going to do without her or how I was going to manage Janie on my own. I wasn't going to be able to keep up with school, that's for sure. The only reason I was even able to go back was because of Lillian. I wasn't even caught up yet. The thought of being totally responsible for Janie again gave me that walls-are-closing-in-on-me feeling. Part of me felt guilty because I'd never been able to take care of her on my own. Was I doing the same thing to her that Cerena had done to me? Depriving her of the care and love from someone who was better able to provide for her than I was?

Janie thrived under Lillian's care.

Honestly, so did I, which only made it hurt more.

We'd just gotten back from a Target run that I'd successfully maneuvered without Janie throwing a single fit. I was feeling quite proud of myself over it when Lillian set the bags down on the counter and announced, "I've decided to leave Thursday morning." She paused with her hand in one of the bags, waiting to see my reaction.

"Oh, that's too bad," I said, tilting my head to the side to look at her and shutting my emotions off. Years of cosplaying with Cerena activated immediately. "You've done so much for us, and I'm incredibly grateful. I can't thank you enough." I gave her a huge smile and never took my eyes off her. Batted my lashes for good measure because I didn't want her to know how much this crushed me. "We're really going to miss you, but I want you to know"—I reached out and gave her hand a little squeeze to emphasize my point—"you don't need to worry about us. Not even for a minute. We'll be totally fine without you."

She looked away and returned to putting away the groceries. I stared at her back, doing my best not to cry.

Just because she couldn't have Janie forever didn't mean she couldn't see her. She had the money to fly back and forth if she wanted to. She could come visit as often as she liked. So, what was the big deal with Janie? She wanted all of her or nothing? That was incredibly selfish. Seemed spoiled and entitled, which was exactly how Cerena had described her. Maybe Cerena wasn't so wrong after all.

Lillian left early again tonight. Just like she had the last three evenings. She didn't hug me, like she'd done every single night since she got to the hospital. She'd pulled her love away as punishment. I felt so betrayed.

There'd only been one other time that I'd been hurt this bad, and that was because of Cerena. I've never forgotten what happened with Mr. Harris when I was seventeen.

(THEN)

Mr. Harris's blood stained the front of my shirt. It was splattered on the wall behind my bed. All over my hands. Even on my shoes. I didn't know it'd spray that much. He was rolling around on my bedroom floor, holding his face in his hands and screaming like he was being murdered.

Good.

I hope he loses his eye. I kicked him hard. Right in the gut. Then, another quick kick to the head before racing down the stairs and leaving him there howling.

I ran into the kitchen. Cerena's back was to me at the sink. She was washing dishes.

"Cerena! Cerena! I stabbed him! What do we do? What do we do now? He's up there bleeding EVERYWHERE!" I clutched my torn T-shirt around me. Tried to ignore the throbbing in my head from when he'd smacked me. The redness around my wrists. His skin underneath my fingernails. His hot breath still felt like it was in my face. I could still feel his sweaty, gross hands all over my body.

Cerena didn't turn around. She just bopped around in front of the sink with her headphones on, listening to music. I raced over and grabbed her shoulders to get her attention. She turned around and slipped off her headphones. Her face flashed with annoyance, then quickly switched to alarm as Mr. Harris's screams registered.

"HELP! SOMEBODY HELP ME!" he hollered from above us.

"I stabbed him in the eye!" I yelled, trying to be louder than his screams. All our neighbors had to hear.

"What? Are you . . . I don't . . ." Cerena's eyes widened. She looked back and forth between the stairway behind me and at my bloodied, tattered self. She brought her hand up to her mouth like it was finally registering. "Oh my god . . . I—I don't understand."

"He tried to rape me, and I stabbed him! That's what I'm saying, and he's bleeding everywhere upstairs. What are we going to do?" Emergencies were the one thing that always brought us together.

She shoved me aside and raced up the stairs to the second floor. I followed behind her as she whipped open my bedroom door. Mr. Harris was writhing in the same place where I'd left him. There was even more blood on the floor. She ran over to him and kneeled down. She placed both hands on his shoulders like she was still trying to assess the situation. That's when she noticed the pencil sticking out of his eye. It was really far in there. I'd gotten him good.

"Call 911!" he screamed at her. His face contorted and covered in blood. "Why are you just standing there staring at me like that? You don't see this goddamn thing in my eye? That little bitch did it. You said she was fine with this."

Cerena's entire body stiffened. She turned around slowly and glared at me. She spoke through gritted teeth. "You worthless piece of trash. Why do you always ruin everything?"

"What? Cerena? No . . ." I just kept shaking my head. She wouldn't. She couldn't. This was too much. Not even Cerena could do something this cruel. No one was this evil.

She told me before school that Mr. Harris was coming to take my picture this afternoon. That he was some famous photographer who wanted to use me in his exhibit. It was weird. Nothing felt right about it from the beginning, especially when she wanted him to take the pictures in my bedroom, but she'd nodded at me like it was fine, so I'd followed him in there. I was more worried about her being mad at me for not going along with whatever scheme she'd concocted than anything else.

"I can't believe you did this," she said. Rage filled her face. She rubbed Mr. Harris's back while she slipped into a sweet voice to talk to him. "Should I call 911? Do you want me to take you to the hospital?"

He started crying and blubbering. "What are we going to tell them?! We can't tell them how I got hurt. You don't just accidentally get a pencil stabbed in your skull." He gripped his chest. "I think I'm having a heart attack. Oh my god. Oh my god."

I felt sick. Even more disgusted than earlier. Pathetic little man.

Cerena let go of him and stood up. She put her hands on her hips and squared off with me. "You worthless piece of trash. You ruined everything," she hissed at me. "Get the fuck out of my house." She pointed at the bedroom door behind me.

I stumbled backward. "What? Cerena? No . . . Where will I go? What will I do?"

He was so gross. That'd been my first thought when he walked into the house earlier. His belly fell over his pants. He looked like the kind of grown man that picked his nose and ate his boogers when he was a kid. I didn't want him anywhere near me, but I didn't have a choice. Living at home again meant doing what Cerena asked. I promised her I'd let him take a few pictures of me. He reeked of broccoli and cheap cologne. She gave me that look. The one she gave me that meant *Remember your promise*. That was my condition of living at home. Doing as she commanded.

The moment he shut the door behind me and turned the lock, my insides seized with anxiety. He didn't have a camera set up on a tripod anywhere, and he wasn't wearing one around his neck. Odd behavior, when the whole point of us being together was for him to take my picture. That's when I noticed his eyes. They were a dead giveaway. The sick, twisted, perverted stare. I'd recognize the look anywhere. After you've seen it once, you never forget.

"Don't touch me!" I said the moment he took a step in my direction.

But it was already too late.

His hand shot out, and he grabbed my wrist so hard, I thought he crushed my bone. He gripped my throat with his other hand and shoved me backward onto the bed. I lost my balance and fell onto it. He pounced on top of me, pinning me down, and ripping my shirt. I writhed underneath him. Kicking. Biting. Scratching. Clawing. He was breathing hard. His sweat burned my skin. He smacked me on the side of my head to get me to be still. I threw my knee into his groin as hard as I could.

He'd screamed like he was going to die. That's when I saw it—the pencil on my nightstand. It was a split-second decision. I grabbed it and stabbed it straight into his eye. If I could've, I would've stabbed it straight into his heart, but it wasn't strong enough to pass through the chest bone and I had one shot to hurt him. He let out another bloodcurdling scream and released me.

I shoved the memory down. Focused on Cerena. Really paid attention to her. And that's when I noticed.

She was wearing headphones. The music still blasting from the speakers. She'd ignored it all. That's why she hadn't heard my screams. She knew it was happening. She'd put her headphones on to drown out the sounds of my cries.

I stumbled back again. My hands over my mouth. I wish I had another pencil. I'd stab her in the eye too. That's the moment I knew it was over. The moment I knew I was leaving and never coming back home.

HIM

(NOW)

Vega sat at his desk, sifting through everything they'd gathered for what felt like the thousandth time. Orion Ellis had a record, but not the kind that kept you out of job interviews. A few bar fights. A trespassing charge from when he was seventeen, but nothing that ever stuck. Nothing that screamed *dangerous* or *killer*. But Vega had been a detective far too long to trust clean files.

There was so much—DMV databases, employment records, and the few addresses that had ever been attached to Orion's name. Most of them were old. Some had been homeless shelters. Others were halfway houses. The most recent address on file was in Champaign. It was a unit on the second floor of a run-down apartment complex with peeling paint and a half-collapsed fence.

Last week, Vega called the local police department and asked them to do a quiet drive-by. No flashing lights. Just eyes. His phone had buzzed an hour later.

"The apartment's empty, Detective Vega. I spoke with the neighbor, and he says the guy that lived there skipped out months ago. He left in the middle of the night with just a duffel bag, and he hasn't been back since."

"Was he alone?" Vega asked.

"No. They said he had a woman and a little girl with him when he left. The woman was totally losing her shit over something."

That lined up with what Tawny had said about the photo of the child Orion had sent her last winter.

"What about the woman and girl? Did any of the neighbors say anything about them?"

"Nope. Just that they kept to themselves and rarely came out of the apartment. Apparently, they came back a few days after they were spotted getting into the truck. But not Orion. Nobody's seen him since. Just the girl and her baby along with some other woman. By the looks of it, they're gone now too. The place is vacant."

It'd been another dead end. Why was this guy so tough to track down?

Vega opened Orion's employment record again. He mostly worked graveyard shifts as a security guard. Four jobs in three years—he never stayed long. His last job was at Northview Medical Campus, where he'd left without warning. There was no forwarding information.

He picked up the phone and dialed the number listed for the hospital's human resources department, even though Santos had already called. He figured he'd give it a shot too. He might get someone more willing to talk than whoever she'd spoken with.

"Hi, this is Detective Vega with the Waldorf County Police Department," he said once he had someone on the line. "I'm looking for employment verification on a former security staffer. Orion Ellis."

The voice on the other end grew cautious. "He hasn't worked here in months. He left without giving notice."

"Did he leave a forwarding address?" Vega asked.

"Nope. He just didn't show up one night for his shift. He didn't respond to any calls or emails. Security found his badge in his locker."

"Anything else unusual?"

There was a pause. "He was . . . jumpy. I don't mean drugs or anything. He was just always nervous and on edge, no matter what. But he was a hard worker. No complaints there. Really, he just kept to himself. The kind of guy you don't realize is gone until someone says his name out loud."

Vega hung up and jotted it down: *No ties. Jumps town. Fades into background.*

He clicked back through the CPS files until he found the original Miller-house complaint logs. He'd read them so many times. Earl's name was there over and over again. So was Orion's. He was always nearby.

Vega pulled the map back up on his monitor. He googled the distance from Waldorf to Champaign. It was far enough to disappear without being noticed. He grabbed his coat. If Orion was still in the area, he was going to find him.

TWENTY-TWO

The click of the lock jolted me awake. Every sense keen and on high alert. Muffled movement. A shape trying to shut the door without making a sound. Someone was in the apartment. Quiet footsteps. I didn't move. Barely breathed. My heart raced in my chest. I shifted my eyes back and forth, trying to adjust and make out the figure. The hammer was tucked underneath the mattress. I shifted toward that side of the mattress as the person stepped quietly into the room.

The light from outside seeped through the window, revealing Lillian's petite figure as she tiptoed into the studio. She was wearing sweatpants, a hoodie, and tennis shoes. A pink baseball cap pulled down over her face. She crept over to the other side of the room.

What was she doing? How did she get inside? She was so close to me now. Within feet. My muscles twitched with the desire to move. To jump up and tackle her. I tried to slow my breath. She looked over at me. I snapped my eyes closed. Did she see that I was awake?

I shifted another few inches toward the other side of the mattress. The futon creaked. I froze. Even with my eyes shut, I could feel her looking at me. She'd heard the sound. I let out a deep sigh and rolled over like I was having the best sleep of my life and completely oblivious to her presence in the room. Did she believe it?

A few seconds passed.

And then the shift in her energy. I sensed her movement away from me. I barely cracked my right lid to peek at what she was doing. She was bent over Janie's Pack 'n Play. Was she stealing Janie?

No way.

I lay there pretending to sleep in the same way I used to pretend to play dead when I was buried in the wooden chest as a little girl. Janie stirred in her Pack 'n Play.

"Lala?" she asked sleepily. Her voice full of confusion.

"Shh . . . shh, honey, yes, Lala's here. Don't you worry about anything, okay? You just go back to sleep for Lala." Her voice was syrupy sweet. Still barely a whisper.

"I'm not seepy," Janie said stubbornly, not even trying to whisper.

"Okay, okay, honey," she said quickly, obviously trying to think fast on her feet and to keep Janie from getting upset. "How about you lay your head down and just rest for a couple seconds while I put some of your things in your backpack, okay? As soon as I get everything packed up, then I'll take you out of there and read you another story. How's that sound? You want another bedtime story from Lala?"

A few beats passed. Janie must've nodded her agreement to the plan.

"Okay, sweetie. Just lay right there then. There you go." I could hear Lillian moving Janie around and adjusting her blankets as she spoke. "Give Lala one second to get all of this together, okay? You're being such a good girl. Thank you so much, my sweet darling."

I felt Lillian looking at me again and squeezed my eyes shut. I forced myself to keep them closed while my mind raced. I listened to the sounds of Lillian as she packed Janie's backpack. Probably the same one that they took on all their grandmother-granddaughter excursions. It was the pink My Little Pony one that she picked out from Target after she earned a reward for going number two on the big-girl potty the first time.

This was unreal.

Lillian was actually kidnapping Janie. That's how she'd decided she was going to handle this situation? I was beyond shocked. She wasn't the sweet, innocent Southern girl she'd pretended to be all this time. She'd set her sights on Janie and was determined to have her no matter what. Probably since the very beginning.

Wow.

I had no idea she had this in her. What was she going to do with Janie?

Part of me wanted to jump up and confront her. Accuse her of being an incredibly selfish and fake person. Ask her if she really cared about me at all or if it had only ever been about Janie. Then I'd grab Janie. Take her back. I could fight Lillian for Janie, and I'd probably win. I was stronger than she was.

But I didn't move. I just lay there. Still. Thinking . . .

What if I just let Lillian take her? Kept pretending to be asleep? I could let the two of them walk out of the door together without either of them knowing I was aware of what happened. They thought I was asleep. When I woke in the morning, it would be like it'd never happened and they'd both be gone. Off to a new, beautiful life in sunny Florida.

Once Janie left with Lillian, she might never come back. Losing Janie throttled me and filled me with such excruciating pain, but another part of me toyed with the idea of letting her go.

I couldn't help remembering all the late nights alone. The isolation that would come the moment I started raising her by myself again. The rent I quickly wouldn't be able to pay. Groceries that would dwindle in the refrigerator because I couldn't feed her, and I wasn't breastfeeding anymore, so we could no longer get by on that. I'd had more than three years to raise her on my own, and as much as I hated to admit it, I'd failed her in so many ways. These past months with Lillian were the only time I'd ever felt like I was truly doing right by Janie. Giving her everything she deserved—a safe, clean home with food, clothes, and shelter, surrounded by people that cared about her. I loved her with every part of my being, but I couldn't even provide for her basic needs.

Lillian was calm in a way I'd never be. She didn't flinch when Janie screamed, or cry when Janie threw her tantrums. She didn't take any of it personally. That's how motherhood was supposed to be. Not whatever I was. Shame flooded me.

What kind of mother even *thinks* about giving her child away?

But the answer was right there in front of me: One who loves her enough to wonder if someone else might do it better.

That's when I knew.

I was just going to lie here and let Lillian take Janie. I wouldn't try to stop her. Conversely, I wouldn't tell her I was okay with it and give her permission. I couldn't do either. Acknowledging this moment meant saying goodbye to both of them, and I wasn't strong enough for that. My insides flooded with so much grief, it hurt to breathe.

I listened as she snuck around the room making barely perceptible sounds. She was good at this. So quiet. I knew what she was feeling. The adrenaline shooting through every part of your body because you're doing something wrong. Heart racing. Everything tingling. I could feel her energy from here.

Then, in the next breath, there she was. Right near me. A force field hovering over me. It took every ounce of willpower not to open my eyes, but I didn't want to break down. If I opened my eyes and saw Janie in her arms, I might change my mind, and despite how I felt, I was doing the right thing. Was Lillian having as hard of a time with this as me? Were tears lodged in her throat too?

Lillian was close. I could hear her breathing. Almost feel it. Janie too.

Suddenly, cold metal slammed hard against my temple. Same spot that Janie hit me with a hammer. My eyes snapped open. Stomach in my throat. Lillian stood next to me, holding a gun to my head.

"Get up and don't make a sound," she ordered.

"I . . . what? Lillian . . . ? I just . . ." I shook my head, trying to make sense of what was happening. Everything whirling and spinning. "I don't understand."

"Get up!" she said, even louder this time. Pressed the gun harder against me.

I scrambled out of the bed with my hands raised above my head. "Okay, I'm up. What do you want me to do? Just tell me what this is about."

"You're going to walk with me to the car and you're not going to say a word. Do you understand?" Her voice was hard and unflinching. Janie stood wide eyed next to Lillian, in her purple dinosaur pajamas, clutching Lillian's other hand in hers—the one not holding the gun pointed at my head.

I kept my hands raised, so Lillian knew I had surrendered. That I didn't want to fight her. "Please, Lillian, just tell me what's going on. I don't know what's happening. Why are you doing this?"

"Oh honey, you think I don't know you killed my daughter?" She looked me straight in the eye. "Did you really believe I was here for you?"

PART THREE: The End

TWENTY-THREE

I desperately tried to adjust my eyes to the darkness. I passed out from sheer exhaustion after Lillian dragged me into this room and tossed me on the ground. I woke up a few minutes ago, wishing it were all a dream. But it's not. I listened for the sounds of something, but there was nothing except the ringing in my ears from straining so hard.

Was Janie here? Lillian?

The ceiling was high. Blankets or some kind of padding hung from the walls. The air stale and thick. Everything was sealed tight. Even the crack in the door, so there was no light or air. It was hard not to panic.

Lillian had locked me in here as soon as she pulled me out of the car the night she broke into the apartment, even though technically it wasn't breaking in, because she had a key. Problem was, I'd never given her a key. At some point, she must've had one made. She'd thought all this through. That much was clear.

Did she spend her nights creating this place after she left us? When I thought she was tucked in bed watching bad reality TV at the bed-and-breakfast in Waldorf? Had she ever been staying in Waldorf? I didn't think to question it or ask. I'd never called her at the hotel. Only on the cell phone number she'd given me. That's how we kept in contact. We'd never gone over there to visit either. She might never have stayed there, because she didn't just throw this place or this plan together in the last week.

She'd forced me out of the apartment and into the car with the gun pressed hard into the middle of my back. The parking garage was empty because it was so late. What would she have done if we'd seen someone outside? How would she have explained herself? I'd considered yelling and screaming for help, but I wasn't sure if she'd shoot me or what was going on. However, I grossly underestimated the severity of this situation or I would've created a huge fuss before we got to the car. Definitely would've screamed, but I'd never imagined she had this in her or what would happen next.

She'd parked in my parking spot in the garage next to the units like she always did. She carried Janie on one hip and her other things stuffed in her My Little Pony backpack. Janie stared at me, wide eyed and unblinking, watching me the entire time, but she never said a word. It was like she knew to be quiet even though Lillian hadn't told her to.

Once we got to the parking garage, Lillian set Janie down next to the car without ever taking the gun off me. Before I knew what was happening or could fight back, she shoved me against the car and whipped out zip ties from the back seat. She quickly tied my hands behind my back, then grabbed a motorcycle helmet and slid it over my head. She'd taped the front visor with black duct tape, so it was pitch black inside the helmet. Foam speakers pushed against my skull. Suddenly, she turned them on, and loud heavy metal music screeched in my ears. She kept the music turned up as she shoved me into the back seat of the car and kicked me to the floor.

If she said anything, I wouldn't know. The music was blasting too loud.

Panic roared through me. I was instantly terrified that I'd run out of air and suffocate. You could go three minutes without any air. I'd looked it up once when I was younger. That wasn't very long. I fought the fear the same way I'd fought it as a kid. With logic and facts. The parts of my brain that weren't panicked. That's how you kept it at bay. Prevented it from taking over your brain and overpowering your senses.

The wheels thrummed underneath me, making me instantly nauseous. I was terrified that I'd throw up in the helmet and choke on my own vomit. All my years doing math to calm myself with Cerena immediately kicked in.

I was too terrified for equations, so I just started counting. Yell counting. Like a drill sergeant.

"ONE! TWO! THREE! FOUR! FIVE! SIX! SEVEN! EIGHT!" I screamed into the abyss of the dark helmet.

Somewhere around 3,400 seconds, my head stopped feeling like firecrackers were going off inside it, and I slid into the realization that counting might actually be helpful in the situation. Knowing how many minutes we drove would give me an idea of how far away we were from home. It'd also give me something to focus on instead of the fear. I kept calling out the numbers to the beat of the music thrashing my ears.

I'd counted to a thousand three times. Fifty-six minutes total. That meant we couldn't be all that far away from Champaign, especially because we hadn't driven fast. That part was easy to tell once I calmed down. Lillian had dragged me out of the car and inside still wearing the helmet. I have no clue where I'm at. I was turned completely upside down and disoriented, which was probably the point.

I fought my fear in the room like I'd been fighting it since the moment Lillian pulled out the gun and said she knew about what happened with Cerena. That was the most terrifying part of all this, even more frightening than the helmet or the gun. There was no way she knew what happened to Cerena, though. How could she?

I shook my head. It was impossible. I killed Cerena as silently and as quietly as I'd slipped out of grocery stores with food stuffed in my pockets.

(THEN)

I crept into Cerena's bedroom. This was only the second time I'd ever done it in my whole life. Every alarm bell went off inside me. Triggering all the memories of that night. Being four years old and stumbling into her bedroom sick. My stomach had been so upset, and I had such awful cramps. We probably ate bad food, but I was four and felt like I was dying. It was so much more than feeling like I was going to throw up. I was on fire with fever. My entire body shook, and all my muscles ached like they were being twisted.

Cerena had been livid when I woke her up, and smacked me across the face, sending me flying against the wall. I tumbled to the ground and tried to get away from her before she could hit me again, but not fast enough. She sprang out of bed and jerked me up by my T-shirt, clutching it in her fists while she screamed, "What the hell do you think you're doing, coming into my bedroom in the middle of the night and waking me up?"

"Mommy—" *Erp!* Vomit sprayed from my mouth and splattered onto the brown carpet.

"Ew! That's disgusting! Get away from me!" Cerena pushed me off her, which only made me heave again and spew more puke on the ground. I couldn't help it. The vomit just kept coming in violent spasms. Over and over again as I clutched my stomach. I puked so hard I popped all the blood vessels in my right eye.

She'd been so angry, and gone on an explosive rant. She was always one short step away from a rampage. She made me wash up the puke on the floor as if I'd done it on purpose. My teeth chattered so hard while I cleaned because my fever was so high. I kept biting the insides of my cheeks. Sending the metallic taste of blood down my throat. I'd had to take breaks or I would've passed out.

I shoved the memories down and stared at Cerena lying flat on her back. Her mouth was open wide and her arms flopped to the side like she didn't have a care in the world. She was getting the most peaceful rest. Hours after she offered her daughter's virginity to a pedophile. Still, there she was. At ease. Her chest moving up and down as she slept. Half a smile on her face.

I walked over to the side of the bed and stood above her, looking down and examining her face. Every single detail. Marveling at her features the same way strangers in the grocery store or random people we passed on the street did. She looked so beautiful when she was asleep. I found myself wondering, like I'd done so many times before, how someone so pretty could be so poisonous.

She'd beaten me to a bloody pulp tonight for stabbing Mr. Harris. Smacking me in the chest. Kicking me in the ribs over and over again while I lay curled up in the fetal position. She hadn't brought her belt out in a long time, but she'd resurrected it from the dead tonight. Yanking my pants down and covering my backside with angry, nasty welts. I wouldn't be able to sit down for days.

Apparently, Cerena had been selling my virginity on Facebook. Mr. Harris was the highest bidder. Ten thousand dollars. In the end, that's what I was worth to her. She'd been sending pictures of me in the shower to him for months. I couldn't stomach the idea.

She didn't say a word when she got home. Didn't even check to see if I was here. That's how little she cares. I've taken way more Tylenol than I probably should've and have been sitting on a bag of frozen peas for the last hour, but everything hurts when I move. Even breathing. Maybe I should wait until I healed. Until I was stronger.

No.

The next immediate thought, as soon as that one hit.

Fuck her.

Blankets twisted around her legs. Her nightstand was covered in all its usual filth. Cigarettes snuffed out right on the wood because she was too lazy to put them in the ashtray. Burnt wax from candles she left burning. Fast-food and candy-bar wrappers. Not just on the nightstand but scattered on the other side of the bed too. The floor was covered in piles of dirty clothes. Condom wrappers. Purses. Belts. All of it disgusting.

I stood over her, holding her pillow in my right hand. My ribs ached and throbbed. Pretty sure my nose was broken again. It'd taken forty-five minutes for it to stop bleeding. My wounds were definitely worse than Mr. Harris's. I probably should've been the one at the hospital.

Instead, I was here. About to put the pillow over Cerena's head. I was going to kill my own mother, but she deserved to die. That's all there was to it.

I moved as quietly as possible, doing my best not to make a sound. Ignoring the protests of my injured body. I straddled her, trying to put the least amount of pressure down. I had no idea if she was a heavy sleeper and didn't want her to wake up before I was in proper position. She might easily overpower me, given my wounded state. That's why I had to be firmly planted on the bed. I burrowed each knee into the mattress for balance.

I gripped the pillow with both hands and gently placed it over her head. Not hard at first. Barely any pressure. I didn't want to startle her awake with a dramatic blow to her lungs and face. She might hurl me off her just from the adrenaline.

Instead, I just kept it over her face, slowly blocking her air, to make it difficult to breathe and get her nice and lightheaded before I applied any pressure. Her body started to shift and move uncomfortably underneath mine. She let out a groan. Tried to move from underneath the pillow.

Go!

I smashed it down, completely covering every part of her face, and held it there.

She was awake immediately. Writhing and bucking underneath me. I braced myself against her on the bed with my legs and held on for dear life. She was strong. Much stronger than I anticipated, especially for being so petite. But I didn't let go of the pillow and I didn't take it off her.

I headbutted her. Even with the pillow over her face, it knocked her back against the bed. Her chest heaved as she struggled to breathe. Hands clawed at her neck and the pillow as she desperately fought to stay alive, but I could feel the fight finally leaving her body. Her twitches coming slower and slower. Less and less strength behind them. Until finally her body stilled, then slowly stopped moving at all. Followed by her chest. Then, one last convulsion, as if that was the moment her spirit left her body. I stayed there on top of her for a long time, unmoving, just to be sure she was gone.

Was it really over?

I finally released my grip on the pillow, but I didn't take it off her face, just in case. My body slowly relaxed on top of hers, and I rested my head on her chest, listening for the sound of air in her lungs or a heartbeat. There was no air. No pulse. Nothing but warm skin underneath mine. I left my head down on her chest. Atop her still-warm body. This was closer to her than I'd ever been in my entire life. She'd never once laid me across her chest while she was alive, but that's where I fell asleep that night, still clutching the pillow over her face while she slept in eternal rest.

TWENTY-FOUR

The room flooded with harsh fluorescent light as soon as the door opened. Lillian stepped through carrying a plastic bag. I held back the urge to lunge at her. I'd never be able to overpower her. Not right now. I was too weak. She'd only come in once since we arrived and given me two bottles of water. No food.

She looked ragged. There were bags underneath her eyes. She hasn't been sleeping either. Fresh worry lines creased her forehead. She worked her jaw as she studied me, trying to assess the shape I was in since the last time she'd seen me.

I didn't know how much time had passed since she'd been here last, but I'd gone without food enough to know it'd been more than a few days since she forced me into the car and dragged me to this room. There's a weird delirium that sets in after you haven't eaten for days. When your body starts feasting on itself. No matter how rough Lillian looks, I'm sure she's eaten. That's why I have to wait to attack until I build up my strength.

I pulled my knees up to my chest. Where had she been all this time, and what had she been doing? Where was Janie? I hadn't heard Lillian coming, so I didn't have a chance to look before she'd slithered through the door and quickly slammed it behind her.

Lillian pulled out a sandwich and tossed it to me. I grabbed it from the floor and fought the desire to smash the entire thing into my mouth all at once, devouring it in one bite. Instead, I took the sandwich out of the Ziploc and pulled off a small chunk from the corner. It was peanut butter and jelly. Smelled wonderful. My mouth watered instantly. I took a deep breath and stuck that piece in my mouth. I counted to thirty in my head while I chewed. It tasted like heaven. I sat the rest of it down next to me on top of the bag.

Lillian was clearly taken aback. "You're not going to eat the sandwich? Is something wrong with it?"

"It's delicious. That's why I'm keeping more for later." This might be her first time with a prisoner, but it definitely wasn't my first time being held captive. I didn't know when she'd feed me next, and I'd learned how to ration my food by the time I was eight. I could tell my behavior had thrown her off guard, and that made me secretly proud, like I used to be with Cerena when I'd do the same thing to her.

We sat in silence. Just staring at each other and waiting for the other one to speak or make a move. Neither of us wanting to reveal our hand—as if I had anything in my hand to hide. Except I might. If this entire thing was about Cerena, then I had information there was no way Lillian knew. At least I didn't think so, because it was impossible that she knew what had actually happened.

Finally, she broke the silence. "I'm sorry it has to be this way."

"Lillian, what's going on? It doesn't have to be this way. What are you doing?"

"Taking back what's mine," she said determinedly, like I was supposed to know what that meant, but I had no clue what she was talking about.

"I'm so confused. You didn't even know Janie existed until I called you from the hospital." You couldn't miss what you didn't have to begin with. She'd just been secretly pining over a great-granddaughter? Wishing she had one?

"You have no idea what I've been through or what it felt like to lose Cerena." Her voice hitched like she might cry.

"Well, I'm a little confused why you kicked her out of your house, then." No matter how I felt about Cerena, abandoning your child—even as a teenager—was wrong. I refused to feel sorry for Lillian, *especially* after this.

She threw her head back and laughed. "Is that what she told you? Your mother was so dramatic."

The air thickened. A knot of anxiety immediately balled in my stomach. "She also said you cut her off."

"We didn't kick her out of the house or cut her off. Ever." She rolled her eyes. "We took Cerena back home immediately. The moment the school told us she was pregnant and before she ever started showing so that we could spare her any embarrassment. Were we disappointed at first? Absolutely! We tried talking to her about different options, but she wasn't interested in anything besides keeping the baby. And so, you know what we did?" She paused and gave me a pointed look, making sure I wouldn't miss what she was about to tell me next. "We got her situated with the best doctors in the state. Your pawpaw got her one that specialized in teenage pregnancy, and he even found a homeschool program for teenage mothers that she could attend so she wouldn't fall behind in her classes and could graduate on time. None of that was easy to do then, but see, honey, we were fully prepared to help her raise the baby. We didn't want that baby—you—" She glanced at me, as if there were any mistaking who she meant. "To ruin all of her hard work. It didn't have to derail her hopes and dreams. We even would've let her keep seeing her boyfriend. But you know what she did?"

My stomach sank. This wasn't how Cerena explained things. She said they kicked her out in the middle of the night when they discovered she was pregnant. Made her leave without even taking a suitcase. My throat felt like it was closing up. I reached for one of my bottles of water and took a sip.

Lillian was still on the verge of tears. "Your mama disappeared. One day, she was just gone. She was supposed to show up at her doctor's appointment, and she never did. For a second, we actually thought she was missing. That's what your mama did to us, Becky. We were so scared. We filed a missing persons report with the police and everything. Your pawpaw was the one that tracked her down with that boy—your father. They were living with his parents. That's why Cerena gave you their last name. But I bet she didn't tell you that part, did she?" She peered at me as I sipped my water, grappling with this new information that didn't fit with anything I'd heard from Cerena. "Your pawpaw begged and begged to get the two of them to come home with him, but they refused. They didn't want anything to do with us. Cerena only likes to share certain parts of her history, and I'm the villain in every single one of her stories, but trust me, sweetie, I was the best thing she ever had. There was nobody who did more for that girl or loved her more than me and your pawpaw."

"What happened with my parents?" I asked. I'd spent many sleepless nights wondering who my father was and what happened between him and Cerena. Sometimes I pretended my dad was dead and that's why he wasn't rescuing me. Other times I imagined he had an entire team of people out searching for me. My maternal family had been easy to find online, but he'd been impossible. Not when I only had a last name and no other information.

"He left her for another young girl when you were just two months old. She'd never admit it, but she was too embarrassed to come home after that. She lived with his mother, Ruth, instead." There was a slight smugness to her expression that was impossible to hide as she said it. Part of her was happy my father hurt Cerena, which didn't fit the image of someone that was supposed to love her the most and be the most supportive.

No wonder Cerena never mentioned my father. His rejection would've destroyed her fragile ego. Lillian knew that too. "But I don't understand . . . you just let her go live on her own, then? Wasn't she seventeen?"

"She was, but like I said—she didn't want anything to do with us. Didn't even claim us. She told everyone Ruth was her mother. Even put that on all her medical and legal paperwork. That's why y'all share the same last name too," Lillian responded, like she didn't see anything wrong with letting her teenage daughter fend for herself as a single mom.

Cerena had been on her own since she was a teenager too. Was she in so much pain that she had to hurt other people? Is that why she was so awful to me? I quickly erased those thoughts. Those kinds of thoughts got me in trouble. You couldn't think of Cerena like a regular person. The same was probably true for her mother. I couldn't let my emotions influence me the way that they had before. I was so mesmerized by Lillian's love-bomb spell that I hadn't noticed anything that fell outside that magic. The signs were probably there all along. God, I hated myself for being so weak, but there was nothing I could do about it now.

"I still can't believe you just let her go," I said.

"You think I was going to let the most precious thing in my life just disappear? Oh no, sweetie." She shook her head. "Not my baby. I always knew what was happening with her." Her eyes narrowed. "How do you think I know you killed her?"

That was impossible. I gave her a blank stare.

There was no way Lillian knew what happened to Cerena or that she was even dead. I'd been so careful. Absolutely meticulous and so patient, from start to finish. Lillian was playing a game with me. Just like Cerena. They were master manipulators. You couldn't trust what either of them said. Lillian might have me in check at the moment, but she better never underestimate me. That's the mistake Cerena had made, and look what it cost her.

HIM

(NOW)

The address came from a payroll stub buried deep in the files of a temporary employment agency headquartered just outside of Champaign. Vega had flagged all the agencies within a fifty-mile radius for alerts matching Orion to a job. Yesterday, they got lucky. It was a three-week job as an overnight warehouse security person down in Mount Vernon. Vega and Santos made the drive and turned off the headlights the moment they turned down the long driveway and into the parking lot. They didn't want to let him know they were coming.

But he must've been watching the security cameras because he was in the parking lot before they were even out of the car. Standing there like a soldier, in his navy blue uniform. The company name embroidered in white on the pocket. He looked even leaner than his old driver's license photo, and it was hard to believe he'd pose any kind of intimidating physical threat if someone tried to break into the warehouse. Santos eyed him to see if it was an armed security position, and it was. A Colt .45 was clipped to his belt.

"Boss," she said without taking her eyes off the weapon. It was their code word for alerting the other when they noticed someone was armed.

Vega gave her a brief nod before turning his attention back to Orion. "Are we just going to sit out here in the parking lot, or are you going to be a gentleman and invite us to come inside?"

Orion shook his head. His eyes swept over them. Top to bottom. "Here's just fine. I'm not allowed to have anyone in the facility after hours, and I don't want to lose my job."

Santos and Vega glanced at each other, quickly nodding their agreement to appease him, even though the place was an aluminum warehouse that was likely rented off the books. Never mind that they were the police and could force their way inside if they really needed to.

"Are you Orion Ellis?" Vega asked, but it was only a formality. Orion looked just like his pictures. There was no mistaking he was their guy. It felt so good to finally be standing with him face-to-face.

"Yeah." His voice was hoarse, like he had a cold or was a smoker. Maybe both.

"I'm Detective Vega, and this is my partner, Detective Santos. We're with the Waldorf County Police Department. Do you have a few minutes?"

Orion's eyes flicked to their badges, then back to Vega. "Sure," he said politely.

"We're investigating a commercial development site on the old Miller property on the east side of Waldorf," Vega explained. "A few human remains have been found, and we're trying to identify them. We were hoping you might be able to help us."

Orion's jaw clenched just slightly. "I saw something about that on the news."

"We've talked to some of your friends and former residents. You were there around 2007, correct?" Santos asked, jumping in for the first time.

"Maybe." Orion shrugged. His face benign, revealing nothing. "I was in a lot of different places when I was a kid, so it's hard to keep them all straight."

"Fair enough," Santos said with a clipped nod. "How about when Earl Miller went missing? Were you living there during that period of time?"

He took a few beats to consider his response.

"Yes." His voice terse.

"Do you have any idea what happened to Earl?" Vega stepped back in.

Orion shrugged for a second time. Completely noncommittal. "Helen told us he was having an affair and took off to be with the other woman. I never thought anything different."

"Do you remember a boy named Brock?" Santos asked next.

Orion paused for a few seconds, considering his answer. He rubbed his jaw before slowly answering, "Yes."

Vega and Santos waited for him to say more, but that was it. He shifted back and forth on his feet. His eyes skirting around them.

"Do you know what happened to him?" Vega asked after a few more awkward beats passed and he still hadn't spoken.

"Rumor was that he ran away. Lots of kids ran away from that house, but I'm sure you already know that." He gave them a pointed look, then quickly went back to his expressionless face.

"Yes," Vega said, frowning. "It's really sad what Earl did to all those foster kids."

"But Brock wasn't reported missing or as a runaway," Santos said. "Not officially."

Orion didn't flinch. "Doesn't surprise me. Lots of things weren't reported."

"We'd like you to come down to the station with us. It'd be helpful if you could walk us through everything you remember. Give us a better idea of the layout of the property. Any other staff there. Things like that." Vega studied him as he said it.

"I don't know how much help I'll be," Orion replied, shaking his head. "It's been years since I lived there, and I barely remember the place."

"Even small pieces of memories can help us figure things out, and you probably have no idea what information you have that might be useful," Santos added.

Orion looked nervously behind him at the warehouse like someone might be watching him from the window. "I can't leave right now. I'm working."

"Come on, it'll be quick," Vega said, motioning toward the car.

"Do I have to?" Orion asked.

"It'd be really helpful to the case," Vega said.

"Do I have to?" Orion asked it again. Locking eyes. His nice way of asking him if they had a warrant.

Vega and Santos both knew it. They had no choice but to shake their heads in unison.

"Then I'm not going down to the station to talk with you, and I need to get back to work now," he said, stepping back from their car.

Santos quickly handed him her card before he could walk away. "Why don't you give me a call when you get off, and we can schedule a better time to come by?"

He reluctantly took the card and nodded. He shifted back and forth on his feet, shoving his hands into the pockets of his pants.

"We'll be in touch," Vega said before they turned around and got back in the car.

They sat in silence with the engine idling for a moment, watching Orion walk back inside the warehouse. He flung a look over his shoulder right before shutting the door behind him.

"He's not going to talk." Vega stated the obvious.

"No," Santos agreed. "But we're going to find a way to make him."

TWENTY-FIVE

I flattened myself against the wall next to the door. Every sense on high alert. All my muscles hurt from being in this same position for so long, but Lillian could come through that door at any second, and when she did, I'd be ready. I'd been strategically rehearsing how many steps it took to get to the door so that once the light went off and she was gone, I could be there. She only turned the light on when she was in the room. Four and a half steps to the door. Two over to the side. And then once I felt it, shimmying over.

The plan was to knock her down and run. It wasn't much, but it was all I had. It felt like I'd been waiting there forever. Then, suddenly, the door opened.

I rushed at Lillian in a flying tackle, slamming her back against the wall. I hit her before she knew I was coming and shoved my knee as hard as I could into her stomach. The air left her lungs, making an *oof* sound. Lillian dropped everything she was carrying and fell to the ground. I kicked her so hard in the face, it snapped her whole head back. I bolted out the door as she screamed.

Blinding fluorescent light hit my eyes.

A double-wide trailer. All the windows covered in tinfoil.

Mirrored walls everywhere. A barre. Raised wooden floor.

And there was Janie.

Standing in the center of the room, wearing a black leotard. Her wrist handcuffed to the barre. Was she wearing a dog collar?

My brain took in everything in quick snippets, but there was no time to process. I had to get out of there, so I raced for the door. I'd come back for Janie once I got help. Lillian grabbed my hair from behind and yanked me back. I twisted around and punched her already-bleeding face. She screamed and stumbled backward, but she refused to release her death grip on my hair. She almost pulled me down with her, but I fought my way out of her hold and ran for the door again.

A gun cocked.

"Don't you move!" she yelled. The fear in her voice gone.

I froze.

Within seconds, the gun was pressed into my back. That's what I'd been afraid of. The biggest risk to this plan, but it was the only one I had. "Take your hand off that door. You're not leaving." She pressed the gun harder into me.

My hand was still on the knob. Both of us breathing hard. Would she actually shoot me? I was afraid she might, and even if she didn't kill me, a bullet to the back would likely paralyze me. I dropped my hold on the door. My shoulders sank in defeat.

"Turn around," she ordered.

I slowly turned around, even though I didn't want to. Her left eye was already swollen shut. Her nose looked crooked and off center like I might've broken it. Hopefully I did. The entire left side of her face was distended and turning colors already. Her lower lip cracked and bleeding.

She wrestled me back inside the dark room, with the gun pressed tight against my side. Just like she'd done to get me out of the apartment and into this place. "I really didn't want to tie you up, but now I'm going to have to." Her breath was ragged. There was so much blood on her face. She was going to be swollen for days. She hadn't taken the gun off me.

"What are you doing with Janie?" I asked. Was there another bedroom on the other side of the trailer where they stayed? I hadn't seen anything besides the makeshift dance studio, but my focus had been on getting out of here as fast as I could.

"I'm just trying to give her the chance at life that we could never give you," she said in a nasally voice, stuffed up from the blood and a probably broken septum.

"Give me, or give Cerena?" I wasn't sure she had any of us girls straight in her mind. Whatever they were trying to do out there, it clearly wasn't going well because she had Janie in handcuffs with a dog collar around her neck.

"Oh, you, sweetie. Have you not been paying attention to anything I've said?" She shook her head. Immediately winced from the pain. "We gave Cerena everything. The best schools. The most decorated coaches. We showered that girl with love and opportunities. She just never appreciated a single thing we ever did for her. So, when she decided to leave us for that loser and strike out on her own, we let her go."

"If you really cared about her that much, you wouldn't be able to just let her leave with another family like that. She was only a teenager!" I snapped. I couldn't help myself.

Lillian gave me a pitying stare. "You really don't know, do you?"

I didn't like how she was looking at me. I was immediately nervous. "What do you mean?"

She shook her head and sighed. "Your mama was something else, you know that."

"What are you talking about?" I rubbed my hands up and down my arms. Why was she messing with me like this?

"How do you think your rent got paid and you had food on your table growing up?" she asked next.

"That's not possible. No way. Cerena never had money." I pointed my finger at Lillian like she'd done something wrong. She was just trying to trick me. Playing mind games. "We were always poor and broke. I spent half my childhood starved."

"I know, honey, and I'm so sorry she did that to you. That's why it broke my heart to hear you talk about what it was like for you because we sent your mama lots and lots of money over the years," she said, giving me a knowing nod. "She contacted us when you were about two years old and said that she was in big trouble. She'd still been living with Ruth and said she needed to get out of there. She wouldn't say what or why. Just begged us to wire her money or the two of you wouldn't be safe, so of course we did. We couldn't tell her no after hearing that. She was somewhere in Alabama then. Shortly after, she called again, but this time, she wanted to talk about you." She paused, giving the information a chance to settle with me before continuing, but I couldn't register what she was saying. It didn't fit with any narrative I'd ever been told. "She was crying so hard, saying she was in over her head and wanted to know if we would take you for a while so she could go back to school. That's one of the things we offered to do for her when she was pregnant before she even left home, by the way—we said we'd raise you and let her go back to school. She'd refused then, but said she'd changed her mind, and we were so thrilled. She said she needed money for the school-tuition deposit and to send you home." Her voice slowed. "This part is so embarrassing. We sent her both. She used the tickets. Just had them switched to Hawaii. She—"

"Stop!" I screamed, raising my hand in the air. I couldn't handle anything more. That was too much. I remembered a picture Cerena kept on her nightstand for years of her in Hawaii with a lei around her neck holding a coconut drink. She said she'd gone there with a guy named Jerry when I was a baby. I didn't want to imagine who she'd left me with while she was gone.

"I know this is so hard. It's the whole reason I never talked to you about it before. Why I always avoided this conversation." She took a step closer to me like we were suddenly friends again and she was considering touching me.

"Please, just get out of here. Leave me alone." I didn't want her anywhere near me. Why would she tell me all this now? How could she have kept something like this to herself?

"She sold you to us so many times over the years, and each time she offered you to us, we paid the price. When I tell you we wanted you, sweetie, we wanted you. And we paid a lot of money for you too. We sent her plane tickets. Bus tickets. Gas money. Once she even came to Florida and said you were with her. That time she showed up at the house and your pawpaw wrote her a big check. We followed through on our end of the bargain. She just never did."

How could Cerena have kept me away from people who would've loved me and taken care of me? In the next instant, I looked around and remembered where I was at. All the things I'd just been through with Lillian. The hurt so fresh. The women in my family were awful.

"We sent you Christmas presents every year. Cards on your birthday. Same as we did her. We never stopped loving either of you." Her voice wavered with emotion. She looked like she was going to cry, but I didn't trust her tears any more than I would Cerena's.

"I don't believe you," I spat at her. It couldn't be true. Cerena wanted nothing to do with them or their money. She swore she'd rather die than ask them for anything ever again.

I'd never gotten a birthday gift, and Cerena told me we were Jewish so we didn't celebrate Christmas. We didn't celebrate any of the Jewish holidays either, but that was because Cerena said they'd gotten too commercialized over the years.

She shrugged. "I have pictures of when she came to visit us. Would you like me to show you?"

"What?! No. No! I don't want to see." I was reeling and couldn't handle anything else. This was an entirely different level. I was involved in every single scam Cerena ran. How many others were out there that I didn't know about? Where did she go when she disappeared? She could've had a nice, beautiful house somewhere else that I knew nothing about. Anything was possible. I clearly didn't know her as well as I thought.

Lillian nodded. "In the end, she was just playing us. The older we got, the less we were interested in playing her games. She never intended to come home. She wasn't ever going to give us you."

The room pulsed with the leftover energy from our fight. The door was still wide open. I could make out Janie. She looked so skinny in her black leotard. All her ribs were sticking out. Collarbone protruding. Her face was gaunt. Painted up like a clown. I no longer needed to wonder if she'd been here as long as I had. By the looks of things, I'd fared better than she had in this mess. Maybe than any of us, actually, because Lillian had never looked so awful as she did right now.

I pointed out the door at Janie without taking my eyes off Lillian. "What's going on with Janie?"

She frowned. "She doesn't like to dance."

So, it was a dance studio. She was teaching Janie ballet? She was obviously trying to turn her into Cerena all over again. "That must be so hard for you," I said, trying to connect with her.

"It is." Her face softened.

"What are you trying to get her to do?" She didn't have Janie tied up out there without a reason.

"Here's the thing." She waved her hands like she always did when she talked, except this time, she still had the gun in her right one, and it was making me nervous. "Okay, I always wanted to be in your life, and you know how much I loved my baby girl. It's like I lost my whole heart when Cerena left, and when you called from the hospital, I finally got it back. It's too late for me to raise you, but I can get a second chance with Janie. She looks so much like your mama did when she was that age too. Sometimes I just look at her and I think, *Wow, a mini Cerena.* I'm so lucky for this opportunity." Lillian's eyes filled with tears.

It all sounded so loving and kind that it was easy to forget Janie was in handcuffs twelve feet away from us. But if anyone understood the need to tie up Janie, it was me. Just because she was skinny didn't mean Lillian was starving her. For all I knew, Janie could be refusing to eat.

"Are you having a hard time with her?" I asked softly.

"I am." She nodded. "She's not adjusting well to the move and our new routines. She's turned into a different little girl ever since we got here. She doesn't want to do anything I ask. Just like you always said she did. She's *so* defiant. And stubborn! Oh my goodness. I've never met a little girl that's more stubborn. I just don't know what I'm going to do if I can't get her to cooperate with me."

Bingo. That was it. All I needed.

I couldn't focus on the sting of her betrayal or Cerena's. That was thinking with my emotions, and if I did that? I might curl up in a ball in this corner, start to cry, and never move again. But thankfully, I didn't think with emotions. I would do whatever it took to get us out. To survive. To free Janie and me from Lillian's clutches the same way I'd freed myself from her daughter's. She'd just given me the golden key.

"Let me help you. I can help you with Janie," I said.

(THEN)

I didn't open the door right away when Orion knocked. Just stood there with my hand on the knob and my forehead pressed against the peeling wood. I found him at lunch and told him I needed him to come over after school. I'd never invited him to my house before, so he knew it was serious. He promised to come over as soon as he finished his shift at the Dairy Queen.

The apartment was so quiet now without Cerena. The TV that was usually blaring 24-7 was gone too, since everything had been shut off again. We didn't even have hot water. When I finally let Orion in, I couldn't look him in the eye because I was so embarrassed about the state of things. I just stepped aside and let him experience it himself.

He walked in slowly, taking it all in—the piles of junk, the empty beer bottles stacked in the corner, the dishes caked in old food. He grimaced from the smell. Not from the food, but the smell of death that had taken over the apartment. He stood in the middle of the living room with his hands shoved deep in the pockets of his hoodie. He didn't say anything for a long time. It felt like forever before he finally spoke.

"Is your mom dead?" he asked like he already knew the answer.

I nodded.

He didn't ask how, and he wouldn't look at me. He just stared at his tennis shoes.

"I didn't know what else to do," I said quietly.

"Did she hurt you?" His voice was raw.

I nodded again. Slower this time. A lump of emotions lodged in my throat.

Orion looked at the apartment again, and then back at me. "Okay."

That's all. Just *okay*.

The same thing I'd said to him a few weeks ago when the police started asking questions about Earl and where Orion was the night Earl went missing. Orion told me to tell them that he was with me, watching old movies, which is exactly what I'd done when it was my turn to be interviewed.

"She's in the bathroom. Do you wanna see her?" I asked, hesitant and unsure how to proceed with this situation. I was only a petty criminal—just a shoplifter, not a murderer. At least not until last week.

I put Cerena in the bathtub to control the smell. I folded her into a tight ball with her knees pressed tight against her chest, and tied a jump rope around her so she'd stay that way. I put her in one of those heavy-duty lawn bags. Double bagged her just in case.

Orion nodded and followed me down the hallway to the bathroom. Neither of us spoke. I opened the door and motioned for him to go inside. I stood in the doorway while he moved past me. After I'd dragged her in here, I shut the door and kept it closed until I could decide my next move.

In the meantime, I'd just pretended that she was away on another trip. I'd created an entire imaginary scenario about it. One where she married a billionaire tech guy and they were sailing around the world together on his private yacht. She sent me a million dollars to apologize for how she hurt me and to help me live a good life. I'd fantasize about all the things I'd buy. Beginning with groceries and toilet paper. What would it be like to live in a world where you always had toilet paper?

I wasn't going to stand for anything less than a world filled with toilet paper.

"All of her is in this bag?" Orion asked, finally turning around to face me again.

I nodded, trying not to breathe through my nose and doing my best not to look in the direction of the tub. "I googled it, and the smell is supposed to go away in a couple weeks, but it's so strong, and I don't think I can wait that long. I'm freaking out that I'm going to get caught. Somebody's going to complain soon. They might've already done it." All of this felt so scary now that he was here. It made the situation entirely too real. "I need to get her out of here, but she's too heavy for me to move by myself, and I have no idea what to do with her once I do."

"How are you planning on getting her out?" he asked, rubbing his jaw.

"That's where you come in." I laughed nervously. My knees weak.

He was silent for a few moments. "Honestly, the best thing to do would be to just burn the apartment down with her in it. No one would suspect a thing because Cerena's accidentally set the apartment on fire twice already, hasn't she?"

I nodded.

The first time, she fell asleep with a cigarette in her hand and burned a hole in her mattress. The other time, she set a frozen TV dinner on fire in the microwave. The fire department only came for the bedroom fire, but the smoke alarms had gone off for both, and they'd evacuated the entire apartment building each time. Nobody would be surprised that she'd finally burned her unit down.

"It'd be a great idea if there weren't other people living here too. The fire alarms work, but that doesn't mean everyone will get out in time." I rubbed my temples and let out a long sigh. "And then I think about the animals . . . I couldn't live with myself if a person or an animal got hurt. We have to think of something else besides that."

He walked over to the sink and opened the medicine cabinet. He stared at the contents for a few seconds before shutting the door. Then, he did the same thing with the other drawers in the vanity. He checked the electrical outlet on the wall next. He moved like he was on a mission, like he'd done this before, but I knew he hadn't. Not this.

"Did she keep the neighbors at a distance?" he asked, moving down the hallway and back into the living room.

"Yeah," I said as I followed him from room to room like he was doing some kind of inspection.

"Any boyfriends who'll come looking for her?"

I shook my head. "No one ever does. She always goes to them or brings them home with her."

He nodded once. "Then we start a fire and make sure no one else gets hurt." He nodded again like he was reassuring himself it was a good plan.

"It just makes me so nervous." I couldn't live with myself if something happened.

"Me too. But check this out—here's what we're going to do. We'll wait until it's the middle of the day during the week because most people will be gone at work. Kids will be at school. I'll knock on every door, and make so much noise screaming and yelling. Set off all the fire alarms. I'll make sure everybody gets out. I promise."

"You don't have to do this," I said.

He smiled and gave me a knowing look. "Yes, I do."

TWENTY-SIX

The second I stepped out of the room behind Lillian, Janie's face lit up. Her mouth dropped open in shock, and then pure joy. She shrieked, high pitched and breathless, and launched herself at me. Her tiny feet slapped the wood as she ran to me with her arms flailing wide like she couldn't get to me fast enough.

"Mommy!" she cried, in a way she'd never said my name before. I wanted to weep at the way she said it, but also because this wasn't how it was supposed to happen.

I barely had time to kneel down before she slammed into me, her body weight knocking me back a little. She wrapped her arms around my neck and held on with full force, like she was afraid I might disappear again.

She was so small. My arms curved around her instinctively. I quickly remembered how Cerena used to say that Lillian starved her to keep her tiny. I thought of Cerena mimicking Lillian's voice—"Ballerinas are svelte"—as I looked down at Janie's thin frame and the way her ribs pressed through her leotard. Something dark crawled up my spine.

Was Lillian doing the same thing to her?

"She's light, huh?" Lillian said behind me with a tight smile like she was reading my mind. "It's all the dancing. She's all muscle."

But none of that mattered right now.

Janie was here.

"I missed you so much," I whispered, stroking the back of her head.

"I missed you *soooooo* much!" she squealed, pulling back to look at me like she used to do when she was a baby. So sweet and innocent. Her face flushed with excitement.

"I know. I'm sorry, sweetie." Her arms went right back around my neck. I felt her fingers dig in. Panicked and possessive. I caught sight of bruises. Faint yellow-green ones around her biceps, and a patch of red skin near her wrist that looked too raw to be old. Cigarette burns on her left hand. I pressed my lips to her temple, gently, so she wouldn't see the way my eyes burned with tears. I wanted to suck up all her pain in my body.

"She's been a little emotional lately," Lillian said, trying to keep her voice light, but I caught the edge underneath it. "She gets overwhelmed. It's a lot for her when things change suddenly."

Right.

But I didn't push. Not yet. I couldn't afford to spook Lillian. If I wanted to get us out of here, I needed to be careful. Find a way to make this work and get on her good side. Make her think we were a team.

Janie pulled back again just far enough to cup my face between her hands. Her little fingers were cold, pressed on my cheeks. "Are you staying, Mommy?"

I nodded. "I'm not going anywhere."

She let out a deep sigh and buried her face in my chest again. Her body melted into mine. I held her tight next to me. Just as afraid to let her go as she was to release her grip on me.

Lillian stood in the center of the room with her arms spread wide. Her chest puffed out with pride like she was introducing me to the finest dance academy. I took in the space. Finally able to really look. There was no living room or kitchen. Had she bought an empty trailer and made the studio? Or gutted what was here before? Either way, that took time—reconfirming she'd been planning this for a long time.

The entire living area was set up as a dance studio. A padded wood floor was laid out in the center of what would've been the living room. It was made up of interlocking wooden floor panels. Full-length mirrors lined the entire wall. A mounted barre in the middle. Huge black speakers framed either side. Clamp lights hung everywhere. All pointed to the dance floor.

Lillian finally spoke. "I've been working really hard on her posture and keeping her core engaged so her back stays straighter when she's doing her pliés. This girl has such terrible posture." She gave Janie a knowing look like this wasn't the first time the two of them had talked about her posture, but Janie didn't even notice. She was too busy clinging to me. "Anyway, this morning I thought I'd have you take her through a couple combination routines that we've been working on for her next audition. Let's start with five demis with the arms in second position, grand plié, grand plié, and then two jetés. Cambré forward to second."

My head spun. What kind of messed-up ballet language did Lillian just speak? And auditions? She was taking Janie on auditions? Where? Nobody talked about ballet like that in Champaign, and we hadn't gone far enough away to be in the city. Did she actually take her into Chicago? Maybe Lillian didn't stay here. This might just be where they did all their ballet training.

Part of me still couldn't believe all this was happening and why.

I'd made Lillian leave the day she told me about Cerena and sending her money. I refused to believe it was true the next time she'd brought it up too. But she was relentless. A few days later, she had come back and shown me a bunch of old bank statements, and there they were—all the cashed checks:

4/12/2005 Cerena Beaumont: $1,000
11/4/2005 Cerena Beaumont: $400
6/23/2006 Cerena Beaumont: $2,000

They spanned over a decade. I was stunned. Whatever money Lillian had sent her, I'd never seen any of it. Cerena had ransomed me to my grandparents multiple times and never followed through with her end of the deal. Lillian owned me. That's what I was doing here. In her mind, I was bought and paid for. Obviously, she'd come to collect.

That's also how she'd known Cerena was dead. When she stopped cashing the checks. Lillian told me that the following day, once I'd finally accepted the truth. I'd had no choice then.

Lillian had never intended to go back to Florida. I didn't know exactly what she wanted from me yet, but I knew this much—it had nothing to do with healing and reconciliation. It might not even be about ballet. Whatever plan Lillian had spun in that twisted mind of hers, I was part of it, though. Not as a mother or a daughter, but as a tool. Something she could use. No doubt I served a purpose.

I held Janie tight against me. Tears lodged in my throat, but I didn't have time to fall apart. I couldn't waste time figuring out what this place was or how long she'd been building it. The only thing I needed to focus on was keeping my daughter alive. I needed to play the part. Be the doting assistant. The ballet mom. The reformed prodigy. Whatever it took to get us out of here.

TWENTY-SEVEN

We'd been in this trailer for months now, and Lillian was spinning more and more out of control. She locked Janie in my room with me again today. I had a really bad feeling about this. Fear inched from my stomach into my throat.

"Mommy?" Janie's voice broke into my thoughts. She was so scared. I could hear it in her voice. Starving too, because Lillian forgot to feed us again. "I don't feel good."

Today was brutal. It's been that way for a long time, though. Each day bleeds into the next, especially since Lillian started giving us the pills. There's no separation between day and night when you can't see out the windows. We only slept in small intervals. They're more like naps. We're like rats on a wheel, running as fast as we can but getting nowhere. On a maniacal merry-go-round.

"It's okay, Janie," I said, trying to sound so much braver than I felt. Janie sat on her side of the bike rack, and I was on the other. After I attacked Lillian all those months ago, she'd come in the room the next day with a drill and bike rack. She'd drilled the bike rack into the floor and put a padlocked leash around my ankle and chained me to it. She did the same thing with Janie whenever she brought her in here.

Bugs felt like they were crawling all over my scalp again, and I dug into the bites as much as the bugs dug into my body. They burrowed under my skin. Even though my mind knew it was a trick, my body felt the experience as real. "I'm going to figure a way out of this."

"Why is Lala mad at us?" Her voice wavered like she was going to cry.

Us.

Finally, the two of us had become a team, and the way she said it made me want to cry. The bonding I'd been waiting for had arrived. Janie was officially attached to me. But it wasn't supposed to happen this way. This was all wrong. A nightmare wasn't supposed to be the thing to bring us together.

I'd pulled Lillian off Janie today when she was beating her with the belt. I was sure she was going to kill Janie that time. She'd come close before. Janie's shoulder was still messed up from when she'd pulled it out of socket last week when Lillian yanked her off the barre. Lillian had forgotten that she'd locked her up, and she'd been furious that Janie wouldn't come to her when she called, so she'd stormed over there to make her. Janie had sat there crying and trying to tell her that she was still locked, but you couldn't talk to Lillian when she was in one of her rages.

Lillian kept Janie in her dog collar and fed her the same nasty dog food Cerena used to feed me. Now I knew where Cerena got the idea from. So much of what Cerena had done to me was what Lillian was doing to us. They were practically the same people.

Everything itched. These damn bugs.

Lillian was tweaked again tonight. She was taking the same pills she forced down our throats. I was terrified she was going to kill all of us just by accident. She paced in circles while we worked, waving the gun around in the air. Screaming and barking at us if we tried to stop. I stepped in for Janie whenever I could, but it was a fine line. I didn't want to get myself sentenced back to my room, which is what usually happened if I pushed too hard. I had to stay on Lillian's good side if I wanted to help us.

I tucked my hand into Janie's and stroked the top of her palm with my thumb. The closest I could come to giving her a back rub when we were locked up like this. "Just try to sleep, honey, okay? Mommy's going to figure out a way to get us out of here. You don't worry about a thing."

She smells so bad again. Lillian put her back in diapers. Not because she was having toileting accidents, but to humiliate her. She also refused to allow her to take our scheduled bathroom breaks. That was the other bizarre thing Lillian had started doing, just like Cerena said Lillian had done to her—scheduled bathroom times.

Janie and I were on the same schedule. Except, for the last few days, Lillian no longer allowed Janie to go during our scheduled times because she was punishing her for talking back. The alarm would go off on Lillian's phone, signaling it was time, and both my body and Janie's automatically responded with the urge to pee. We'd turned into Pavlov's dogs that quick. Then, Lillian would take me to the bathroom. Ever since she stopped allowing Janie to relieve herself, she made me leave the door open while I went so Janie could hear the rush of the liquid as it came out of me and blasted into the toilet. Eventually, Janie had no choice but to soil herself. And when she did?

Lillian ridiculed her.

"You're so disgusting. How could you do something like that?" She'd get right down in her face. Same gnarled expression Cerena used to wear.

I hate this.

For so long, I'd thought this was all about turning Janie into Cerena. Re-creating their childhood experience—a corrective experience—gone horribly wrong. It's possible that's what it was in the beginning, but it'd morphed into something else entirely. I was starting to suspect money was involved. Same as it'd been with Cerena.

Even in the dark, I could feel Janie's eyes on me. Watching. Hesitating. She didn't trust me completely yet, but that was okay. She didn't know me—not really. She didn't know what I'd survived. I could figure my way out of anything. I'd claw my way through drywall if I had to.

TWENTY-EIGHT

"Demi plié and up, demi plié and up!" I called it out like a song while I walked circles around the dance studio, snapping my fingers. Treading the same worn path on the cheap wood like I did most days, for countless hours, hating every moment. But I didn't have any other choice if I wanted to be out of my room and on Lillian's good side. Janie jerked up and down like a puppet to my movements. Her stringlike arms out. Back straight.

Lillian sat on the aluminum folding chair next to the trailer door with the gun on her lap. She carried it with her at all times, but I didn't think it had anything to do with Janie and me anymore. People were coming and going from our place constantly, even though she never let anyone inside. She'd made a peephole in the tinfoil on the living room window so she could see if anyone was out there while still keeping an eye on us.

She tapped away on her phone like she did most days. Stepping outside to take phone calls. She never talked to anyone in front of us other than to say hello before dashing outside. A few times we'd heard the sounds of a car picking her up. We'd learn to spot the difference between Lillian's own car and someone else's. Once, when she went outside, I'd gotten Janie to start screaming. Lillian never even came back inside to tell us to be quiet. Our cries for help didn't faze Lillian in the least, which meant we were somewhere that she wasn't worried about people hearing us or complaining if they did.

Lillian was still furious from yesterday. Her lip was swollen and distended. She had four black stitches on the bottom.

What did she expect? I'd told her to stop giving Janie the pills. That they made her violent and unable to sleep, but she wouldn't listen to me. She never does.

"I need her to work! She has auditions!" she screamed frantically.

Except so far, she'd never taken Janie out of the trailer. Maybe she did before, but she didn't now. I didn't know what kind of auditions she meant. She filmed our sessions constantly for the reel she was forever creating for Janie. Kept her in full makeup for the photographer she said was coming, even though no one besides us had ever taken her picture. Lillian was the one constantly filming and taking pictures.

She gave us our pills every morning. Placed mine gently on my tongue. Chopped up Janie's and gave it to her in a bite of applesauce, like you bury medicine in peanut butter for dogs. I didn't want to take that first one, but I didn't have any other choice. Not when I was trying to get on her good side, and especially because things with Janie were worse than they'd ever been.

It was obvious Lillian had been taking the pills herself and was just as strung out. She worked her jaw while she spoke to us. Eyes huge and bulging out of her head. Her movements jerky. She couldn't stay still.

That first time she gave me the pill, she said, "Baby girl, I'm gonna let you in on a little secret. None of us get through this life without a little help from a friend, especially when things are tough, and things are real tough on all of us right now." She'd said it with the most empathetic smile. Her arm around my shoulder, squeezing me tight like we were suddenly friends again.

I'd taken the pill and dropped it on my tongue. She handed me a bottle of water. She never broke eye contact while the cold liquid washed the pill straight down my throat.

And it was magic. My hair tingled. Body buzzed. I wanted to run a marathon or write the world's most brilliant novel all at the same time. But I didn't do any of that. Lillian put us to work. Hours upon hours without rest or sleep. Chanting out ballet positions. Different combinations.

When Janie would screw up, or sometimes just randomly for no reason, Lillian would stop in the middle of Janie's routine and race over to her. She'd grab Janie and make her stand right in front of the mirror with her nose almost touching the glass.

"Say 'I'm the best ballerina in the entire world,'" Lillian would order.

When Janie didn't respond immediately, Lillian would go ballistic.

"SAY IT!!" she'd scream right in Janie's ear, her lips pressed against the skin at the top. Then she'd smash Janie's face up against the glass and scream, "'I'M THE BEST BALLERINA IN THE ENTIRE WORLD!'"

Janie wouldn't move. She'd just stand there. Arms at her side. Face stone. Never flinched, even when Lillian's spit hit her face because she was so close to her and yelling so loud. The harder Lillian pushed Janie, the harder she fought against her. It was a dangerous power struggle, and you never knew who was going to win on any given day.

Janie was regressing. Moving back to the way she behaved when she was a toddler. It was the pill's fault. That's what happened yesterday.

We were midway into practice when Janie collapsed. She started shaking on the ground.

"She's having a seizure!" I yelled, and Lillian came running across the room.

She bent down next to Janie and turned her on her side. Janie kept trembling. Her jaw chattering. Knees clacking against themselves and the raised wooden floor.

"Call 911!" I yelled at her, but she wasn't doing anything, and Janie just kept seizing. We needed to call for Janie, but this was also our chance to get help. The EMTs would take one look at this place and know something was up. They'd ask questions when they saw us.

How else would we explain the locks? All the marks on Janie's body? "I'm calling 911!"

I grabbed Lillian's phone from her, and she quickly swatted it out of my hands. "No! We're not calling!"

Just like that, Janie's trembling stilled. She rolled onto her back. Her eyes slowly opened. Had she been faking it? There was no way . . . but maybe . . .

"See?" Lillian turned to me with a huge grin on her face. "She's fine. Probably just got a little bit dehydrated, didn't you, baby girl?" She patted her head. The most affection she'd shown her in ages. "Give Lala a big kiss so your mama stops worrying." Lillian planted a smooch on Janie's mouth, and then suddenly, "Aaah!" A bloodcurdling scream as Janie bit into her lip. Blood gushed down her chin. I raced over and pulled Janie off her.

Lillian held her hand up to her mouth. "She bit me. Oh my god. That devil child just bit me."

Janie grinned. Blood stained her lips.

Lillian bolted outside, shouting something I couldn't hear and waving the gun around. I pushed Janie off me, forgetting her episode that quick, and lunged for the phone I'd dropped moments ago. My hands shook so badly I almost fumbled it. When the screen lit up, I swiped—no password.

Thank god!

I didn't think. I just tapped out 911.

The dispatcher picked up on the third ring. "Nine-one-one, what's your emergency?"

"I don't have time," I whispered, crouching low and keeping my eyes locked on the front door for any sign of Lillian. "I don't know my address or where I am, but it's a trailer somewhere about an hour outside of Champaign. One with metal siding, I think, maybe? At the end of a gravel road. I don't know . . . please trace the call. There's a child, and she's been hurt. I think she's being trafficked. There's blood everywhere too. Please. Just come. Hurry!"

"Ma'am, stay on the line—"

But I couldn't stay on the line. I might never get another chance to call anyone else.

I put the dispatcher on hold and lowered the phone from my ear. I quickly opened Lillian's contacts. Just numbers and other names I didn't recognize. Except one—Gloria.

The social worker from last year. It was worth a try.

I tapped her name. It went straight to voicemail:

"Hi, you've reached Northern Country Child Services Department. If this is a medical emergency, please hang up and dial 911. For everything else, please leave me a message with your name and case number, along with a brief message about the reason for your call. Someone will get back to you as soon as possible."

I leaned in close to the speaker and kept my voice clear and steady while I spoke. "Hi, Gloria, it's Becky Watson. From Champaign. You came by the house last year. I don't have our case number, I'm so sorry. I wish I did. But you told me to call if I ever needed help. Well—" I swallowed hard. "I do. Things are really bad here, and I need help with Janie. I don't know what to do. We're not at the same house anymore, though. That's the only problem. We're in a trailer court somewhere in the country, I think. Probably listed or rented under my grandmother's name, Lillian Beaumont. You remember her, right? She should be in the report. Please try to find us! Please!"

I hung up. Deleted the call log. Flipped back to the keypad.

Texted the only number I knew by heart—Orion: Find me. Emergency!!!

I deleted the text, then tossed the phone back on the ground just seconds before the front door opened and Lillian raced back inside. She was still furious. I jumped to my feet and stood with my arms crossed and a blank face. Janie hadn't moved from her spot by the barre, but she was watching me, and her eyes narrowed slightly. Did she know what I'd done?

What if nobody came to help us?

I pushed the thought down.

Stop.

Someone will come.

Orion will find me.

But what if that wasn't his number anymore or his phone got shut off because he didn't pay the bill? I shook my head. I still had Gloria. She'd follow up. She had to, didn't she? 911 might trace the call. Someone had to come by and check on us. They had to, especially since I said there was a child involved. I just had to be patient.

And to stop taking the pills. I had to do that too. They were fogging up my head. Scrambling everything and slowing down my thinking. I couldn't have that. I'd already started missing doses. Lillian hadn't noticed yet, but I had. Pieces of myself were knitting back together again. Clarity was slowly returning, and the truth was crystal clear.

Ballet was over. Janie wasn't built for it. Whatever Cerena was when it came to dancing, Janie wasn't. She had no flexibility or coordination. Absolutely no rhythm. And she was unraveling more every day. She'd faked a seizure and bit Lillian. Whether it was trauma or brain damage didn't matter anymore. Lillian's fantasy was a delusion, and dragging Janie through it was a slow destruction that wasn't going to end well for any of us.

We needed a plan B.

HIM

(NOW)

Santos was already pacing in circles when Vega came through the door of the precinct. She didn't need to say it—he could see it in her eyes. A huge grin spread across his face. This was the part he lived for.

"Confirmed?" he asked.

She held up the CSU report from the lab like a flag. "DNA match on the fiber from the grave. Partial hit. It's degraded, but it's enough. It puts Orion at the site."

She was rightfully pleased with herself, and so was he. She'd spent three nights outside the warehouse waiting and watching for Orion to give them something. On Wednesday night, he'd discarded his leftover Subway sandwich in the trash on the way out to his truck. It was exactly the break they needed.

Vega took the report from her and scanned the paper anyway. He couldn't help himself. The fibers pulled from the army blanket had yielded skin cells—sweat, maybe blood. Whatever it was, it had Orion Ellis's name stamped into it now. Along with his past: violent incidents, sealed juvenile charges, and an ex who once filed for a protective order and later dropped it without comment.

"It's thin," he said, handing it back to Santos. "But it's enough for a judge to sign off?"

"Judge Dalton already did," she said, smiling wide. "Thirty minutes ago. Let's go." She grabbed the keys from the top of his desk, and they headed out the door. They were mostly silent on the drive over.

They pulled up to the last known address for Orion on file, the one they'd gotten from the temporary employment agency. It was a one-story rental off a cracked two-lane street. The place was a converted garage behind a boarded-up house. A half-broken mailbox duct-taped to a chain-link fence that encircled the front. The curtains were drawn. There was no movement.

Vega turned to Santos. "Ready?"

But she was already out the door and headed down the sidewalk. This was what she lived for too. They approached the front door with caution. Hands on their weapons. Vega could feel the neighbors' eyes on their backs, even though no one was outside. Santos knocked hard on the wood.

"Orion Ellis? This is the Waldorf police. We have a warrant," she bellowed into the door.

No answer.

She knocked again with the same declaration.

Still no answer.

Vega stepped around back and surveyed the house. The empty driveway. His gut screamed that Orion was already gone. He circled around the back through the rusted gate left open on the side. There was a single boot print in the soft dirt near the back porch. He ducked his head and jiggled the screen doorknob. It was locked. He punched his hand through the screen and easily unlocked it.

"Going inside." He spoke into his walkie-talkie, alerting Santos. He kept his other hand on his gun.

The door opened into the kitchen. Empty except for a coffee mug on the counter. All the lights still turned on. An overhead fan whirring in the living room. A mattress in the center, stripped clean of bedding.

The old wooden dresser pushed up against the wall had all the drawers pulled out. Nothing in them.

He radioed Santos again. "He's gone," he said, even though he hadn't searched the rest of the house yet.

Her voice crackled back. "I just spoke with one of the neighbors next door, and he said the same thing. That he left two days ago. He had a big backpack. No car."

"Left where? Did he say?"

"They didn't ask."

People never did. They minded their business on this side of town.

Vega walked back out to the front and stood in the center of the yard with his hands on his hips. He looked out over the house toward the pine trees. Of course, Orion was a runner. He hadn't pegged him to be anything less. Santos came up and stood beside him. He could feel her disappointment without looking at her. He felt the same way.

She patted his back. "I guess he knew we were coming."

Vega didn't answer. He was already calculating their next move. Strip malls. Bus depots. Halfway houses. Whatever was waiting in Orion's wake, this wasn't over.

Not even close.

(THEN)

It was hard to believe it'd been almost a month since Cerena had died. I tugged at my backpack. I had the three most important things inside it—my birth certificate, my emancipation papers, and my government-issued ID. That's all I needed for a new start. I didn't need Cerena. I never had. I now existed in a world where there was no one abusing me, and that felt incredible. Buffered me against any guilt I felt over what I was about to do.

Everything I've done up until this point has been to survive. Period.

Orion squeezed my hand. Neither of us slept last night. Not wanting to waste even a single minute of our last few hours together. After today—especially after today—we couldn't be associated with each other. We were connected to too many crimes. The police were really starting to pressure him about Earl, especially since Brock went missing too, and he'd been Orion's roommate for a while at the Millers'. Orion planned to leave town tonight.

I'd gotten a small apartment through the Sacred Heart Fund. They helped pay for the first month's rent and deposit for transition-age youth in danger of homelessness. On Monday, I was going to a warehouse to pick out furniture. It sounded way more glamorous than it was. The warehouse consisted of all the leftover furniture from the Salvation Army and Goodwill that didn't sell in the store. We got to pick through their leftovers with furniture vouchers from the county. I planned on being the first one in line.

It was wrong to kill—I knew that—but I couldn't help smiling to myself as I twirled the matches in my hand. Cerena had always underestimated me. I was so much smarter than her, and she'd been too conceited to ever even notice.

"Are you ready?" I asked, turning to Orion.

He nodded solemnly back at me as we stood in the doorway of Cerena's bedroom. We'd dragged her out of the bathtub yesterday and laid her on the bed. Doing our best not to choke on the smell. It was so much easier to move her with his help. The plan was to make it look like she'd fallen asleep with a cigarette in her hand again, and we couldn't do that if she was in the tub. Plus, we had to make sure her body was disintegrated enough to hide any evidence of what really happened to her.

The air felt different in the apartment, like the walls were holding their breath and waiting for what they knew we were about to do. Orion and I went to work silently. He cut the trash bags from her body and pulled them out from underneath her while I grabbed the sheets to tuck in the doorway to keep the smoke from traveling too fast. The windows were sealed. We checked all the outlets again.

Orion covered Cerena with the old blanket from the closet, and I stepped over to the bed next to him. I struck one of the matches and grabbed the ashtray off the nightstand. I started one of the cigarette butts on fire, quickly followed by another. They were so stale and old that they ignited immediately. I took the ashtray and tossed it upside down on Cerena's covered body. I struck another match and threw that one on the mattress too. It took a second, but the mattress finally lit and started burning.

I stood there watching as the flames engulfed her body, then licked the walls. The heat rose in waves, scorching my skin and making my face hot. I couldn't look away as the entire room ignited.

"Let's go," Orion said with his hand on my back. He gently guided me out the door and into the hallway.

I quickly knelt and tucked the rolled-up sheet into the doorframe crack. He pulled me up when I finished. The smoke started to swirl and leak underneath almost immediately.

He tucked my hair behind my ears. "You need to get out of here."

"Promise me you won't let anyone get hurt." My voice shook with emotion. I didn't want to leave him, but there was no other choice. This was the plan. We had to stick to it.

He tilted my chin up and gazed into my eyes. "Becks, I promise." And then he kissed me softly, like an angel, barely brushing my lips, and pointed at the front door. "Now go."

I stayed rooted to my spot. Frozen. I couldn't move. Not yet.

He motioned toward the front door again as he walked into the living room. He took one of Cerena's old T-shirts and twisted it tight. I watched as he stuffed it into the mouth of a half-empty vodka bottle.

He stood still for a moment, then touched a flame to the shirt. It caught instantly—*whoosh*—a low roar that sucked the oxygen right out of the room. He tossed it at the foot of her recliner, and it shattered, sending fire spiraling across the floor. "GO!"

I had no choice now but to run.

I darted out the door and down the hallway, pulling every fire alarm as I went. Their wails screaming behind me. I shoved open the lobby doors, and the cold air smacked my face. I leaned over, breathing hard. The smell of smoke heavy in the air. People started pouring out of the apartment building almost immediately, and I ran across the street, disappearing behind a car. I pictured Orion running up and down the hallways and floors, banging on all the doors and screaming, while Cerena's body burned.

I looked up to the sky and whispered a prayer to all the gods in the entire universe. "Please let everyone get out safe. Please."

Then I ran away as fast as I could and didn't look back.

TWENTY-NINE

I squatted and hoisted Janie on my shoulders. She wrapped her scrawny legs around my neck and pressed on my head for balance. "Okay, here we go," I said, holding on to her legs as tight as I could. "Are you ready?"

"Let's do it, Mommy!" she said, tapping on my head and squeezing her legs tight around my neck. We'd been practicing for hours. It was harder than I imagined it'd be, to put her on my shoulders and stand up in the dark. Even harder to stand on my tippy-toes so that she could reach up to the light bulb.

The success of the plan hinged on her, and I wasn't going to give it a green light until I was 100 percent sure she was ready. We only had one opportunity to get this right. We needed the light bulb to be intact. We couldn't have her drop it and the pieces randomly shatter. We needed to break it a certain way so that we could use the piece of glass as a knife.

Lillian only locked us in my room together occasionally, and I hadn't thought of the light-bulb idea until recently. I'd been kicking myself that I hadn't thought of it sooner. There was no telling how long we'd been in here. Weeks bled into months bled into . . . years? Could it have been years? The drugs made it hard to keep track. But this was our chance. I've been eagerly waiting for Lillian to lock us up together again so I'd get the opportunity, and now, here it was.

We had to seize the moment.

Lillian was frantic and desperate. There were so many oozing sores on her arms from picking her skin, and her face was a mess too. I was so glad I'd stopped taking the drugs, even though she thought I still was. I tucked my morning dose into my cheek every morning and spit it out as soon as I could. Janie was still taking them, and I had no idea if she would listen to my instructions for the light-bulb plan. She was as wildly unpredictable as Lillian.

Lillian and I had started making GoFundMe videos with Janie. So far, the videos were going much better than her ballet lessons ever did because all we really had to do was make her look pathetic and take her picture. The videos definitely brought in money, but Janie was still really tough to control and manage. We were pretending that Janie had cancer, so we had to shave her head yesterday, and she's been impossible ever since.

Lillian gets frustrated trying to post Janie's videos on social media and YouTube, so she's always asking me for help. Whenever she does, I use the opportunity to sneak texts and videos to Gloria down at social services, begging her to come and help us. I snuck in another 911 call once, when Lillian went to the bathroom. I've texted Orion three other times, but he's never responded to anything, which means his phone is probably cut off.

Janie and I have only been locked up together a few other times, but suddenly, today, Lillian put us in here together twice. Once, it was because she'd brought that preacher man by, and she actually let him into the trailer while we were out. That was the first time she's done something like that and why I'm so nervous.

She's plotting her next move, and whatever plan she has with that preacher isn't good. He barely looked at me, but I didn't like the way his eyes slid over Janie. They'd gone outside afterward, and when Lillian came back inside, she put both of us in the room again. What was she planning? Every one of my internal alarms was screaming. Along with my will to survive.

I had to get Janie to focus. Pay attention. Do exactly what I asked of her.

"Here's what you have to do. Are you listening, Janie? This is super important." I knelt down next to her. She was pressed up in the dark with her back against the wall. Tired and worn out from practicing.

"I am, Mommy," she said in the kindest and most serious voice.

"I'm so sorry Lala treats you so bad and hurts you. She's not well. She's sick in the head. Like people get sick in the body? Well, Lala is sick in the head. The thinking part. That's why she acts the way she does, and I'm so sorry, honey," I said. This wasn't the first time she'd heard it from me. I explained this to her all the time, especially when Lillian was barking ballet orders at us that made no sense. But this was different. We were finally going to do something about the way she treated us. "Sometimes, when you're in a bad situation, like we are, you have to do things you wouldn't normally do to get out. Like hurt someone."

I couldn't see her face. So, I reached for her hand instead. "Do you want to get out of here?"

"Yes!" she squealed. Instantly excited.

"Okay, me too. I have a plan that could get us out of here, but I'm going to need your help. You're going to need to be a big girl and listen to Mommy. Can you do that?"

"Yes, Mommy. I'll help you." She gave my hand a gentle squeeze. Her tiny frail hand in mine. Fingers cold. The trailer was always freezing. The temperatures had fallen. Things would only get worse as we edged toward winter. We had to do this now.

I gave Janie's hand another squeeze. "All right. The only way for us to get free is to hurt Lala. I know you love Lala, but right now she isn't treating us right. She makes us do all these things we don't want to do, and she hurts us. Hurting people is never okay, but we have to hurt her so that we can get away. It's the only way we can escape. Do you want to know how we're going to do that? Can Mommy explain the plan?"

Her chain clanked as she crawled up into my lap. "Okay."

Lillian still didn't come near me. Other than when she helped Janie, she never took her eyes off me. But she didn't watch Janie in the same way she watched me, and she handled her physically all the time. She didn't ever get close to me, but she often got close to Janie.

I'd explained to Janie how we needed a weapon to hurt Lillian and that we could make a weapon out of the light bulb in the ceiling for her to stab Lillian with. The plan was to put her on my shoulders and hope that would make her tall enough to reach it. I didn't want her to unscrew it until we were sure she'd be able to do it without dropping it on the ground. We've been practicing ever since.

It was easy to hoist up Janie, and she was so light. Up and down we went, until we had every single step worked out to perfection. Her getting on my shoulders. The hold. The lift. I just wished there was a way for her to practice unscrewing the light bulb, since she'd never unscrewed anything before and her first time would be in the dark, but it wasn't feasible. Too risky.

We were finally ready.

"Okay, Janie, this is it. This time when I put you on my shoulders, you're going to get the light bulb out, just like we practiced. Are you ready?"

She clapped and squealed. "I'll get the light bulb, Mommy. I will. I'm not going to break it, I promise."

"Let's do it then. Teamwork, Mommy and Janie!" I bent down, and she scrambled back onto my shoulders. She slid into her position. A professional at this point, since we'd practiced it so many times. She was so much better at this than she was at ballet. She tapped my head.

"Ready."

"Here we go." I stood like I had been for the last two hours, but this was the real deal, and my heart was thudding like it was going to burst out of my chest. Janie was trembling. She was just as nervous as I was. I got us up. She had a hard time reaching even on my shoulders, but she could do it. "Okay, Janie girl, you've got this. Just like we talked about. Put your hand around it and turn it like a doorknob. Real soft. Gentle."

"Okay, Mommy."

She hoisted her legs up. Stiff. Completely focused. All I could hear was her labored breathing through her nose. I didn't dare say a word for fear that I'd break her concentration. She was concentrating so hard. And then just like that, her body relaxed.

"I did it!" I'd never heard her sound so happy.

I whipped her off my shoulders and spun her around while she gripped the light bulb in her hand. "Oh my god, Janie! You did it! You did it! I'm so proud of you!" We hugged and danced around the room, jumping up and down. Both of us squealing with delight.

The light bulb was easy to break. Much easier than I expected. It gave us the perfect piece. I handed it to Janie.

"Remember what we talked about," I said. "This is how you hold it."

She'd taken it from me, and we'd quickly settled into our respective spots. That's how Lillian expected us to be when she came back inside. I didn't know how long she'd be gone. It could be minutes. It might be days. Either way, Janie had to have the weapon so that when Lillian did return, we'd be ready. Lillian always unlocked her first. Janie was so excited she could barely contain herself. I was thankful it was dark, because if Lillian got close to her in the light, she'd recognize something was up immediately.

I couldn't sleep, though. Not when Janie had a weapon. There was a tiny part of me that worried if I did sleep, she might try the piece of glass on me first. Just for fun or to see if it worked. So, I stayed awake. Eyes wide open and my senses turned all the way on.

And waited.

THIRTY

Lillian unlocked the door and came in carrying Janie's bowl of dog food. She unshackled Janie, and Janie sprang from her ties like a beast, screaming at the top of her lungs while she stabbed Lillian in the neck. In the exact spot that I'd showed her. It was a perfect slice.

Lillian's eyes went wide. She dropped everything. The bowl clattered to the floor, spilling all the dog food. She brought her hand to her throat, blood spilling through her fingers.

Janie stuck her tongue out at her. "Evil bad witch, Lala."

"Janie! Janie! Good girl," I shouted, trying to get her away from Lillian and over to me like we'd planned. She had to unlock me. This was going to be the hardest part. "You did a great job. Just like Mommy asked you to. Now grab the keys from Lala's hands and come over here, okay? Come over here, sweetie, and unlock me. Mommy will show you how to do it."

Janie ignored me. What would I do if she left me alone in this room? She couldn't. She wouldn't. My pulse quickened. Panic thrummed through me. She was a wild card.

Lillian dropped to her knees. Face white. The blood draining the life force out of her body and onto the floor. Janie took another step closer to her. Close enough to step on her. Her eyes were filled with fascination. She wasn't intentionally ignoring me. She was too mesmerized by what was happening with Lillian to pay attention to anything else.

"Janie!" I smacked my legs and hollered at her again to get her attention.

She finally turned around. She was wild-eyed. Pupils dilated. Hair everywhere in tufts from how we'd shaved it. A soiled diaper hanging off her skeletal frame. Pale skin speckled with Lillian's blood. She smiled.

"Good job, good job! You did such a good job, Janie. I'm so proud of you, honey. Mommy is proud. Now let's do the next step, huh? Just like we talked about," I said in the sweetest and kindest voice. "I know you can unlock me, and then we can go get ice cream. You want to go get ice cream? We can get the kind with sprinkles. The rainbow ones. Just the way you like."

It'd been years since she'd had ice cream, and she'd only had it once, when we were trying to get her to eat. She probably didn't even remember what it tasted like, but she was smart enough to know she couldn't get out of here on her own. She hurried over to me while Lillian collapsed in a heap on the floor, struggling for breath. I ignored her painful gasps. There was only one chance to get it right.

Janie had stabbed Lillian. She actually stabbed her. I couldn't believe it!

"Honey, grab the keys that Lala uses to unlock Mommy and bring them here." I needed the keys to get out of my lock and to start her car. I hadn't driven in years, but I wasn't worried about it. Had to be just like riding a bike. "They're right there by her head."

Janie bent over Lillian's body to grab the keys from the ground. Immediately distracted by what was happening to Lillian. Gurgling sounds came from Lillian's mouth, like she was choking on the blood. Janie crouched down. Not to grab the keys, but to look closer. Lillian reached over to grab her leg.

"Ah!" Janie yelled when Lillian's fingers grazed her ankle.

I lunged as far as the chain would let me and tried to kick Lillian.

"Not this time," I hissed.

Lillian's fingers twitched around Janie's ankle, but there was no strength left in her grip, and Janie easily slipped out of her hold. I didn't want Lillian to grab her again. Not when I couldn't reach her.

"The keys, honey. You have to hurry. Right there, Janie," I said, again in a sugar-sweet voice as I pointed to the key ring half hidden under Lillian's blond hair. "Grab them and bring them to Mommy. Please. You can do it. I know you can."

She crouched down and grabbed the keys from underneath Lillian. She hurried back over to me and dropped them in my hand like a prize. Her hands were slick with blood.

"Good girl, Janie! You did such a good job!" I squealed. My fingers were shaking so bad I could barely hold the keys. "Find the little silver one with the square head," I said, handing them back to her. She easily found the correct one.

"Good. Now put it in the tiny hole. Turn it toward the door. Hard," I instructed as her forehead creased in concentration while she worked the lock.

She fumbled once. Then twice. On the third try, the cuff gave with a wet, metallic *click*. Pins and needles screamed through my hands as the blood rushed back. I yanked the other cuff loose and let the chain fall. I scooped Janie up from the floor along with me and twirled her around.

"We did it!" I smothered her face with kisses. Her cheeks still speckled with Lillian's blood, but I didn't care. We were getting out of here.

HIM

(NOW)

Vega leaned back in his chair, rubbing the bridge of his nose with his thumb and forefinger. His desk was buried in folders, evidence bags, and maps of the Miller property. Recently, they'd added the photos taken from Orion Ellis's apartment. He needed to give it a rest and call it a night. He'd barely been home all week.

But just as he was getting up to leave, Santos entered his office. She dropped a thin manila folder on top of the mess. "You're going to want to see this."

He raised his eyebrows before opening it. It contained copies of photographs of a young woman and a scanned evidence report along with a couple of receipts. "Where'd this come from?"

"The bottom of a shoebox. It was tucked under the floorboards behind Orion's dresser. He must've forgotten about it when he took off. CSU almost missed it. But we got a hit on the woman in the pictures." She gave him a full smile. This was the first lead in the case since Orion had skipped town a few weeks ago.

Vega sat forward in his seat. "What kind of hit?"

Santos pointed to the name on the top document: **Beatrice Watson.**

"Who's that?" he asked. "Should I know her?"

She pulled a stool closer and perched on the edge. "She's the woman at his previous residence. The one Tawny mentioned and whose picture he sent to her. I already confirmed it."

"She's the one in these pictures?" He pointed to the photocopies taken from the shoebox.

She grinned. "Look through the file. You'll see. We found her in the system, and she did a very brief stint at the Millers'. Same time as Orion. All the Polaroids are mostly when they're teenagers probably around that time, but there's also a few that look semi-recent, like they've been in touch again in recent years."

Vega tapped a photo. Beatrice and Orion standing on a beach. There was no time stamp, but from the way he held her close and the wind-tangled hair falling across her smile, it wasn't a random vacation shot. It was intimate. "We're sure she was at the Millers' at the same time as Orion?"

"It's all there. That's where the two of them met. She was on our original list of kids at the Millers', but we didn't follow up because her time there was so short and inconsequential. Or so we thought."

He narrowed his eyes. "Beatrice Watson. You think she's the missing link?"

Santos nodded. "And here's the kicker. I pulled fire records for the address Beatrice was living at before she moved into the Sacred Heart Fund building when she was seventeen. Her apartment burned down six days before she was granted emergency placement. Fire marshal report says suspicious origin, but it never went anywhere. No suspects. No follow-up."

"That's convenient," Vega muttered. "Let me guess—Ellis wasn't listed on the lease?"

"Nope. But guess who ran off to Texas shortly after that?"

He exhaled sharply. He pushed back from his desk and stood. "We've been looking at him like a lone wolf. But this"—he tapped the file again—"means he might not have been working alone."

"You think she helped him?" Santos asked. The bodies on the property just kept multiplying. They'd pulled another one last week.

"I don't know yet," Vega said. "But we need to find her, because if Ellis is on the run, there's a good chance they're together. She might be with him, and even if she's not, I'm willing to bet she knows exactly where he is."

Santos hesitated. "You think she was involved in what happened to Kyle? What about Brock?"

"I think," Vega said slowly, like he was still trying to formulate his own hypothesis, "that Beatrice Watson is the key to solving this case."

He crossed the room to the whiteboard. In black, he wrote Beatrice's name beneath Orion's. Then he picked up a red marker and drew a heart around them in a thick line.

THIRTY-ONE

Dispatcher: Nine-one-one. What's your emergency?

Becky: [trembling] I'd like to . . . I'd like to report a toddler. [sounds of traffic in background] She's wandering alone in the Walmart parking lot.

Dispatcher: A toddler? Is she in danger?

Becky: No . . . yes . . . I mean, she's a toddler, and she's alone in the Walmart parking lot. There's nobody with her. Something's wrong.

Dispatcher: Are you in danger?

Becky: No, I'm fine. I'm okay. She's the one that needs help. You have to help her.

Dispatcher: Ma'am, I'm here. Your voice is trembling and you sound really afraid. Stay on the line with me, okay? I'm here to help.

Becky: Don't worry about me. I'm fine. Just go help her. Please, she's just a little girl and all alone. She's only wearing a diaper, so she's obviously in trouble. Please hurry!

I ended the phone call before the dispatcher could ask any more questions or trace my location. Panic gripped my chest. Sweat dripped down my back. I forced myself to keep walking away. Not to turn around and go back for Janie. Tears and snot covered my face. Mouth tasted like vomit. I'd cried so hard, I threw up. My stomach was still twitching.

I crossed the street and hurried back to Lillian's car. Glancing over my shoulder for Janie every two seconds—torn between running away and going back for her. I hadn't planned on leaving her in the parking lot. Not at all. She was my daughter. My heart. The whole point of getting us out. The entire reason we'd killed Lillian.

What'd I just do?

My mind reeled. Emotions throttled. An involuntary sob escaped. I stifled the urge to scream.

A few blocks away from the trailer, with Lillian's body stuffed into the trunk, I felt the same moment of clarity hit like it had all those years ago when Lillian broke into the apartment: Janie didn't stand a chance at a good life if she stayed with me. The realization had pummeled me. All I could do was stare at her in the rearview mirror, watching me from the back seat, just like I used to do with Cerena. She was wide eyed and clutched her teddy bear. Lillian's blood dotted her face like freckles.

Janie had big problems long before Lillian took us hostage, and she was going to have even more now. She'd had no prenatal care. Drugged with Tylenol as a baby. Still hooked on what was probably Adderall. Horrifically abused. She was going to need so much support to learn how to be a regular kid. She'd need so many doctors. Specialists. Therapists. I would never be able to pay for all that. I couldn't even feed her. We had nothing. Literally nothing. Only the clothes we were wearing, and those were filthy. We didn't even have shoes. How would I ever be able to get her the help she needed?

There was something wrong with the women in our family, and she was already exhibiting signs. Maybe if she was on her own—cut off from our toxic family tree—with another family to take care of her, she'd learn how to recover from our generational trauma. She was still so young, and there was plenty of time to fix what was broken. I had to believe that, but she might not ever get that opportunity if she stayed with me.

I was her mother, and sometimes that's the greatest gift you can give your child—knowing when you're not the one that's best for them. And Janie deserved the best. The best parents. Home. Education. Teachers. Friends. Life. All of it. So that's what I'd just given her. Maybe that was my part in breaking the cycle.

I looked behind me. Still no red lights. Where were the police? What was taking them so long? Would they come with their sirens? I wished they'd hurry. Janie was probably freezing on top of being terrified.

I hurried down the block, darting into the shadows before anyone could see me. The same one I'd dragged Janie across seconds ago. What if she was coming after me? *Please don't let her get hit by a car.* Could she see me? I furtively glanced over my shoulder to make sure nobody was there. I tossed the phone into the ditch. Practically running, but I didn't want to draw any attention to myself.

I'd parked Lillian's car four blocks away from Walmart and on the other side of the street. I didn't want to take the chance that there were cameras and someone would get our license plate number. That'd ruin everything.

Janie had fought me the entire way. "Mommy, you're hurting me! Stop hurting me! Mommy!" Janie screeched from behind me as I dragged her across the street and toward the parking lot.

I ignored her cries and kept moving. I wasn't hurting her, but we had to move fast.

Her experience won't be like mine. There are good people in the system. That's what I kept telling myself over and over again, trying to prepare for what I knew was coming as soon as I found the right spot.

She was young. They'd treat her differently. Some loving family would want to save her. That's how it was when you were a young kid in the system. Their experience was totally different from when you were older. She wasn't going to go through what I did. I refused to let those thoughts terrorize me.

I'd finally stopped when we reached the middle of the parking lot and knelt down in front of her, panting and out of breath.

I gazed into her face, hoping she could see how much I loved her. That's the only reason I was doing this. Her big blue eyes were filled with confusion and tears. "I'm so sorry, baby. I know this doesn't make any sense to you right now, but I'm not going to be able to be your mommy anymore. I'm so sorry." I choked back the sobs. Shoved down the wails of anguish threatening to erupt from my body. "I want you to know this, Janie, okay, honey?" I furtively looked around. Making sure nobody was coming yet before continuing. I gripped her shoulders. "I'm always going to love you, and I'm always going to be in your heart. No matter what. That never changes. Even when I'm not around. Anytime you think about me or want to talk to me, you just put your hand right here." I grabbed her tiny hand and held it over her heart with mine. "That's all you have to do, and you'll feel me with you. Just like your heartbeat. You feel that? I'm always going to be with you even when I'm not here, but I want you to find a new mommy and daddy, okay?"

She looked at me, bewildered. Shaking her head slowly. Like nothing I'd just said registered. How could it? This came out of nowhere.

"Janie, sweetie, you have to go in that store behind you, just like we went in the grocery store with Orion. Remember how we did that? Someone inside will help you find new parents. I know this doesn't make sense. I'm so sorry. I'm so sorry, baby." I grabbed her and pulled her against my chest. Her body was rigid with shock. I had to stay strong. "Please, listen to me, okay?" I brought her off me and held her at arm's length. Tears streamed down both our faces. "Don't be scared. They're going to take so much better care of you than I can. I promise. They'll have a nice house. Lots and lots of toys. Probably real Barbie dolls. I'm sure they have real ones! Can you imagine? And so much food in the refrigerator for you, okay? You're never going to be hungry again, and you'll like your new parents. It'll be so much better there. I promise. They might even have a puppy." I motioned behind us again. "I want you to go inside and tell the first person you see that you need a mommy. Right now. Okay—go!"

"No, Mommy. No! I don't want a new mommy. You're my mommy. I don't wanna go to the store! I don't want a new mommy. I want you." She frantically shook her head and grabbed me, wrapping herself around my legs. She held on tight. "Mommy, please. I don't want to go in there. Mommy!"

"No, Janie. No. You have to let go. You don't understand why I have to do this, but someday you will, I promise. It's because I love you. I'll always love you. Mommy loves you, but I can't be your mommy anymore. Please, Janie, just go! Be a brave girl. It's going to be okay, I promise!" I cried. "But you have to let go."

She just kept shaking her head and clinging tighter. Her hands clutching the fabric of my jeans, like that would anchor her to me. I didn't know which one of us was crying harder. The sound of tires crunching broke through the night air. Headlights glared. Another car was turning into the parking lot. I had to move. There was no more time.

"I'm so sorry," I whispered, and then I wrenched her off me. Hard. She pawed at me, desperately trying to grab me again. I flung her toward the blue glare of the storefront.

"Go!" I screamed, already backing away. "Go, Janie! Run!"

Then, I turned and ran.

Sobs tore through me as I sprinted across the parking lot. Past blinking neon signs and other parked cars. I didn't look back. I couldn't. Because if I did—if I saw her face or heard her voice again—I wouldn't leave. And I had to.

This was the last good thing I'd ever do for her.

THIRTY-TWO

I just saw on the news that Janie's living with the Bauer family—Christopher and Hannah. He's a surgeon, and she's a nurse. Could there be a more perfect couple? What an incredible fit. I couldn't have done a better job finding her a set of parents if I'd picked them out myself. I still couldn't believe what I'd done. Placing her in someone else's care came out of nowhere, and even though I didn't regret my decision, I might never get over it. I missed her every day. More than I'd ever missed anyone else in my life, even Orion.

Janie's case was a media sensation overnight. People went crazy for her story. Of course they did. An abandoned child found wandering in the Walmart parking lot wearing only a diaper? How could they not? She tugged at every single one of America's heartstrings. The entire country was swooning over her.

Therapy every week was the biggest help in moving through all this. I found a new therapist as soon as I got to Florida. I wished I could go back to therapy with Maura, but I couldn't. She was too far away, but also I couldn't go anywhere I used to be known. Because as far as anyone knew, I was dead.

The thing about Lillian, and the same with Cerena—they'd both underestimated me. There was a lot to be said about intelligence. And my intelligence would always trump their psychopathy. So would my ability to feel for other human beings.

I've been talking to my new therapist about the Janie story. Everyone's watching and gripped by what's going to happen to her next. I told my therapist that the reason it's so triggering for me is because I gave my daughter up for adoption years ago. I made her believe I dropped off Janie at the fire station, like I'd wanted to do in the beginning. The story worked because it allowed me to process my feelings about abandoning Janie without incriminating myself. We've been doing some great therapy work around it.

I'm going to go back to school, but I'm not sure I still want to become a medical doctor. I was thinking of being a psychologist. Getting my PhD in psychology instead. Technically, I'll still be a doctor. I think I'll be good at it. Maybe even better than I'd be at being a medical doctor because I was so good at being nonjudgmental and enjoyed studying people. Psychologists make a lot of money too.

No one will ever know that Lillian was in the trailer, or that I'd been the one who gave Janie the piece of glass to kill her. They'll assume the blood in the trailer is mine after they find my teeth in the backyard. That's the last thing I did before leaving town. Yanked two of my molars out with pliers. I'd chewed on cotton for three days.

They'll find my teeth underneath the oak tree. Make the logical conclusion that I'm dead. That the rest of my body had decayed or other parts of it had been eaten by animals. They'd wonder about me. Try to put the pieces together, but they would never for one second wonder if I was alive. What would Janie tell them about me?

It didn't really matter. She has new parents now. Good ones. I hope they heal all the hurt we caused her. I have to believe they can. They seem so lovely. That's what I tell myself every time the loss of her threatens to overtake me. Some days are easier than others.

None of this would've happened if I hadn't called Lillian from the hospital. She must've thought she'd hit the jackpot when I did. She had control of me when I was on drugs, but I'd tricked her and bled that poison out of me. Hiding all of it from her the entire time. Because the thing about my will? It's ironclad. Cerena used to hold cigarettes to my flesh, trying to get me to cry, and if I could keep a straight face while my skin bubbled, I could surely keep a straight face while the diarrhea burned its way through my system, which is exactly what I'd done.

The look of utter shock on Lillian's face when Janie came at her with the glass and sliced her throat made all the pain that she'd put us through feel a little bit better.

Turns out, Lillian was as big of a liar as her daughter. Her husband—good ole pawpaw—didn't die of a heart attack. He'd jumped off the Sunshine Skyway Bridge in St. Petersburg, Florida. He was one of the few who'd made it over the prevention fences. He'd been a stockbroker his entire life, and made a bad deal. He was headed to prison, and the feds had seized every single one of his assets. They were completely broke. All their money gone. The pieces of jewelry she wore on her body were the most expensive things she owned. They were all she had left.

She'd come back to make money off Janie. Turn her into a child star for profit. That's why she'd jumped at the GoFundMe-account idea. It added another revenue stream. I still didn't know what she'd actually had planned for me, but it no longer mattered. None of it did.

Lillian made getting rid of her body so easy for me, given what happened to my grandfather. After leaving Janie in the Walmart parking lot, I'd taken Lillian's car, with her in the trunk, and driven it all the way to Florida. I found the cheap apartment in Gainesville that she'd been staying in ever since he'd taken his life and she lost their home. I pulled her out of the trunk and placed her in the driver's seat. Stuffed a sock in her gas tank and started it on fire. I burned her car down in the parking lot like I'd burned Cerena's place. I left a note inside her apartment explaining what she'd done. How she'd played a part in her husband's deception and couldn't go on without him. Everyone would think she'd followed suit. No one would think to dig any deeper.

My therapist says that it's time to stop watching all the media and news coverage on Janie's story, especially if I'm trying to move forward. That all it does is trigger me. She wasn't wrong, so that's what I'm doing now.

I finally got ahold of Orion on social media. We've been talking for these past few weeks, and as always, it's like we've never been apart. That's what happens every time we reconnect. We fall right back into each other so easily. I told him everything that happened with Janie and Lillian. I was afraid to tell him about abandoning Janie because he was abandoned almost the same way when he was a little boy, but he didn't judge me. He never does. That's what so special about us.

The police were questioning him after the bodies on the Miller farm started rising from their graves, so he's in North Carolina, living under a different name. He doesn't know I took care of Brock for him. Maybe someday I'll tell him. Maybe not.

Orion never said anything about Brock hurting him, not really. But I noticed the bruises. The sudden winces when I hugged him too tight. The way his body flinched at certain words or sounds. I thought it was Earl. So did everybody else. But it was Brock. He'd turned into Earl. Become just like him, and Orion was his first victim.

One night, I asked him outright—just blurted it out while we were eating cold soup from the can—and he froze. His eyes dropped. He gave the smallest nod.

The next night, I found Brock behind the Miller property. I'd told him I scored some cheap booze and a joint, and he followed me like a dog. That's what men like him always did—chased the scent of something they thought they could take.

I brought him out to the old tractor trailer behind the sheds. The one with rust along the door hinges and the nasty mouse droppings in the corners, but Brock didn't even notice. He was too busy thinking he was going to get down my pants. I handed him a beer and lit the joint, passing both back and forth between us. I waited until he got nice and buzzed. Then, I told him—flat out—to leave Orion alone and to keep his hands to himself.

He laughed in my face and said Orion liked it. Said he begged for it sometimes. That was when I saw it—that flash in his eyes. The same one Cerena had. The one that said *I enjoy hurting people.*

I told him to shut up. That I'd kill him if he ever touched Orion again. That's when he grabbed me and pinned me against the wall. He called me crazy and told me I'd like it, just like Orion did.

I still didn't remember reaching for the knife—I'd taken one from the Millers' kitchen earlier that day for protection. Just in case. I only remember the sound. The wet squish of the blade entering his stomach. Then again. And again. Until he slid down the wall and I was on top of him. Hands soaked in his blood.

It wasn't clean. Nothing about it was. But he didn't get back up.

I stumbled outside. Breath heaving. The cold air slapped my face. My hands trembled as the world spun. I dropped the knife into the snow. Everything warped and wobbly.

That's when I saw her.

Helen.

Standing by the edge of the trees with her arms crossed. She didn't scream or ask what happened. She just looked at me like she'd known this day was coming.

"Go home, Becky," she said after a long silence. "I'll take care of it."

I started sobbing, the kind that buckles your knees. I told her I didn't mean to do it. That I didn't want to go to prison. She walked over and pulled me off the ground. She gripped my chin in her hand and said, "You saved Orion, and that's all that matters. You're a good person."

She buried Brock while I took a shower in her bedroom. It felt so odd, being in there. Uncharted territory for any other foster kid. She gave me a pair of her sweatpants when I finished and promised to get rid of my clothes. She logged Brock as a runaway. It fit. No one looked twice. Runaways were normal at the Millers'. No one ever came looking for the broken ones. And as we got older? The closer we came to aging out of the system? They were secretly glad when we disappeared because that meant they no longer had to deal with us.

I never told Orion about that night. And he never asked.

I'm not a killer. Which feels strange to say, because technically I've been involved in three murders. Some people might even call me a serial killer. But if I had to do it again, for him? Or to free Janie so she'd have a chance at a good life?

I would. It's hard to feel bad about getting rid of people that deserved to die.

Yesterday I bought a bus ticket to Raleigh, North Carolina. I've never pictured myself as a Southern girl, but apparently it's in my blood, so we'll see how it goes. I leave tomorrow at nine and should be there by Tuesday. I can't wait to see Orion again. It's time to start moving on with my life. Everyone deserves a fresh start and a new beginning. And technically, I was dead, so I could be whoever I wanted to be. Now *that* was true freedom.

EPILOGUE

He hurried back to the apartment with the creamer they'd forgotten to grab earlier. It'd been three months since he picked Becky up from the bus station, and for the first time in his life, things felt like they might just be all right. At least headed in that direction.

The first month had been really hard. Becky spent most of it crying, too depressed to even get out of bed. She'd made the hardest choice a mother could make—walking away from her daughter in that parking lot, not because she didn't love her but because she did. He didn't know how to fix her pain other than to hold her and tell her that she wasn't alone. He couldn't take the hurt away. She'd carry what she'd done with her forever. Same as him.

They were both learning to forgive themselves.

He'd known he was going to take off the moment those police officers showed up at his job. He slipped out once he'd collected his last paycheck. He'd been holding his breath for years, so he already had a plan. He shaved his head and his beard as soon as he crossed the Illinois border. Got colored contacts in Kentucky once he'd saved up enough money. Settled in North Carolina and told everyone his name was Jake.

He wasn't a killer.

He'd never laid a hand on Earl, despite what the police thought. Brock was the one that pushed him down the stairs that night. Brock might've killed him, but they all wanted him dead. Including Helen.

She was the first one down the stairs after Brock shoved him. She didn't scream or cry. Didn't even make a sound. Just stood there staring at Earl's contorted body as the blood grew in a puddle around his head.

The sound Earl's head made when it hit the basement floor had never left Orion. A sickening crack. Final and hollow. He was already dead by the time they got down there. Brock didn't say a word either. He just backed into the corner while everyone else panicked. It was Helen's idea to bury Earl behind the shed underneath the poplar tree.

Within minutes, they'd wrapped his body in blue tarps and were dragging it across the property. They dug through the frozen soil without saying a word to each other. It was cloudy, so they took turns holding the flashlight all night. Soledad didn't help at all. She stayed in her room, along with a couple of the younger kids. But most of them helped bury Earl. Helen cooked everyone a full breakfast afterward, right as the sun was coming up. Then she sent them off to school.

He told Becky the truth about that night on the drive home from the bus station. Same as she'd told him about Lillian. No lies between them—that was the first rule of their relationship. Always had been. He had no idea what happened to Brock or the other two kids they found buried next to him. Kids disappeared from the Millers' all the time. He'd bet there were more on the property they hadn't found yet.

Becky had never asked about Kyle, so he didn't tell her anything. Technically, he wasn't violating their rules about honesty. She'd already been through so much. He'd carry this part alone, to protect her.

He'd never meant to hurt Kyle. It was an accident.

Kyle was his friend, and the only person in the world who ever made him feel halfway normal. They'd worked together at the Dairy Queen. Their nights closing down the restaurant where they turned the radio up as loud as it would go while singing into chocolate ice cream cones like microphones were still some of his fondest memories. They always laughed so hard at the customers, and Kyle made Orion feel like he could be more than just a foster kid. He could be a regular one too.

The night it happened, he was wiping down the counters, and Kyle came up behind him—unexpectedly and by surprise—just like Earl and Brock used to do. Kyle put his hands on the back of his neck and whispered something dumb. Maybe a joke. Maybe flirting. He couldn't even remember.

Because something inside him snapped in that moment.

Orion's fist was through Kyle's face before he even knew it was happening. The sound of cartilage breaking and the warm spray of blood. And then, he just kept going. Kicking. Punching. Pummeling him. Red everywhere. Kyle's face wasn't Kyle's anymore. It was Earl's. Brock's. Every night in that house. Every scream he swallowed. Every shame he buried. It was all of it. And he couldn't stop.

When it was over, he couldn't breathe. The panic hit like a tidal wave. He'd buried Kyle the same way they buried Earl. Fast and clumsy in the middle of the night. Just past the tree line in a shallow grave, wrapped in an old army blanket. He hadn't even thought about the driver's license. The same way he hadn't thought about leaving behind any possible evidence when he moved Kyle's body after the news first broke. He didn't think along those lines because he wasn't a killer. Any more than Becky was. That's why they were the perfect couple.

They were finally going to be together and put all this behind them. A real shot at a normal life. Maybe someday they'd have a baby of their own. Becky didn't need to worry about him, even though he could tell she sometimes still worried about his temper. She would be safe. He'd never do anything to hurt her. He felt confident that you couldn't snap like that on someone you loved, and he loved Becky. More than anything or anyone else in this world.

And at the end of the day, that's all that mattered—love.

About the Author

Photo © 2025 Jocelyn Snowdon

USA Today bestselling author Lucinda Berry is a former psychologist and leading researcher in childhood trauma. She's written multiple bestsellers, reaching millions of readers worldwide. Some of her bestselling works include *The Perfect Child*, *Saving Noah*, *When She Returned*, *The Best of Friends*, and *Keep Your Friends Close*. Her books have been optioned for film and translated into several languages.

If Berry isn't chasing after her son, you can find her running through Los Angeles, prepping for her next marathon. To hear about her upcoming releases and other author news, visit her on social media (@lucindaberryauthor) or sign up for her newsletter at https://lucindaberry.com.